I0525095

68

A NOVEL

JIM TRAINOR

UpNorth
Press

By Jim Trainor

Grasp: Making Sense of Science and Spirituality (2010)

Waverly's Universe (2012)

The Sand People (2013)

Up North (2014)

The Mountain Goat (2017)

68 (2018)

68

A NOVEL

68 is a work of fiction.
Characters, places and incidents are the products of the
author's imagination, and any real names or locales
used in the book are used fictitiously.

68: A Novel
Copyright © 2018 by Jim Trainor.
All rights reserved.
No part of this book may be used or reproduced in any manner
whatsoever without written permission except in the case of
brief quotations embodied in critical articles and reviews.

For information contact
UpNorth Press
www.JimTrainorAuthor.com

ISBN-13: 978-0-692-18537-7

For Khalil, Liam, Isla and Jackson

Reality is a multiverse instead of a simple universe.
John Polkinghorne

We have a few minutes at sunset time
when the whole world has a glow.
Georgia O'Keeffe

Chapter 1

E d Turner almost didn't go in. The massive carved-oak entry doors of the Golden Foothills Inn were fanned open, like welcoming arms, so there was no problem negotiating the entrance with his cane. The background music—Dionne Warwick's "Do You Know the Way to San Jose," from 1968 he assumed—was soothing, and a path of Spanish tiles leading around a gurgling fountain provided a hospitable greeting.

Still, this was a bad idea, he thought. If Ship hadn't hounded him after he'd showed him the invitation, he wouldn't be here. A large plastic banner pinned above the entrance read, "Welcome to the Sentinel High School 50th Reunion! Go Titans!" This made him even more nervous. He should have been excited about the reunion, anticipating rekindling old friendships, sharing memories of the good old days. But he hadn't been to any of his previous reunions, hadn't kept in touch with even one student. Good God, he didn't know any of these people. Even fifty years ago, he didn't know them very well. Would anyone even remember him?

Ed hobbled his way inside, where a cheery woman sat behind a folding table, with an array of name badges in front of her. It was silly, he knew, but he'd imagined that they'd all look just like they did when he'd last seen them, half a century ago. This woman—on Medicare and Social Security and probably someone's grandmother—was one of his former high school classmates, now in her late sixties, just like him. He let out a quavering sigh.

The woman beamed. "Hey there, welcome! I'm Dottie Arnold. Last name's Brighton now. Remember me?"

Of course he remembered Dottie. Who wouldn't? Dottie, the bouncy, popular cheerleader. He doubted if she remembered him.

Ed manufactured a grin.

Dottie fumbled through the printed name tags, glancing up periodically with a peppy smile. "Oh, good grief, remind me who you are."

"Ed Turner."

Dottie leaned back, folded her arms and looked hard at him. "Say again?"

He said it a little louder. "Ed Turner. Maybe you've got me as Eddie Turner. I went by Eddie back then."

Dottie was shaking her head. "That's not funny, you know." Her smiling face had turned sullen.

"What do you mean?"

"I mean it's not funny." She forced a smile. "Okay, let's start over. I must have your tag here somewhere."

"It's Ed Turner." He leaned in for a closer look at the name tags. "Do you need to see my ID?" This was getting ridiculous. He reached for his billfold, then remembered it was gone. Damn, it had also contained his invitation.

Dottie stopped again. "Just a minute," she said, now turning businesslike. She scowled at him, then stood abruptly and darted around a curtain behind the table. She returned a moment later with a big hulk of a guy. He'd probably been a football player. Ed didn't recognize him, and the man didn't introduce himself.

"Excuse me, sir, but your humor's a bit off base," the man said. "Why don't you just head on down the road? Okay?" He placed his hands on his hips like a bouncer who wasn't in the mood to take any crap.

Ed felt his face redden with a mixture of confusion, embarrassment, and anger. He wasn't one to make a scene, and it was tempting to just leave. But hell, he'd come this far. He leaned forward over his cane. "Look," he said, "I'm here for the fiftieth. I was a student at Sentinel, class of sixty-eight. Ed Turner. I received an invitation. I don't see what the problem is."

The big guy raised his eyebrows, ran a hand over his crew cut, then blew out a big breath. He leaned over the folding table toward Ed, a lean that could be taken as aggressive. "The problem is, you're pulling our chain and you know it. Now, please—"

"I'm sorry," Ed interrupted. "I'm just here for the—"

"Look, buddy, do you think we don't know that Eddie Turner died fifty years ago?"

Chapter 2

Ed backed away from the table, stunned, as the football player glowered at him and Dottie turned her attention to another senior citizen checking in. Needing air and feeling suddenly shaky on his feet, he made his way to a folding chair and sat down, leaning forward onto his cane.

This was the culmination of a lousy day. He never should have taken this nonsense about attending the reunion seriously. A week ago he'd decided not to go, but Ship just wouldn't drop the subject.

It had been at breakfast yesterday, at Sarah's Cafe, in Cloverdale, California. Shipley Jameson taught physics at Muir College and was one of Ed's few friends. His wild, shaggy hair—now white—conveyed an Einstein-like image, which fit Ship well. Even though Ed had retired from the Muir physics department two years ago, he still met Ship here almost every morning for breakfast. The noisy ambiance of laughter, rustling newspapers and clinking dishes required them to talk loud, but they didn't mind. The bustle of a busy coffee shop is a soothing balm for loneliness.

"Frankly, I wouldn't be caught dead at that reunion," Ed had said. He'd received the invitation two months ago and still hadn't responded. "I really didn't know anyone very well in high school, never dated. Back then I was such a shy dork, and—"

Ship's burst of laughter was so intense that he almost spit out his mouthful of oatmeal.

"What?" asked Ed.

"You a shy dork? How come I find that so easy to believe?" Ship was a small man, perpetually hunched over, like he'd spent a lifetime in some musty library poring through journals. His eyes twinkled with mischief.

Ed decided to ignore Ship's nasty remark. "Anyway, there'll be all these people there who were good friends, part of all the cliques that I wasn't a part of, all these people who've probably kept in touch with each other over the years, gone to every reunion. Pretty sure I wouldn't fit into any of that."

Now Ship set his fork down, dabbed at his mouth with his napkin, and folded his hands in front of him. "Still, that was all a part of your life, Ed. It was a long time ago, yes, but I think it would be important to have one final connection with that important time."

Ed nodded, considering this. Then he said, "I hear you, but I'm not sure any of those people would even remember me, much less want to have anything to do with me."

Ship shook his head. "You might be surprised. Look, Ed, I'm almost as old as you, and I've learned that time has a way of changing things. A way of leveling the playing field."

Ed wondered if Ship was referring to his own early years, to the hidden tragedy that had brought him from one of the most prestigious physics departments in the world to a third-tier, four-year college like Muir. Long ago, Ship had been a hot shot in grad school at MIT, then seemed to be headed to the top as an assistant prof at Chicago—Ed knew that much. How Ship wound up here at Muir was still a mystery to Ed, and one that Ship, despite their thirty-year friendship, was unwilling to discuss. Ed produced a weak smile and said, "Leveling the playing field? You mean because we'll all soon be six feet under the playing field?"

Ship bellowed with laughter. "Obviously, all those people who said you have no sense of humor were wrong."

Ed laughed, too.

A few hours later, just yesterday—it seemed so long ago now—Ed stood in the midst of his garden, a twenty-by-twenty space that filled the courtyard of his tiny condo, reflecting on what he'd done. Following the pep talk from Ship, he'd texted the chairperson for the reunion—someone he'd never heard of—saying he'd come. He'd reserved a room for the next night at Villa Solana, where the reunion would be held, and tomorrow he'd make the seven-hour drive from northern California down to Riverside County. It wouldn't be easy getting away. It wouldn't be easy leaving his garden and its wealth of color that always lifted his spirits: the peonies, roses, gardenias, hyacinth, hibiscus, and camellias—the place where he'd spent much of his life, down on his knees on the foam kneeling mat, weeding, fertilizing, pruning. And he'd have to pack, a struggle for even a one-night trip—he didn't travel much—and it would be hard to say goodbye to Carmen, what with her current health problems.

But by this afternoon Ed had arrived in the parking lot of Villa Solana, where he sat for a long time in his old Volvo, still shaking from the long drive and uncertain about going in. He checked the time again on his Garmin exercise watch—he was already a half-hour late, and this wouldn't make his entrance any easier. He could just head home right now. That's what he wanted to do—he was worried about Carmen, he wanted to retreat to the sanctuary of his garden. Sure, he'd lose his money for the room, but that mattered little. He felt a bead of sweat form on his forehead and he was suddenly unable to get enough air. He loosened his tie and unbuttoned the top button of his shirt. Ship would never let him live this down. He sighed.

Ed pulled his two forearm crutches from the back seat, eased himself out of the car and stood motionless in the parking lot for a while, as a deep-orange sun ball, filtered through haze, was setting behind a row of eucalyptus trees. It was a beautiful sunset, but it was the product of air pollution. He recalled playing kickball in the fifth grade, running hard, and his lungs burning from the smog. Those smog alerts from his childhood—first stage, second stage and so on—did they still have them in LA?

Freeway noise was a steady, dull roar in the background. He couldn't remember that annoying drone from when he'd lived here—that was a long time ago—maybe he'd just gotten used to it back then. He exhaled a shaky, troubled breath. This had been his home, and yet it felt strange to be here. Had it changed that much? But then his eyes found the familiar gray silhouettes of the high peaks of the eastern end of the San Gabriel Mountains, off to the north. He'd never hiked up in those mountains—other kids in school talked about it—but those big peaks, unchanged after all the years, brought a smile, and he could still name them: Ontario, Cucamonga and the tallest, Old Baldy.

Now he turned toward Villa Solana, sprawling across one edge of the parking lot, a low, rambling earth-tone structure built to resemble an ancient hacienda. The red Spanish-tiled roofline was beautiful, but Ed was certain that inside it would be just another Best Western.

In the foyer, he heard the laughter on the other side of the dark-glass entry doors. There were lots of people in there.

He stopped to study himself in a tall mirror. Good Lord, it was the stereotypical retired college teacher, a crusty old curmudgeon in a well-worn corduroy sport coat with leather elbow patches. He was at least fifteen pounds overweight, in spite of his daily exercise on the treadmill, but seriously, how many calories can you burn when you can barely move your legs?

His features were wooden. Large green, impassive eyes hid the emotion that was inside, and an expressionless mouth made him look like he was reserving judgment, even when he thought he was smiling—the curse of an introvert. *Thanks for the encouragement*, he thought. He pointed at himself in the mirror. *You're your own worst enemy, you know that.* He smoothed his gray, thinning hair; cleaned off his wire-framed glasses on his shirt; and practiced his smile again—it still looked stiff and forced. He took a deep breath and headed toward the doors, determined to give this his best shot.

What the hell just happened? Ed lay on the floor, against a wall. Had he passed out? He felt okay, but then quickly realized that his crutches were gone. *Shit.* He grabbed his wrist—the Garmin watch. *Gone.* He checked his pockets. His iPhone, his wallet, car keys. *Gone. Damn.* He'd been mugged.

But there was no memory of an attack. There was no pain, no sore bump on his head, no bruised ribs. As far as he could tell, he was fine. Could this be another TGA?

This would be a terrible time for a TGA attack. The first one, three years ago, occurred after an especially intense workout on the treadmill. He'd gone to the ER immediately, afraid he'd had a stroke, but a neurologist had explained that he'd experienced a TGA—an attack of transient global amnesia. It was transient in that it lasted only a few hours and global because during the episode Ed couldn't remember even simple things like his birth date or his home phone number or what street he lived on.

Ed had learned that TGAs are fairly common after the age of sixty, but that there was no understanding of what caused them or how to prevent them. The good news was that they are apparently not life-threatening. The doctor had also told Ed that he could expect a TGA to reoccur unexpectedly during times of intense physical activity or during moments of extreme stress. *That must be it*, Ed concluded, *a TGA*. But somehow, he'd passed out—how long had he been unconscious? Certainly long enough for someone to help themselves to his belongings.

It was now quiet. The noise behind the doors had subsided. That was odd. But Ed needed to get help. Without his crutches, he could barely move. He rolled over onto his knees and crawled to the glass entry doors. With considerable effort he got one door open enough to wedge his body through the opening. The large lobby was empty. *Where is everybody?* What about the laughter he'd heard before? Had he been unconscious so long that he'd missed the whole thing? His eyes found a large clock against a far wall. Only a few minutes had elapsed. *What the hell is going on?*

"Can I help you, sir?"

The voice caused Ed to jerk around quickly, ready for another attack. A young guy, probably in his early twenties, wearing the red double-breasted jacket of a bellhop, stood over him, his long blond hair falling over his face. He extended one hand toward Ed to help, while he brushed the hair away from his face with the other hand. Then he said, "Sir, are you okay?"

There was no one else in the lobby area, except for a half-asleep clerk behind the registration desk. "I'm not sure what's going on. I think I've been mugged."

"Holy crap." There was alarm on the young man's face. "Want me to call the police? Or an ambulance?"

Ed shook his head. "No ambulance—I think I'm all right. And let's hold off on the police for a bit, okay? I first need to figure out what happened. Did you see anyone suspicious in the last few minutes?"

The young man shook his head. "Nothing, sir. I've been here all afternoon. Haven't seen anyone recently, until you crawled in through the door. Oh, I'm Cody. Welcome to Villa Solana." He gave out a little laugh. "I guess."

"Look, I need my crutches. Might you check around here for them?"

Cody glanced around the room, then poked his head out through the entrance doors. "No crutches anywhere," he said.

"Damn. I'm pretty helpless without them."

Cody scratched his head. "Geez, I don't know what I can do to … wait a minute, I've got an idea." He disappeared into a room behind the registration desk, then a moment later he returned carrying a metal quad cane. He was beaming. "I just remembered that we have a few items back there for residents who sprain an ankle or need a little extra help. Would this work for you?"

"Yeah, it just might. Can you help me get up?"

Cody placed two hands under Ed's arms and lifted him to a standing position. Now Ed shifted his weight onto the cane and took a few tentative steps. "I think this might work. Thank you."

Cody beamed with pleasure, as he again brushed his blond hair back from his well-tanned face. "What can I help you with now, sir?"

Ed surveyed the quiet lobby. "I'm not sure what's going on. I'm here for a high school reunion, but I don't see anyone. Maybe they're down the hall?"

Cody, who looked like his main vocation was surfing, seemed puzzled. "No reunion here tonight, sir. In fact, no special activities at all. You sure you got the right place? This is Villa—"

"I know where I am." On top of everything else, he was suddenly feeling like an idiot. "Villa Solana. It's right here on my invitation." He reached for his wallet. *Shit.*

"What's the reunion?"

"My fiftieth at Sentinel High School."

"Fiftieth? Wow." Cody now seemed to be studying Ed's face closely, probably wondering how anyone could be this old. Then he gave Ed a big grin. "Sentinel, huh? Cool. I just graduated from there two years ago. Great place." He turned serious again. "But they're not having any kind of activity here tonight."

Ed leaned on his new cane with both hands. He shook his head but said nothing.

Then Cody raised an index finger like he'd just had a great idea. "Sentinel fiftieth, you say? Let me check something." Cody pulled out his phone and typed quickly with his thumbs. He shook his head, then typed some more. He muttered something to himself, then looked up at Ed. "Okay, I found it. Your reunion is indeed tonight, but it's not here. It's at the

Golden Foothills Inn. Easy to get these places mixed up. It's only a few miles from here."

Ed never made mistakes like this. His invitation had in fact said it was at the Villa Solana. Could the organizing committee have made a mistake? Unlikely. And what about all the voices he'd heard before the episode? Or maybe that was all a part of the episode. He wasn't sure about anything right now. Finally, he said, "I've got a reservation here tonight. Can someone check on that? It's under Ed Turner."

Cody stepped over to the registration desk, where he spoke with the clerk. They both turned their attention to the computer monitor. Then Cody shook his head. "I'm sorry, sir. No reservation for an Ed Turner in the system." He gave Ed a sorrowful look.

Ed licked his lips, then looked down at his wrist where the watch should have been. He gave out a little laugh. "I'm not sure what to do now."

"Look, Mr. Turner, here's what I'd do. I'd head over to my reunion. Just five minutes away. Worry about all this other stuff later. You got a car out in the lot?"

"Yes, but … crap, they took my keys. I hope that doesn't mean they got my car, too."

"Let's go look," the helpful Cody said. He held the entry door open for Ed, who was still trying to master the new cane.

The parking lot was emptier than it had been when Ed had arrived, which was odd, and it only took a few moments to discover that the Volvo was indeed gone. Ed shook his head. "So, I guess I'm not surprised. Maybe now we should call the cops."

Cody waited in the parking lot with Ed until the police arrived.

That turned out to be another unpleasant situation. After Ed gave the cop all the relevant information—model and license number of the vehicle, his name and address, and so on—the officer, a woman at least forty years his junior, spent way too long back in her patrol car verifying the information.

When she finally returned, there was suspicion written all over her face. Thumbing through a small notebook as she spoke, she said, "So, Mr. Turner, there seem to be a few issues here. It would have really helped if you'd had some ID with you. You see, I can find no record of your vehicle in the system. Furthermore, I can find no record of you in the system." Then she closed the notebook and looked hard at Ed, so hard that he squirmed uncomfortably and had to look down.

Damn, he thought, *the TGA. I've obviously got all the information wrong.* He gave Cody an apologetic smile, then said to the officer, "Look, I suffer from periodic episodes called TGAs. They're—"

"Are you having a medical emergency right now?"

"No, but—"

"Have you talked with your doctor?"

"Well, no, but—"

"Excuse me, Mr. Turner, or whatever your name is," the officer interjected, "but the city didn't send a police officer over here to hear about your health conditions. I have some more questions, Mr. Turner. Have you been drinking? Or maybe taking something?"

Ed opened his mouth, but no words came out. He glanced over at Cody with a pleading 'help-me' look.

Cody spoke up. "Look, officer, I'm on the staff here at Villa Solana, and I can assure you that Mr. Turner is not under the influence of any kind of substance. He's been under a lot of stress today. So, look, we're very sorry to have dragged you out here, and we appreciate your coming, but now I'm going to get Mr. Turner back inside and he'll soon be okay. I don't think we need any further—"

"Okay, okay," said the cop, backing away toward her car, shaking her head slowly, no doubt wondering about the kinds of weirdoes you run into these days.

Back inside, Ed said, "Cody, I'm really thankful for your help out there. I really do have a condition that—"

"It's okay, Mr. Turner, I sized you up as okay from the get-go. I don't need any explanations if—"

"But I feel I really do need to explain," said Ed, and with that gave Cody a quick description of the TGAs.

When he was done, Cody said, "Holy crap, amnesia, huh? I thought that stuff was just in movies, you know, Jason Bourne." Then he laughed and reached over and laid a hand on Ed's shoulder. "Look, let me call you an Uber, just take a minute. Then—"

"But I don't even have the money to pay for—"

"It won't be much. I'll take care of it. Then after your big party, you can come back over here. We've got lots of rooms available. You probably noticed—the place is hardly booked up tonight."

"Yeah, and how will I pay for a room?"

"I'm sure we'll figure out something, Mr. Turner."

Sure, Ed would go to the reunion, or whatever awaited him over at that other hotel. What else was he going to do?

Chapter 3

Ed squirmed in his chair and gazed past Dottie's table into the large meeting room, where a huge crowd was exchanging hugs, laughing, reconnecting. He didn't belong here. He should leave, but where would he go? After all the other crap that hadn't made sense this evening, this was the icing on the cake: *do you think we don't know that Eddie Turner died fifty years ago?*

He needed time to think this through. *Died fifty years ago? No, I didn't die fifty years ago, but I almost did. Sure, that's it. The only explanation that makes any sense.*

He'd moved with his parents up north, right after high school. His dad had been out of work for nearly a year when his brother-in-law told him about the opening with a construction crew in Santa Rosa. In the fall Ed began classes at Sonoma State University—it was called Sonoma State College back then—while living at home, just ten miles away. But he didn't get very far into his studies.

Late in the fall, Ed's dad had allowed him to take the family's old Plymouth Valiant—a '63—for the day, and he drove alone up toward the Sierras, toward Lake Tahoe. The roadmap had convinced him he could make it up and back in a day, and if he could glimpse the beautiful lake and the mountains for even a few minutes, the long drive would be worth it. Ed still hadn't made many friends at college, and a getaway, even if he was going alone, felt good.

But just east of Sacramento, he ran into rain, and an hour east of Placerville, where US 50 began to climb up into the Sierra, he saw the first snowflakes. He pressed on, but within ten miles cars were stopped, and police were turning back vehicles without snow chains. The old Valiant didn't have chains. Disappointed, Ed turned around and headed home. Already the roads were icing up, and the driving had become treacherous. Ed had relived that drive over and over the past fifty years, because it had shaped his life.

Somewhere along US 50, on a curve, he apparently hit a patch of black ice and the car went into a skid. Ed had clenched the wheel tight, started to hit the brakes, then remembered what he'd heard about maneuvering a car on ice. *Turn toward the direction of the skid.* Too late for that—he was out of control. The car sideswiped a guard rail, which popped the driver's side door open. Ed didn't have his seat belt fastened— mandatory seat belt use had only recently become law—and the thought of jumping out flashed through his mind.

But another car was coming toward him, and a collision seemed imminent. The next few seconds seemed to pass in slow motion, as he calmly observed the impending tragedy. Somehow, he was able to steer the car away from the oncoming vehicle, but that took him off the road directly into a dense forest. The impact with a tree must have knocked him unconscious. When he came to, he smelled gasoline. The driver's side door was still sprung open, but he couldn't move. His legs wouldn't work. He recalled looking down at them, but all he could see was the steering wheel and dashboard crumpled down upon the lower half of his body, amid a sea of windshield shards.

It had taken superhuman effort, no doubt fueled by a massive adrenalin infusion, to pull himself out through the driver's side opening and drag his broken body away from the wreck. Ten yards from the car, he was nearly blinded by light and singed by a blast of heat, as the car was engulfed in flames.

The next thing he remembered was being in a hospital in Placerville, as a nurse told him he was lucky to be alive, lucky he hadn't gone through the windshield and that his parents were on their way. Ed spent the next two months in the hospital—in Placerville for a week until it was safe for him to be moved, then seven weeks in Santa Rosa. When he was finally discharged, he and his parents were told that he would never walk again.

Even now, all these years later, the memories of that day caused him to shake.

Ed lifted himself off the chair and onto his cane and made his way back over to Dottie. She gave him an uncertain look, but said nothing.

"I think I can explain the mix-up," he said, then told her about the accident. "Clearly," he said, wrapping up, "the news that got back down here had erroneously reported that Eddie Turner had died. Yeah, I almost did." He gave out a nervous laugh. "But, as you can see, somehow I didn't."

Dottie continued to eye him with skepticism, but then she seemed to melt. "Oh, my goodness, Eddie, I'm so sorry. You can understand, though, how we'd be suspicious." She gave him a tender grandmotherly look and reached out and touched his hand. "I'm so glad you're still with us. And I'm so glad you're here."

Chapter 4

A half-hour later, Ed had found another chair against a wall next to one of the refreshments tables at the rear of the Grand Ballroom, a large, high-ceiling multi-purpose meeting space, illuminated by a dozen chandeliers. Didn't such rooms always have grandiose names to help the hotel promote itself as a conference center? It looked like a cross between a dining room at Buckingham Palace and a high school gym. Balloons and colorful ribbons hung between the chandeliers, and the room was abuzz with the chatter and laughter of at least a hundred attendees, almost masking the background of Otis Redding singing "Sittin' on the Dock of the Bay."

He had tried to mingle when he'd first come in. Although there was seating at tables around the periphery of the room, most of his classmates were standing, gathered in small, animated, laughing groups. He'd gotten a cup of fruit punch from the refreshments table, so he'd have something to do with the hand that wasn't grasping the cane, then made his way from one small group to the next, where he'd stood nodding and smiling, trying to fit in. But for the most part, no one took much notice of him. This would have been a good time to check his phone—pretend there was an important text or incoming call—if he had his phone.

Now in his chair in the rear, he felt relieved to have the pressure to mingle lifted from him for the time being. He closed his eyes and sang quietly, transporting himself to that lonely place on the dock, with Otis, wasting time.

His mind returned to his stolen car. What was he going to do about that? He sighed and ran a hand through his hair. He pushed this worry away by surveying his surroundings. Reunions are odd things, he thought, perhaps the closest thing to a time machine that we can experience. They're like a movie played backwards until all the characters are where they were at the beginning, except they've all aged fifty years. All together in one place again, perhaps in the same relationships, or at least hoping for that. All together: the beauties and the bullies, the bashful and the brains. *But can everything be rolled back so simply?*

He wondered what Ship would say about this. Ship taught the only upper-level quantum physics course at Muir, and students raved about his lectures. He was always talking about time travel, black holes and dark matter. Ship understood such things at a scholarly level, and even though there was no research ongoing at Muir, he kept abreast of the hot physics topics in *Physical Review Letters* and all the most important physics journals. Sure, Ed had taught physics also, but after he got his master's at Davis, he dropped out of the doctoral program when the teaching opportunity at Muir opened up. He considered himself a moderately competent physicist, did a passable job teaching the freshman survey courses for non-majors, although he had seldom been entrusted with one of the upper division courses. He wasn't in the same league with Ship.

No, reunions are more than time machines, Ed concluded. But just what they were, he wasn't sure. It's hard to understand how that small four-year slice of your life could be so important, even to a guy like Ed, who'd had a very limited social life in high school. He could still remember the names of many of his fellow students, could remember events and teachers, like it was yesterday. In the years since, he'd known many people and experienced many things. But the memories of these events had mostly faded in comparison with his memories of high school. What was he doing between the ages of thirty and thirty five? That period was just a blur now. But he could still remember with clarity that day in PE when he'd hit the home run, the time Laura Brantley blew him a kiss in geometry, getting a perfect score on the US History exam. He could see the faces of almost all of his teachers: Mr. Sloan, the brawny assistant football coach who also taught chemistry, probably reluctantly; Mrs. Jarvis, the jovial civics teacher; and Miss Stewart—ah, Miss Stewart—his highly tense but brilliant senior English teacher.

Ed took another sip of the fruit punch, as the MC for the evening stood at a floor mic across the room. The woman, wearing a long gown that seemed too formal for the occasion, said, "Hey, Titans, welcome to this long-awaited evening!" A smattering of applause. "Sherrie Blanton here—oh, I used to be Sherrie Lewis back in school." She laughed nervously and pushed her pink cat-eye glasses back up onto her nose, then said, "Anyhoo, glad to see you all again. I've been put in charge of collecting memories from '68 for tonight—you know, movies, music, news from back in the day and all that— and I'll be sharing some of them as the night goes on. Jerry over there—" She gestured toward a bald guy in the corner, who waved enthusiastically—"he'll be playing some of our golden moldies from 1968. Hope you enjoy. And maybe there'll even be some dancing later on.

"So, anyhoo, I'm up here a little sooner than I expected to be, because I've got a very special announcement. An awesome announcement, really."

One guy hollered out, "We're going to be eighteen again?" The room roared.

Sherrie raised a hand to quell the laughter, then said, "No, seriously. One of our fellow Titans, who we thought had left us fifty years ago, just out of high school, is actually here tonight. Eddie Turner, everybody!" Suddenly, a spotlight came out of nowhere and found Ed. "Turns out he was only injured in a car accident all those years ago up in Northern California, and somehow the news had reached us that he'd died. Let's give him a big Sentinel High welcome!"

Good grief, how he wanted to crawl off into a hole right now. Everybody applauded.

Ed stood, with considerable effort, feeling unstable on the new cane. He did his best to offer a carefree, sure-glad-to-be-here smile and hoisted his punch cup in a toast.

While the spotlight was still on him, Sherrie said, "So, Titans, what with Eddie's appearance tonight, I thought it would be a good time to remind everyone that 1968 was the debut of the movie, drum roll please, *Night of the Living Dead*!"

The room exploded with laughter. Eyes turned toward Ed again, and he wished he knew how to walk like a zombie. He swayed slowly side to side, doing his best imitation—pathetic, he was sure—of a stumbling zombie. The room roared again. Ed lifted his cup of punch again in another toast.

Then, everyone turned back toward their conversations, and Ed sat back down with great relief, wishing he was home with Carmen or working out on the Precor.

"Man, were you really dead?"

Ed turned toward the voice. A kid in a white smock over blue jeans stared at him, mouth open. "No, it was just a misunderstanding."

"Misunderstanding? Don't see how you can have a misunderstanding about being dead ... I was hoping that maybe you really were a zombie."

"You doof," said a girl next to him. "There's no such things as zombies. You know, Shane, you'd do well to pay a little more attention to school and a little less on your freaking video games." Then she turned toward Ed and said, "Oh, I'm Jazz and this is Shane. We're from Sentinel, and we're here helping with the refreshments tonight. Part of DECA."

"Nice to meet you, Jazz. And Shane. I'm Ed." He stood again and leaned with both hands on his cane. "DECA?"

"Yeah, it's a leadership program at school, focuses of hospitality and stuff like that." Jazz also wore a white smock over black jeans. Her almost-black eyes peered from underneath blue hair, cropped tight around her pale face, and she had multiple small earrings along each ear. She was thin and probably no more than five feet tall.

"So, anyway, I'm afraid I'm not a zombie. Although I feel like one sometimes." He added, in response to the quizzical look from Shane, "Just kidding."

"No problem," said Shane.

"Look, here's the deal. Right after high school I moved up north, north of San Francisco, when my dad took a new job. That fall, I drove up toward Lake Tahoe ..."

"Never been there. Heard it's cool," said Shane.

"Ha, actually, I've never been there, either. Hit a patch of ice. Totaled the car and almost totaled me. Just about died. It's why I still have a hard time walking."

"That really sucks, man," said Jazz.

Funny. Ed had spent so many years teaching kids not much older than Shane and Jazz. He felt more comfortable with them than he did with his own classmates.

Jazz asked, "Was anybody else hurt? I mean, like killed or anything?"

"No, thank goodness. When my car went out of control, I just narrowly missed another car, but they got away uninjured." He closed his eyes. "God, I can still see it in my mind, even after all these years."

"I'm glad you made it out okay." Jazz glanced down at the cane. "Well, almost okay."

"But I'm not gonna lie, man," added Shane, "I'm still a little disappointed that you're not a zombie."

They all laughed.

"Hello there," said the voice behind him.

Ed turned to see Ellen Barnes. He still recognized her, even after fifty years. Sure, she had aged. She seemed shorter than he remembered, probably was, and she was no longer the skinny girl she'd been in high school. But he recognized her eyes, those warm eyes. Her hair was gray and stylishly cut—did they call this a bob? It reminded him of Diane Keaton. She was obviously not into hair coloring. But her skin was smooth and bore few wrinkles. She still had full lips, like he remembered. "Geez, Ellen, it's nice to see you," he said and extended a hand, which she did not shake.

Ellen stepped up close to him and looked hard into his eyes. She was not smiling. "So, who are you really?" she said.

"Huh? Guess I've changed a bit." He forced a laugh.

"All this talk of you only being injured is great, but the only thing is: you're not Eddie Turner." She now pursed her lips, like she was angry. "And that pisses me off."

Jazz and Shane had now headed out into the crowd with platters of hors d'oeuvres. "Ellen, I really am Ed Turner," he said.

While he spoke, she was shaking her head violently. Then she blurted out, "How dare you ...." She stammered for a moment, then added, "I went to Eddie Turner's funeral."

Chapter 5

E d couldn't breathe. *What the ...?* "You went to my funeral?"

Ellen backed away a step. She seemed to be fuming. "No, asshole. I went to Eddie Turner's funeral."

Ed felt a rush of shame that even in this tense encounter he was checking out how sexy Ellen Barnes looked. She wore black tights, with a colorful silk tank top under a soft-gray flowing cardigan. Maroon ankle boots. Tasteful. Professional. Feminine. He cleared his throat. "But, I really am Eddie Turner." He tried to lighten the mood by adding, "Always have been."

Ellen seemed to ignore his words. "I was the only one from Sentinel who went to the funeral, as far as I knew. Your ... I mean Eddie's ... parents were there, sobbing. Eddie's casket was there. There was even a photo, his yearbook photo, in front of the casket." She took a deep breath. "Get the picture, creep?" She paused, perhaps expecting a response from him, but then continued, "I'll admit, you do kinda look like him. You must have studied up. Is this some kind of sick prank or something? Are you filming this?" She looked around the ballroom. "Anyway ... whoever you are ... you need to know that at least one person here knows the truth. You are not Eddie Turner. Because Eddie Turner died."

Then she stomped away.

Ed needed to sit. He was breathing hard as he collapsed back into his chair. *She went to my funeral? She saw my parents? They were sobbing?*

Maybe this was all just a dream, but it was too real. And if this was a dream, it would sure be a good time to wake up. He knew it wasn't a dream. It felt too crisp and clear. He ran his hand over the ridges of his corduroy jacket, watched the light reflecting off the balloons hanging from the chandeliers. No, this wasn't a dream.

But then what was happening? This couldn't have all been caused by a TGA, could it? A hallucination? Maybe. He didn't know much about hallucinations. Or maybe dementia was setting in. He knew something about that. His mother, now 92, had been getting progressively worse for the past five years. During his visits to her at the nursing home, she'd be convinced that she was in some other place, usually a place from her past, that she could still drive, that people long dead were still alive. *That could be it. Dementia.* But doesn't that come on slowly, like over years, as it had with his mother?

Or maybe it was something else. Maybe there really was something bizarre going on with space and time here. How else could he explain what Ellen Barnes just told him? How else could he explain the strange events at Villa Solana? No, this couldn't all be the result of a TGA episode. But maybe a TGA was just the tip of the iceberg, just the hint of a person going into—who knows?—some kind of alternate reality.

He needed to talk to Ship. He understood more than most about all this strange shit. He wished now that he'd paid more attention when Ship would get on a roll at one of their breakfasts, go on and on about quantum entanglement or string theory or a host of other mind-blowing topics with which science was still struggling. He was suddenly aware that his hands were trembling. He lifted his head toward the ceiling and closed his eyes. Maybe he really did die fifty years ago.

Chapter 6

Ed opened his eyes when he heard Sherrie Blanton back up at the microphone. "Hey, Titans, as promised, I'm reminding you of a few of the big events that took place in 1968. Of course, the biggest was all of us graduating." She paused for laughter that didn't come. Just a few polite chuckles. "Anyhoo, yeah, I know there was a lot of bad stuff that happened back then, but I'm not going to talk about all that. There was a lot of good stuff, too." She looked down at an index card in her hand. "You probably don't remember, but 1968 was the year the first Big Mac was served. And it was the year that *Hawaii Five-O* debuted. Geez, I've still got a crush on … on … oh, heck, what's his name?"

A voice from the crowd hollered, "Jack Lord."

"Oh, yes," Sherrie cooed. "Jack Lord. I loved him." She giggled, then looked back down at the index card. "And it was the year that *60 Minutes* first appeared on TV." She paused, checking the card again. "Okay, that's it for now. All I've gotta say is, 'Book 'em, Dano.'" She was still laughing as she sat back down.

Ed shifted in his chair. Big Macs. *Hawaii Five-O*. *60 Minutes*. These were all real things he remembered, part of his reality. Maybe Ellen's talk about his funeral was just nonsense. He had no way of knowing she hadn't become some kind of nut case. But those warm eyes, green and clear. She sure didn't look like a nut case.

The chatter in the room had barely resumed when a man stepped up to the microphone, where Sherrie had just been. "Excuse me, folks. I'm Jeff Marshall. Some of you may not remember me, but I don't really give a rat's ass if you don't." There were a few nervous laughs in the room. Ed remembered Jeff from some class—he couldn't remember which one.

Jeff continued. "Sherrie said she didn't want to talk about the depressing stuff, but for some of us that depressing stuff was really important. Yeah, I don't want to talk about it, either, but that doesn't mean I can get it out of my mind. So, here's some charming little factoids for you. 1968 was when our country's presence in Vietnam peaked. That's right, over a half million of our young people were fighting over there. And nearly 17,000 of them died that year. And, oh yeah, remember the My Lai Massacre? That was 1968, also. Don't want to rain on your parade, but that's what was happening."

As Jeff Marshall began to return to his seat, an angry voice from the crowd bellowed. "Yeah, but your sorry ass apparently survived."

Jeff Marshall returned to the microphone. He looked down for a while before speaking. "So, thanks for that edifying comment." He was quiet for another moment, then said, "Here's the deal. I've got prostate cancer. Now, I know that a lot of you old farts have had prostate cancer, too, so no big deal, really. But mine's Stage 4. And I got it because of Agent Orange in Vietnam. So, yeah, I am a sorry ass, like you said. But I haven't really survived." Then he sat down.

There was quiet in the room. Then the chatter slowly began to build again, and within five minutes it was like Jeff Marshall's disturbing rant had never happened.

Until a woman leaning on a walker made her way to the microphone. "Hello?" She tapped the head of the mic to test if it was on, and it generated a shrill noise that caused several people to squeal in discomfort. "Sorry about that," the woman said. "I'm Vivian Thomas, and after Jeff's comments I just had to say this. 1968 was also the year that Martin Luther King and Bobby Kennedy both were gunned down. Heavy stuff, huh? So, sure, let's not think about all that. Let's all grab another Big Mac, settle in for an episode of *Hawaii Five-O* and chill out. Sorry, but I just had to say that."

Jerry, the DJ, apparently sensing the need to lighten the mood, immediately cranked up the volume on "Harper Valley PTA."

Ed stood and leaned forward onto his cane, stretching his back that had stiffened in the folding metal chair. Vietnam. Martin Luther King and Bobby Kennedy. As sad as these things were, they were part of his reality, more evidence that he wasn't in some scene from *The Twilight Zone.*

He let out a sigh of relief as he began to make his way around the perimeter of the room, pondering the disturbing comments of Vivian Thomas and Jeff Marshall. He had to smile, as he sang along, under his breath, with Jeannie C. Riley, about socking it to the institution.

Then the memory of that night returned, the night Bobby Kennedy was shot. June 5, 1968. It was a Wednesday, just three days before his high school graduation ceremony. It was late, after midnight, and Ed couldn't sleep. He lay in bed, listening to his clock radio. An AM oldies station was playing Patsy Cline's "Crazy," when the music was interrupted with the announcement that Kennedy had been shot at the Ambassador Hotel in LA, just thirty miles from Ed's home.

He'd sat up in bed and dialed through the stations trying to find more information. Then he woke his parents and told them. Kennedy would hold on for another twenty-four hours before dying.

Ed had not followed politics closely when he was in high school, but this event really shook him. Kennedy was so young, was headed for the Democratic nomination, and it happened so close by. He recalled an RFK quote that he loved. "Only those who dare to fail greatly can ever achieve greatly." He shook his head, wishing these words described his own life.

He paused to take in a display of school photos from 1968. Football heroes, prom queens, a group photo of cheerleaders. There was one of the Inklings, a group that produced a poetry journal for the school, and he leaned in close to study the image of Ellen Barnes, sitting behind a desk and holding a pen, looking creative.

Ed moved on to another display of photos, titled Fallen Titans. Here were the classmates who had died. Before he could study the photos, a loud voice behind him bellowed, "Hey, Turner, glad to see you didn't croak."

No one says croak anymore. Ed turned toward the voice. It was Chuck Barlow. He had known Chuck all the way from grammar school through high school. They hadn't been close friends, but then Ed hadn't had any close friends. He remembered Chuck as a big, barrel-chested guy in high school, but now the barrel extended well below his chest. He wore his bright, floral short-sleeve shirt untucked over Levis and held a plastic cup of cola in one hand. "Good to see you, Chuck."

"Bitchin' party, don't you think? Can you dig it?"

Bitchin? Dig? Where's this guy been for the last fifty years? Ed shrugged. "So, what are you up to these days, Chuck?"

"Same ol' shit, man." Ed couldn't remember or more likely never knew if Chuck went to college. "Still live within walking distance of Sentinel," he laughed. Chuck had a full face and a red nose indicative of significant alcohol use. His gray hair looked slicked down with some sort of gel. "How about you?"

"I'm retired now, live up north a few hundred miles."

Chuck grinned as he stepped to Ed's side, so they could face the room together. "Hey, these old chicks still look pretty good, don't you think?"

Ed nodded uncomfortably.

"Hell, is that Brenaman over there? God, check out that babe he's with. Outta sight. Is she stacked or what?"

Ed remembered Roger Brenaman as a political kid. Not that much of a student, but always running for class council or some such thing. And he'd usually gotten elected, too, probably because most other kids didn't want the job. Ed nodded at Chuck and began to edge away.

"Maybe she's his trophy wife. Must be twenty years younger." Chuck shook his head in disbelief as he laughed. "So, three facts about trophy wives. Listen up, Turner, some Barlow wisdom here." He took a big swig from his cup. "First, everybody hates trophy wives. Second, every woman would like to think she could be one. Third, every man would like to think he could get one." Now, he bellowed even harder.

Ed looked around, hoping no one else was listening in. He tried to shift the subject. "So, are you married, Chuck?" *Maybe not a good question.*

"Copacetic, man, copacetic." He took another swig. "Hell, me and the old lady are doin okay. She'd be here but her shows are on tonight." Then he lowered his voice, like he was about to share a confidence. "Party's a blast, but no booze." He frowned, but then a smile slowly broke across his face. "But some of us have taken matters into our own hands, if you get my drift." He lifted his cup, then looked around like others might be watching. They weren't. "Tell you what. We got a stash of Wild Turkey over by my table. Smuggled it in. Come on over if you want a little real refreshment."

"I'll keep that in mind, Chuck."

"Well, gotta boogie. See ya later." He toasted Ed with his plastic cup, then headed off into the room.

Ed shook his head again, unsure of what to make of that interaction. It would be easy to look down on Chuck Barlow, but then Chuck at least had a wife. He only had Carmen.

He turned back toward the display of Fallen Titans. A large tri-fold of posters featured senior class photos of classmates who had died. He did a quick count. *Good God, seventy-four.* He recalled that his graduating class was around 300. Must be a hundred or so attendees here tonight. He wondered what had happened to all these kids—74 out of 300, almost a quarter of his class. That seemed like a high number, but after all they were now 67 or 68, so maybe this was expected.

There were no captions under the photos, just the names, no information about when these people had died or how they died. He thought about Jeff Marshall's words and wondered how many of them had died in Vietnam. He scanned through the photos, shaking his head each time he came to someone he'd known.

There was Evelyn Holiday, the beauty queen and the object of many of the male students' lust. And Ronnie Jefferds, a class clown—Ed didn't realize he'd graduated. There was Sammy Sitzman, who kids had teased. He had been short, with thick glasses and a prominent nose. Ed had joined the others in the teasing; he'd felt bad about it, but never stood up and protested. Years later, he was still ashamed of that. There was Kim Folger, a big, tough bully. Ed had been afraid of him, kept his distance. Jenny Hollingsworth—hadn't she been valedictorian or something? Brilliant, good-looking in a sophisticated, bookish way. And Judy Ishihara, quiet and pretty—she'd been in several of his classes.

Ed had to catch his breath when he came to Danny Rogers. He hadn't seen him since high school. Lost track of him, like he'd lost track of everyone else. He and Danny used to argue about baseball, while they played wiffle ball in Danny's front yard. Danny was a Dodgers fan and Ed was an Angels fan. Ed bit his lip, as the fingers of his right hand instinctively curled into the grip he used to throw his deadly sinker ball. *Oh, Danny.*

Just below Danny's photo, there it was. Eddie Turner. Ed let out a long, troubled sigh, as he gazed upon his own senior photo.

He hadn't seen that photo in years. He leaned in closer. It didn't really look like him. He was wearing a suit. He wasn't sure he'd ever worn a suit before that senior photo day. He was positioned at an angle to the camera, so he'd be looking to his side to see the camera—the effect was like you'd surprised him and he'd turned to see you. He had slicked down hair and black horn-rims, and he was better looking than he remembered. The smile was as phony as they come—he looked confident and sophisticated, ready to graduate and charge off to take on exciting new endeavors. *What a crock.* He looked like a guy who'd be a success, but, of course, his picture wound up on this board.

Sure, it was just an old black and white photo from years ago, but it shook him. Was it possible he really had died? How do you add up all the strange data: the police unable to find a record of his existence, Dottie's conviction that he had died, Ellen's claim about attending his funeral?

Ed turned and faced the room. If it was true that he had died, and yet here he was alive—no, he couldn't buy into that explanation. He was a physicist, and a physicist doesn't accept just any wild idea that comes floating by.

But if it were somehow true, then what about the reality he had lived in for the past fifty years? How many of the people laughing tonight in this room were actually dead in the reality from which he'd just come a few hours ago? And how many of those Fallen Titans on the poster display were, like him, still alive?

He felt suddenly wobbly, and he thought he might faint. He leaned on the quad cane with both hands to steady himself.

Then another thought came to him, and this made him even more unsteady. If this far-fetched alternate reality explanation were, in fact, true, then was he trapped permanently in this reality? Stuck here forever? No home, no identity, no car, no money. Not even a change of clothes. A chill swept over him, like an arctic wind had just blown into the Grand Ballroom. He had no idea how he'd gotten here. He had no idea how he might get back.

Ed was hyperventilating. He needed to get back to his chair. Turning toward the other side of the room, he realized too late that the toe of his shoe was caught in the support legs of the quad cane, and down he went.

He wasn't hurt, but he was embarrassed, which he'd already had enough of tonight. He scrambled to stand, but he couldn't get up.

Suddenly, strong arms lifted him upright. It was the football player type he'd met at the check-in table. "You okay, Eddie?" the man asked.

Ed adjusted the lapels of his sport coat, trying to reclaim some dignity. "Thanks. Yeah, I'm fine. I just got my feet tangled in this damn cane. Kind of embarrassing."

"You shouldn't feel embarrassed."

"Well, you're a strong athlete."

The man laughed. "What you don't know is that I just had both knees replaced last year. Before that, I was worse off than you for ten years."

"You played football, right?" It was a lame question, but it was all Ed could come up with.

"Yeah. Denny Jones." He extended a hand.

Ed shook Denny's hand. He now vaguely remembered him. He hadn't hung out with the jocks. "That's cool. I never played sports in high school."

"You know," he said, "that was a long time ago." There was look of resignation in the man's eyes. "I'm sorry, Eddie, that I came on so strong back at the check-in table. I really believed you had died. I mean, I remember reading about it in the paper, or I thought I remembered it." He shrugged. "So, you can imagine …." His voice trailed off.

Actually, Ed couldn't imagine. He couldn't begin to imagine what had happened to him tonight. And he couldn't imagine what to do about it.

Chapter 7

Denny walked with Ed back to his chair by the refreshments table, keeping a supportive hand, palm up, near his elbow, just in case another fall might be imminent.

"So, this is where I'm hanging out," said Ed, taking his seat.

"Hey, why aren't you out there mingling with the crowd? You're missing out, you know."

"I'll get out there in a bit. I just need to take it easy, after my topple."

"Understood," said Denny. "So how come I don't remember you from high school? I mean, I remember reading about Eddie Turner ... I mean, like I said ... you ... getting killed." He cleared his throat. "This is still kinda weird, if you ask me."

Denny was a huge guy, must have been in the offensive line or something. He was at least six-four, with broad shoulders, but the hint of a flabby gut. "I didn't get around much back then," said Ed. He stared off into the room, like he was sizing things up.

It had always been difficult for Ed to make small talk, especially with strangers. On a screen behind the microphone, a video without sound flashed various clips from the 1968 LA sports scene. The legendary announcer Vin Scully was interviewing Dodger great Don Drysdale after some game. Then a clip showed Chick Hearn doing play-by-play for the Lakers and Jerry West and Elgin Baylor making some fantastic plays. In another clip, Johnny Wooden spoke with an interviewer, probably after his UCLA Bruins had won yet another national basketball title. "Some great sports memories from back then," he said.

Denny was also now caught up in the video. "Dang, those were the days, huh?"

It's funny, thought Ed, how following sports had been such a foundation in his life, how it could provide companionship and connection, even when you were lonely. It also provided a vehicle for men to talk with each other, when more difficult topics might be too challenging. Ed cleared his throat, feeling the pressure to be social. "So, what are you up to these days, Denny?"

Denny returned his attention to Ed. "Retired from the Tustin Fire Department about fifteen years ago. Medical retirement. Damned knees—too much football, I guess. Since then, it's been hard to find something that really challenged me." He leaned against the wall, looking casual and relaxed. He had a broad face with sagging jowls and a red forehead that sloped up into his silvery crew cut. "Hell, I've done a lot of things, volunteered here and there, even been a greeter at Walmart." He let out a big laugh and slapped the wall with a meaty hand. "Tried selling real estate, thought I might be really good at that, you know, meeting people and all that. But I didn't really have what it took to make deals." He shook his head, like he still hadn't figured that out. "Plus, I hated it. Now I work down at Home Depot. I'm the guy walking the aisles in an orange vest. Love it. If you ever want to know about toggle bolts, hey, I'm your guy." They shared the laughter, then Denny said, "What about you?"

Ed squirmed in his chair. His back was already beginning to stiffen up again. "Yeah, as you might imagine, the accident set me back. I'd been enrolled in college, but had to drop out after I'd missed so much time recuperating. Took me a couple of years to get back to college, and that was after several nosedives in my life. But I finally got a degree in physics, went off to Davis, got a master's, then I taught at Muir College. Ever hear of it?"

Denny shook his head.

"Anyway, I taught there until two years ago, when I retired." Ed looked out into the room again, pondering if he should say more. "Actually, I wasn't quite ready to retire, but the powers that be kind of urged me to." He was surprised at how forthcoming he was being, sharing such things with a stranger.

Denny let out a cynical grunt. "Yeah, tell me about it. It's crazy—you spend your whole life busting your ass, never having a chance to really kick back and do the things you'd like to do. You dream about retirement, count the days like the guy in prison who X's the days off on the calendar. Then it finally comes, and suddenly you don't know what to do with yourself. You know what I mean?"

"Sure do."

"You don't have anyone expecting you to be in a certain place at a certain time every morning. People expecting you to show up. From one day to the next, it all changes, and nobody cares. If you're still lounging around in your bathrobe in the middle of the afternoon, nobody gives a shit. Nobody calls you up and says, hey, Denny, where are you? We need you here. All of a sudden, you're on your own, and that freedom may sound nice, but suddenly you've got to figure out what to do with your life. It ain't as pretty as it seems.

"Anyway, pardon the sermon. You said you had some nosedives, Ed. What was that about?"

"So, I couldn't walk. I spent way too much of that time feeling sorry for myself, I guess. Got depressed. Then I had a little struggle with alcohol during those years, too." Maybe he was spilling his guts because it took him away from worrying about his immediate crisis.

"Yeah, I know about that," said Denny, slowly shaking his head. "You noticed they're not serving booze here tonight? Pretty wise move. There's probably a lot of folks here like us."

Ed nodded.

"But it sounds like you whipped those demons, Ed. Good for you."

"Sometimes, it's hard to feel like I've whipped much of anything. But at least, I got up on my feet again, literally. I can drive a car." He gave out a little chuckle. "A helluva lot of PT and exercise. You see me stumbling around here tonight, but actually that's pretty good compared to where I used to be."

Denny's attentive green eyes appeared to be genuinely taking in what Ed said. "You married?"

"No. I was married once. Back in my twenties. Lasted two years. I was a really bad husband." Ed shook his head and gave out a self-deprecating chuckle. "All my feeling sorry for myself. It's amazing that Diane put up with me that long. How about you?"

Denny scratched his chin with a forefinger. "Not presently. Been married twice, divorced twice. Hell, I came from a straight-laced family. I was the first person in my family to ever get divorced." His green eyes twinkled. "And also the second. Got a couple of kids that I'm very proud of, though."

They chatted for a few more minutes, then Denny said, "Well, I think Dottie's probably got some more chores for me. Not sure why I ever agreed to be on this committee. Too much work." He laid a hand on Ed's shoulder, then headed back into the crowd.

Ed sat back in his chair, rocking it slowly on two legs. Jerry had put on "Those Were The Days My Friend." He closed his eyes and sang along softly.

"How 'bout an hors d'oeuvre, Ed?" Jazz held out a metal platter.

"Hmm, don't mind if I do," he said, selecting a small diagonally cut sandwich that looked like it was filled with salmon or pate. "Thank you, Jazz." He took a bite. "Say, Jazz, I was wondering. Might I use your phone to make call? Mine got stolen tonight. I really—"

"No problem, Ed." She handed Ed her iPhone.

Ed had hoped Jazz might step away, so he could make his call in privacy, but she stayed right next to him. He checked his wrist, forgetting again that the Garmin was gone, then he checked the time on the phone. Eight. Ship went to bed early, but hopefully he was still up. He tapped in Ship's number.

"This is Shipley Jameson." His voice sounded sleepy.

"Ship, it's Ed."

"Who?"

"Ed Turner."

There was a pause on the other end, like Ship was uncertain what to say.

"It's Ed Turner, Ship. Can you hear me?" He looked down at the phone to check the signal. Five bars.

"What can I do for you?" He sounded formal.

"Ship, it's Ed. I'm at the reunion. I need to talk."

"Uh … I think you have the wrong number, my friend. I don't know an Ed … uh, what was the last name again?"

Oh, shit. "Ship, listen, it's Ed Turner. I've known you for thirty years. I need to talk to you."

There was silence for a moment on the other end. "Look, I said I don't know any Ed Turner. Why don't you—"

"Ship, you teach upper division QM at Muir. I taught physics there, too. You graduated from MIT. I know who I'm—"

"Okay, friend, this is getting weird. I'm going to have to hang up now, okay?"

"No, wait, Ship. It's your old friend, Ed. I'm in a jam. I think I've gone into an alternate reality or something I can't understand. I—"

"I'm hanging up now. Please don't—"

"Ship, listen, there's some screwy physics going on here, and I need to talk to you about it. Please—"

"Good night." There was a click on the other end.

Ed's mouth hung open, and his eyes turned toward the high ceiling of the room. Without looking at Jazz, he held the phone out for her to take back.

"Holy crap, Ed, you look terrible. I'd be lying if I said I wasn't kinda worried about you. What can I do?" Jazz's black eyes sparkled like polished onyx. She shuffled from one foot to the other.

"I'll be all right," he said. "That was just an uncomfortable call to an old friend."

But it was clear to Ed that it wasn't an old friend he'd been speaking to, not in this reality. And no, he wouldn't be all right.

Chapter 8

He pressed his head between his hands, like he had the mother of all migraines, like somehow he might squeeze some clarity into his beleaguered brain. *I've got to get a handle on this.*

There were the immediate issues he needed to deal with. His stolen things. His car. He sighed, remembering the fruitless interaction with the police. His credit card. He should report it. But he suspected what the answer would be: "Sorry, sir, we have no record of …" *Screw that.*

So, maybe his things hadn't been stolen, after all. Maybe if he did not exist in this reality, there could be no wallet, car, phone, smart watch—things connected to an identity that perhaps no longer existed. He recalled how his mother, as her dementia had first become a problem, used to worry about, in her words, losing her buttons. He almost laughed. He was losing his buttons.

Jazz still stood next to him, probably afraid to leave him alone. He asked to borrow her phone again and called his cell, then called the landline at his home.

No answer on the cell. A robo-voice intercepted his call to the landline: "This number is no longer in service." He pulled the phone away from his ear and stared at the screen. It was the correct number. *What the* ...? Was his home gone? Geez, he had hated that place. The one-bedroom condo, two blocks off the main drag in Cloverdale, was claustrophobic. It hadn't been updated since the seventies, at least. But it was all he could afford on his modest teaching salary and now Social Security and his meager pension from Muir. He had frequently complained about his condo to Ship at breakfast, and Ship always listened patiently, although it was clear that he had little sympathy for Ed's whining. God, how he'd like to see that place right now.

The best part of the small condo was that its almost-non-existent backyard had enough room for a small garden. Enough space for a few vegetables—three Celebrity tomato plants and two cherry tomato plants, a tiny patch of radishes and carrots and a dozen or so sweet potato plants. The tomatoes, especially, needed to be picked, and all the plants needed watering. He'd planned to be away for only a day, two at most—who would care for his plants? But his real showpiece was what rimmed the small vegetable patch—as many ornamentals as he could squeeze in, mostly annuals. He'd spent many peaceful afternoons in the small garden. Even with his bum legs, he could drop down to his knees onto the foam kneeling pad, then lift himself up, when needed, with his forearm crutches. Crutches that no longer existed.

All that may be behind him now, if he could not find his way back—wake up, come to his senses, stumble through some kind of sci-fi portal, or whatever the hell was required to reconnect him with his real life.

He was an intelligent and educated man, even though possibly delusional. He should be able to get a handle on this.

His audible sigh caused Jazz to inquire again about his well-being. "I'm okay, Jazz, really," he said.

It must be related to the stress caused by his arrival at the reunion, but was there more? Maybe going back in time through memory and nostalgia had also taken him back to those defining moments of the accident. There had been a moment on that day—he recalled it with clarity—as he had looked down at his crushed legs beneath the collapsed steering wheel and broken glass, when he considered staying in the car, a brief moment when he feared that by moving, he might injure himself more. That it was better to wait for help to come. But he had rejected that idea. The smell of gasoline had driven him to pull himself out, through pain that even the adrenalin couldn't mask.

Two lives, both ruined. Eddie had stayed with the car and died. Ed had crawled away to live, but with injuries that would make him at times wish he had died.

This all had to be bullshit. Somehow, his mind was being tricked—maybe a bizarre extension of the TGA, maybe a crazy Ebenezer Scrooge nightmare, hallucination, sudden-onset dementia or some weird form of Alzheimer's, whatever. These explanations also offered hope that he might soon wake up, that he might emerge from this terror.

His old life—his boring, meaningless life: he longed for it now.

Chapter 9

Ed again leaned his chair back against the wall and surveyed the room. The crowded room, the noisy people, many of whom were vaguely familiar from long ago, provided a welcomed, if momentary distraction from his predicament. Jerry was on a raised platform across the room, like a real DJ, tapping in selections on his phone. In the old days, he would have been spinning 45s on a turntable. When Jerry caught eyes with Ed, he flashed a hearty smile and waved. Short, stocky and bald, Jerry looked like he smoked cigars and had probably been a hell of a salesman. He wore a white dress shirt—open at the collar and with sleeves rolled up—and wide, colorful suspenders. All Ed could recall of Jerry in high school was that he played trumpet, was a leader of the pep band, and seemed to be popular with the girls. The next song came on. "Mrs. Robinson."

The clusters of people had begun migrating to tables around the room. Ed noticed Ellen Barnes, talking in a group. She glanced his way, as if she'd felt his eyes on her, shot him a menacing glare, then turned away. Ed hoisted his punch glass to no one, as he sang softly, 'So here's to you, Mrs. Barnes ...."

Time to refill the old punch glass. Hell, he was at his fiftieth reunion—he should be out there socializing. Yes, maybe he was in some alternate reality, but these were the people he'd gone to high school with, they were real—he'd likely never see them again. He stood and headed toward the refreshments table. *This quad cane isn't too bad*, he thought. Maybe he should re-evaluate the forearm crutches when he got back. He shook his head. Would he get back?

"Oh, Eddie." He recognized her immediately. Lila Panovsky. He'd been with her in the Shutterbugs, hardly an original name for the photo club. He recalled his senior annual, which had an index of all the extracurricular activities of each senior. The photo club was the only activity under his name.

His first camera was a film camera, a Kodak Signet. It had been his father's and it was old when Ed more-or-less took ownership of it. His dad had purchased it used, years before, but had never really gotten interested in photography, so it sat around the house for a long time. Ed started using the camera about the time he was a freshman, and he would buy film when he could afford the three bucks for a 24-exposure roll of Kodachrome.

He'd joined the Shutterbugs to learn how to use the camera—there was no instruction manual—and that started his love for photography.

Ed turned toward Lila. She'd been an overweight redhead with thick glasses back then, but what was most distinctive about her was that friendly smile and beautiful, perfect teeth. Her dad was a dentist. Tonight she was much more slender and no longer wore glasses. Her hair was colored red and pulled behind her head. The long colorful dress looked tie-dyed. She reminded Ed of the old hippie who ran the bakery in Cloverdale, where he'd pick up fresh bread on his way home from breakfast with Ship. He wouldn't have recognized her tonight, if it weren't for the great smile. "Lila, it's good to see you."

"Eddie, what a surprise to see you, too. Here. Stand right here with me. I want to get a selfie of me with the dead guy." She howled, as Ed managed a weak smile.

After the shot, Ed said, "So, Lila, how have—"

But Lila was already headed back across the room, presumably to upload her photo to social media. Ed continued on to the refreshments table, pondering why he'd ever loved photography in the first place. For photojournalists the goal was recording reality, the unchangeable facts, even though they may be harsh. But photography gave Ed license to soften that reality, reform it into something beautiful. If beauty is truly in the eye of the beholder, then the beholder was the one who interpreted beauty, as well as ugliness, and that gave the beholder great power. If Ed in fact had little power to change the way reality was, at least through photography he could change how reality was perceived.

But the physicist in Ed knew that reality could not be changed. There were cold hard facts that had to be accepted. A shiver pulsed through his body, as he reviewed his situation once more. Cold hard facts, yes, but he—What did Lila call him? The dead guy?—was not yet ready to accept them.

Ed poured another cup of punch, then did a double take when he noticed Jazz sitting next to the refreshments table, reading a book. *What the?* "Jazz, is that what I think it is?"

"What?"

"Your book. It's *The Feynman Lecture Series*, isn't it?"

"You've heard of it?"

"Heard of it? Hell, I read the whole series, but that was a long time ago. Back in the early seventies, I think. Richard Feynman was one of my heroes."

Jazz laid the open book in her lap and looked hard at Ed. "You studied physics?"

"Yeah. I'm a physicist."

"Cool. I've never met a real physicist."

Ed shrugged. He didn't consider himself a *real* physicist. Not like Ship. "So you're reading that book in high school? Geez, I was like a sophomore or junior in college before I read it. You must be really smart."

Jazz rolled her eyes. "Smart? Dunno. It's just volume one. Mrs. Bowman gave it to me to read because I was bored."

"Volume One is the best of the three volumes. Do you like it?"

"I love it. The other physics books I've seen ... they just focus on memorization. Equations for this or that. What's the equation for a falling body? They take the most interesting stuff in the world and make it ... like I said, boring." She closed the book and stared at the cover. "But Feynman. He makes it all so ... what's the word?"

"Intuitive?"

"Yeah, intuitive. He makes it fun." She smiled, a brief smile that quickly dissolved into a serious glower. "So, Ed, what's really going on with you?"

"What do you mean?" He now leaned on his cane with both hands. He wasn't ready to talk to anyone about this mess yet. Except Ship.

"I mean about you being dead and all. I know you gave some lame explanation, and maybe all these people bought it. But then you made that phone call. You were, like weird. Sorry, I didn't mean to eavesdrop."

Ed smirked. Of course she had meant to eavesdrop.

Jazz grinned. "You said something about screwy physics." Her dark eyes bored into him, and she raised her eyebrows, as if she was expecting a non-bullshit answer.

Ed ran his tongue over lips that were suddenly dry. *What the hell*, he thought. *What have I got to lose?* He pulled up a chair and sat next to her, then told her everything: going to Villa Solana, hearing the laughter inside, passing out, thinking he'd been mugged or had a TGA, Cody helping him get to the reunion, Dottie Arnold's shock, Ellen saying that she'd gone to his funeral, Ship not knowing him.

Then he leaned back in his chair. "I don't know what's going on. Maybe I'm having some kind of mental breakdown. Maybe I'll wake up or snap out it soon. Or ..." He shook his head slowly. "Or maybe there's something even more bizarre going on here. Maybe Eddie Turner really did die, and now I'm here, a very much alive Eddie Turner. Cheesh, I'm sorry I told you all this."

Jazz stood, then began to pace. "Sorry, but I can't think and sit still at the same time." She laughed. "First, my real name is Jasmine. Kids started calling me Jazz in school and it just sorta stuck. But my mother named me Jasmine—thought it sounded elegant—so I like it when people call me that. Makes me think of her." She let out a nervous laugh. "Anyway, here's the deal. What if the screwy physics explanation is correct? I mean—look, I know this is freaky and I understand you being scared. But holy crap, Ed, we could be witnessing something totally amazing here, and I've got to admit I'm pretty stoked about that."

Ed had to chuckle. "Sure, maybe you're stoked, but—"

She put up a hand like a stop sign. "Okay. We've got this never-happened-before shit going on, and two physics geeks like us are the only ones who get to witness it. We should be able to figure this out, dontcha think?"

"Look, Jazz ... er ... Jasmine, I like cool physics problems as much as anyone else, but it's my life we're—"

She stopped her pacing and faced him, with hands on her hips. "So, what do you know about imaginary numbers?"

"Huh? What's that got to—"

"I mean like the square root of minus one, you know."

She was talking about the mathematical fact that no number multiplied by itself can be a negative number; simply, a positive number multiplied by a positive number is a positive number, and a negative number multiplied by a negative number is also a positive number. So, mathematicians came up with the concept of imaginary numbers, numbers that when multiplied by themselves would be negative numbers. This would be just an intellectual curiosity, some science fiction thing, if it weren't for the fact that imaginary numbers are necessary to mathematically explain very real phenomena like the propagation of light waves. He let out an impatient breath. "Sure, Jasmine, but where are you going with this?"

"I have no idea." Maybe she should have laughed, but she was deadly serious. "I mean, like when we probe into things we don't understand, that's when we really start to learn things. Right, mister physicist?"

It amazed Ed how quickly Jasmine had accepted his story and was ready to leap into some fantastical, maybe crazy, speculation with him. He recalled reading that when Robert Oppenheimer, the famed Berkeley theoretical physicist and head of the Manhattan Project at Los Alamos, got stuck on some physics question, often he'd bypass consulting a physics colleague and head off down the street to the local schoolyard, where he'd ask children what they thought about his physics problem. Sure, they had no scientific training, but their brains were unconfined by education that oftentimes just taught you what wasn't possible. "Yes, of course, you're right."

"I mean, like there is an infinite number of real numbers, ordinary positive and negative numbers, right? And there is also an infinite number of imaginary numbers. Problem is, the number of apples in the basket is never an imaginary number. Right?" She arched her eyebrows like Ed should be able to see that this was obvious. "And yet, here's that infinite number of imaginary numbers, sitting right alongside all the real numbers. You just don't see them in ordinary life. Hey, I'm just a high school student, so just tell me if I'm full of crap."

Ed smiled. "Actually, you're doing fine. Go ahead."

"So, let's say there's one reality that is defined by real numbers and there's another that's defined by imaginary numbers. These realities could exist side by side, never interacting with each other. Right?"

Ed nodded his head in affirmation, both in amusement and awe.

"So they never interact, unless something really freaky happens, like say, some screwy physics." Jasmine now crossed her arms and smiled like she'd just presented the closing arguments to the case.

"Interesting theory, Jasmine," he said with his patient professorial voice that he'd worked hard to make not sound condescending. "But I don't think that's quite the way numbers work. Imaginary numbers are something artificially constructed in mathematics, a useful tool that helps you make certain kinds of calculations. They're not something that actually exist."

Jasmine chewed the inside of her cheek. "Are you sure?"

Ed let out a hollow laugh. Of course he wasn't sure. Right now, he wasn't sure about anything.

Chapter 10

As Jasmine headed off into the room with another platter of snacks, Ed saw Dottie Arnold heading his way with a purposeful stride. With an extended hand, palm up, her fingers wiggling a come-with-me invitation, she said, "We can't have you just sitting here all by your lonesome."

It would be hard to say no to Dottie. She was like a mother hen rounding up her chicks. She still had that upbeat, friendly look that had guaranteed her popularity in high school and probably her whole life. Her hair, textured in layers of tinted platinum with brown streaks, surrounded her round face like an embrace and dropped to her shoulders—it was obviously an expensive haircut. Her face bore a few wrinkles, sure, and you'd guess she was in her early sixties, but her large blue eyes still twinkled with life. She made you feel good. Ed couldn't help reflecting that he'd never even spoken to Dottie Arnold in high school—she was part of a far more popular crowd back then—and he now regretted this.

"Oh, I'm doing …." Ed began crafting an excuse for his seemingly antisocial behavior, but then said, "Sure, I was getting ready to head over to a table."

Without further words, Ed stood and grasped his cane, while Dottie laced an arm in his. She led him toward the table where Ellen Barnes sat.

Ed stopped before they got to the table. "Maybe this isn't the best—"

Dottie continued to tug on his arm, as she cut him off. "Here's an empty chair, Eddie. Now, why don't you sit down here and enjoy yourself?" She pulled out the chair right next to Ellen.

"Seriously, Dottie, I'm not sure that—"

Dottie gave him a wink, then patted him on the shoulder. "Trust me on this, Eddie. Now have some fun." Before he could further protest, she had turned and left.

Ellen shot him a quick glance as he sat down. "I don't want you near me, okay?" Then she shifted in her chair toward the man on her other side—Ed didn't recognize him—who was talking about real estate investments.

Ed cleared his throat. "Uh, I'm sorry, it wasn't my ..." he said to her back. Her gray cardigan—was it cashmere?—looked soft, and he thought about how it would feel to rest his face against it. He looked for Dottie, but she was gone. He cleared his throat again, then looked around the table with what he thought was his best smile.

"It's good to see you, Eddie," said Frank Castenado, who sat across the table from him. Frank was tall and slender. His brown sport shirt hung loosely on him and his tie was an ultra-narrow model like something out of 1968. Except for the receding gray hair, he hadn't changed much since high school. His dark face, weathered like he'd spent a lot of time outdoors, was serious, a slight upturn at the edge of his mouth being the closest thing to a smile.

Ed nodded toward Frank over the collection of party centerpiece items on the table. Atop a colorful paper table cloth were noisemakers, the kind that blow out a colorful strip; a can of ballpoint pens, each with an artificial flower or tiny hula dancer on its cap; Post-it notes; and an assortment of candies from the sixties—Good & Plenty, M&Ms, Pez dispensers. Ed was sure he'd been in several classes with Frank, but the only memory that surfaced now was playing football in Phys Ed, and how Frank was a speed demon with the ball. If he got the handoff and saw a little daylight, he was gone. Ed was pretty certain that Frank never went out for the football team, and he wondered now why that was. "You're looking well, Frank," he said.

The man and woman to Ed's left, between Frank and him, were caught up in an animated conversation, punctuated with loud outbursts of laughter. Ed couldn't place their faces.

"So what have you been up to for the last, say fifty years?" asked Frank. Again the slight hint of a smile at the edge of Frank's mouth.

In his periphery, Ed noticed Ellen shift in her chair and how her shoulders moved under the soft fabric of the cardigan. "Huh? Oh, um, I've been a physics teacher at a small college up north. Did that for almost forty years."

"You must have liked it."

Ed glanced over at Ellen, who was still pretending, he suspected, to be engrossed in the inner workings of real estate investments. He was aware that whatever he said would probably be heard by her, so he would stay clear of depressing talk about a failed marriage, being forced into early retirement and the like. "Yes, I really enjoyed it. Retired now, though."

He poured himself a cup of water from a pitcher on the table. "How about you?"

"It's been interesting."

Now Ellen reached behind her head with both hands and pulled her hair into a bunch, then released it, briefly exposing the bare skin of her neck. "Say more."

Frank scooped up a few Good & Plentys from the center of the table and popped one in his mouth. "I came from a poor family. Dad had a gardening service back then, and I had to work after school, helping him with mowing lawns, fertilizing plants, and the like. It seemed like an unspoken law that I wouldn't go to college, but that I'd just keep working for my dad and maybe one day take over the business."

So that's why Frank never played football. "Did you do that?" Ellen seemed to be sitting up straighter now. Ed wondered if she felt his eyes on her back.

"Yeah, I did for a while. Then, as I got older, I started thinking about launching out, doing something on my own. So, in my mid-twenties, I headed out for Alaska."

"Alaska? Whoa, that's launching out, for sure." Ed was aware that he'd probably never launched out in his life. "How long did you stay there?"

"Oh, I still live there."

"What do you do?"

"When I left, I had no money, or very little. I hitchhiked, got a couple of bus rides, then in Seattle I snuck aboard a ferry headed for Juneau."

"And they didn't catch you?"

Frank stroked his chin between two fingers and gave that little smile, like this was something he was proud of. "Nope."

"So, what did you do in Juneau?"

"I was there only a short while. Finally made my way to Cordova. Ever hear of it?"

"Uh, don't think so."

"Most people haven't. It's a small town along the coast, between Anchorage and Juneau. No roads or railroads into the place. Gotta fly or take a ferry. Cruise ships don't stop there."

"So what's there?"

"Just a cool little town and about the world's greatest salmon fishery. Kings, silvers, sockeyes, they've got it all. I worked on the fishing boats there for a long time."

"Sounds interesting." Ed was monitoring Ellen out of the corner of his eye. She was mainly nodding, "Uh huh" and "Oh, really," to the guy who was now laying out the ins and outs of foreclosures. "So you became a fisherman," Ed said, basically repeating what Frank had just told him.

"Yes. I lived among the Eyak people. Only a few of them left. Last full-blooded Eyak died about ten years ago."

"That must have been interesting," Ed said, still focused on Ellen. "So you're still a fisherman?"

"Yep, worked the seines and the gill nets for a long time. Then I was finally able to buy my own boat. Then more."

"How many do you have?"

"Twelve."

Holy crap, Frank Castenado is a wealthy man. "That's wonderful, Frank."

"Maybe, but it wasn't what I was looking for."

Ellen now ran a hand through her hair, and he noticed the pink gloss of her fingernail polish. He forced his eyes back to Frank. "What do you mean?"

"I mean, I ran away from my dad's gardening service to find myself, but I never really did. One day, an old Eyak woman said to me, 'Frank, you don't look happy.' I tried to deny her words, but I couldn't. Then she said, 'Frank, never forget who you are.'"

Never forget who you are. Who is Ed Turner? Just some old man, who was either dead or alive? He sagged. For so long it seemed like he had just been a follow-behind-the-plow kind of guy, planning to do tomorrow what he'd done yesterday. Ed cleared his throat. "Did you find out? I mean find out who you are?"

"I'm working on it. I went home to see my parents for the first time in twenty years. I asked Geralynn, my partner in the fishing business, who I'd been secretly in love with forever, to marry me. She said yes. I started going to church. All of those things have made a difference." His lips curled in that slight smile again, then he said, "Sometimes, Eddie, you've just got to go for it."

So why was Frank telling Ed all these things? He'd barely known Frank in high school. Ed remembered giving oral book reports in his English class: standing before the class and sharing about the book he'd read. Not just a rote summary, Miss Stewart always cautioned, but tell us what the book was really about. Maybe that's what was happening here. Late in life, as we've nearly finished the book, there is a need to report back to the class, and reunions provide that opportunity. Not just a rote summary, but what was my life really about? That's what Denny Jones, who he'd never known in high school, had seemed to do. It's what Frank, whom he'd barely known, had just done. The need to give an accounting, to report back on your progress or lack thereof. Maybe he needed to do that, too.

But even more, Frank had somehow reconciled with his past, *remembered who he was*. He had not hidden behind the monotony and predictability of freshman survey courses, never daring to change or even question if that was possible. "Thank you," Ed said. He started to say more, but couldn't finds words to do justice to Frank's profound sharing.

Frank nodded, with that sly smile, as he popped another Good & Plenty into his mouth. Now Ed looked over at Ellen, who was still turned away from him. He spoke to her anyway. *Sometimes, Eddie, you've just got to go for it.* "So, Ellen. You probably don't remember this, but back in eleventh grade, we were in Mrs. Klinewell's geometry class, and you and I were talking during class. We did that a lot in that class."

Ellen turned toward him, her mouth open, her eyes bearing a look of uncertainty. Her face was smooth—soft and white, like she had protected it from the sun—with some wrinkles at the outer edges of her eyes and at the corners of her full lips. Her presence had him off balance. It was like she was someone he'd always known, but at the same time a complete stranger.

Ed took note of the big diamond on her right hand. Did that mean she was divorced or widowed? She wore a slender gold chain with a small gold cross around her neck and a Fitbit on her left wrist. "And Mrs. Klinewell shouted at us. Do you remember that? Then she made me move to the other side of the room. But we kept glancing at each other and tried hard to fight off the giggles. No, I'm guessing you probably don't remember that." As Ed said this, he wondered why nothing more ever came from that friendship, why he never asked Ellen Barnes out. Why he never asked anyone out in high school.

Ellen swallowed, then stammered, "Somebody could have told you that." Her lips were shaped in a slight smile, like she was sharing an inside joke that the others present did not get. Her eyes were green and large, with a devilish twinkle, as if she'd just heard something that could be taken in an off-color way that might cause her to blush, and you, too. But he knew those eyes could flash with fiery anger, also—he'd already seen that this evening. They were lively eyes, not tired and worn down from the rigors of over six decades of life.

"And how about when we were in biology class together? You sat right behind me, and they were teaching us about sex. I remember looking at you, feeling really embarrassed, and you gave out a little giggle and whispered something like, 'Go get 'em, lover boy,' and I must have turned redder than a beet. You had to cover your mouth with your hand to keep from laughing."

Ellen's eyes bored into him, like she was seeing a ghost, and maybe she was. "Okay," she said, breathing hard, "Like I said, somebody could have told you those things. So here's one for you." She looked down, like she was carefully choosing her words. "Eddie and I were in social studies together in the sixth grade. And we made a map together as a term project. Tell me about that map."

"Sure. It was a map of Uruguay." Ellen's mouth fell open, and she placed one hand on the table, as if to steady herself. "It was a paper-mache relief map. I remember you being disappointed about us getting Uruguay, which, as you said, is flat and round, when other kids got countries like Chile, which was long and had high mountains. Yeah, I still remember that."

Ellen looked like she might be about to cry. "So, who are you?"

"Like I said, I'm Eddie Turner, go by Ed Turner now."

Ellen backed her chair a few inches farther from Ed, and she placed a palm against her neck. "So, who was the guy at the funeral?"

Ed looked around the table to see who else might be listening in on this strange conversation. The couple to his left were still engaged in their own lively discussion, Frank was typing something into his phone, the real estate guy was now droning on with the person to his right. He shook his head slowly. "Look, Ellen, I'm baffled about that, too. But I'm beginning to believe that that was Eddie Turner, also."

The color had now gone out of her face. "How could that be?"

Ed bit his lip. "I don't know. Only thing I'm sure of is that I'm here now." *Fairly sure.*

Chapter 11

"Look, whoever you are, I don't know about this." Ellen looked down. "I'm not sure it's good for me to be talking to you." But then she leaned in closer, like she wanted a close-up look, wanted to understand just who this person really was. He could feel her breath, warm and moist. Not minty or mouthwashy, but like the scent of biscuits baking in the oven.

"What about mutual induction?" the voice from behind Ed said.

"Huh?"

It was Jasmine. "Mutual induction. You know, like when two wires are next to each other and one of them is carrying current and that induces a current in the other wire?" She seemed unconcerned about interrupting a conversation.

"Yeah, I know what mutual induction is, Jasmine," Ed said with a hint of annoyance. The topic of mutual induction was a staple of his physics survey course. He had forty years of experience lecturing on mutual induction, and it certainly had no more bearing on his situation than did her simplistic imaginary numbers theory. "So, why do you bring that up?"

"I'm amazed you don't see it, Ed." She stood with hands on her hips, shaking her head. "So let's say your life is like the current flowing in a wire, moving along, doing its own thing. Everything is cool. Okay?"

Ed shot Ellen a glance, then let out a heavy breath.

Jasmine said, "But then another wire—maybe like another life or another reality—is placed near the current-carrying wire and voila, a current is induced in that wire. Now, you've got two realities interacting." She pursed her lips together and waited a moment, presumably to give Ed time to recognize the brilliance of this theory, then said, "So, what do you think?"

"Oh, by the way," said Ed, "this is Ellen, a classmate of mine. Ellen, Jasmine. She's a junior at Sentinel."

"Nice to meet you, Jasmine."

"Likewise, Ellen." Jasmine smiled at Ellen, then quickly returned her attention to Ed. "So what do you think?"

Ed laughed. "What I think is that you're pretty amazing, Jasmine. I'd say you've got the makings for being—"

"No," interrupted Jasmine. "I mean about the mutual induction theory. Well, not a theory, actually. Maybe just an analogy. What do you think?"

"I guess I'm doubtful about it," he said. "Induction is a classical physics concept that applies to electric circuits. Sure, life may have some parallels to electromagnetism, but it seems to me that's too simple an explanation for …" He shot Ellen a quick, slightly embarrassed glance. God, he didn't want her to see him as some crackpot discussing metaphysics with a high school kid. He cleared his throat. "That's probably too simple an explanation … uh …" He didn't finish, just bit his lip and nodded instead.

Ellen had a confused look. So Ed said, "Jasmine's helping out with refreshments tonight." The last thing he needed now was for Ellen to be jumping to some unsavory conclusion about why this 68-year-old guy was hanging out with a teen-age girl.

Ellen looked up at Jasmine. "So you're going into your senior year?"

Jasmine gave a slight nod.

"And you want to be a physicist?"

Jasmine shrugged, then laughed nervously. "I guess. Gotta go to college first."

Ellen was making an effort to be engaged. "Junior year. You need to be applying. Have you taken any of the tests yet?"

"You mean like the ACT?"

"Yeah, and the SAT."

"Not yet. In the Fall, I think."

"So, do you like school?" Ellen asked. Ed thought he noticed Ellen wince, probably aware that she'd just asked the most cliché question that adults always ask kids.

Jasmine wagged her hand in the air, indicating it was just so-so. "Not much, actually," she said.

"Why's that?"

Jasmine scratched her short blue hair. "All the pressure to fit in I guess. Be like everybody else."

"I can relate to that," Ed said.

"I mean it doesn't bother me that much. It's not like the other kids aren't nice. They are. Mostly. Not everyone, but mostly."

Ellen and Ed were silent, so Jasmine continued. "You know what's funny?" She chuckled.

"What?" Ed and Ellen both said, almost in unison.

"I mean, all you people who are really old. Sorry, Ed. But here you guys are, fifty freaking years later, trying to recapture the feelings and experiences you had in high school. And here I am, actually in that place where you all are tiptoeing down memory lane to get to, I mean all the old music and whatever. And I'm actually there and the truth is it's really pretty boring. Kind of scares me."

Ed and Ellen exchanged awkward glances. "How?" asked Ellen.

"I mean, you're all like literally that was the best time of your life, and here I am, going, oh shit, is this really the best time of my life? Makes the future look a little dubious, you know."

A quick chill shot down Ed's spine, as he realized that Jasmine was just a year younger than he had been at the time of the accident. But he quickly composed himself. "Here's what I think," he said, projecting fake confidence. He hadn't really thought about this much until Jasmine's comments just now. "I think there are a lot of good times in your life." *Probably a lie.* "It's just that the high school years were maybe the first ones where you started to feel grown up. Does that make sense?"

"Whatever. I mean, sure. I guess."

"Nice meeting you, Jasmine," said Ellen, apparently ushering in an end to the conversation.

"Yeah," said Jasmine. "So, one more question. How come you're meeting here instead of back at the school?"

Ed and Ellen exchanged glances. *Good question.* Ellen shrugged, "This is the place the organizers picked, I guess."

"Do you ever go back over there?" Jasmine asked.

"You mean Sentinel?" asked Ed.

"Yeah."

"I haven't been back since high school."

"Me neither," Ellen said. "It would probably feel kinda weird."

Jasmine looked from face to face. "Do you want to go?"

Marvin Gaye was wrapping up "I Heard It Through the Grapevine." As soon as the song ended, Sherrie Blanton was back up at the microphone. "Hey, everybody, having a good time?" Scattered applause. "Anyhoo," she said, holding a hand up to quell the applause, "More memories from 1968. Happy memories, I might add." She paused, while a few people applauded. "So, 1968 was a great year for movies. *Planet of the Apes.* Anyone remember that? I know there have been a lot of remakes, but that original was the best, wasn't it? Oh my, Charlton Heston was so handsome." She placed a palm over her chest like she was trying to calm her fluttering heart. "And a real patriot, I might add." Another bit of applause. She looked down at her notes. "And it was the year that *2001, A Space Odyssey* came out. I know that was a big hit, but personally I never went in for the sci-fi stuff."

"Good God," Ellen whispered, leaning toward Ed, "Poor Sherrie's still the same chatterbox she was back in high school."

Ed hadn't known her.

Sherrie Blanton wasn't done. "And it was the year that *The Mod Squad* debuted on TV." She checked her notes again. "Guess that's about it for now." She started to head away from the mic, then stopped and returned. "One more thing," she said, her voice now cracking. "I know some difficult things happened in our country back then. And you're free to say all the bad things you want. Free to criticize our great country. Free to make fun of me. But ... uh ... I'm just saying, I don't like it, not one bit, when you're putting down America, and I think that's just what some people were doing." Her words were interrupted by a smattering of applause, a few boos, but mostly silence. Then she said, "I mean, all those hippies and draft dodgers were protesting back in '68, while our brave men were fighting the enemy. I didn't like it then, and I don't like it now. So, that's just my two cents worth."

Marvin Gaye's words rang through Ed's brain. *Sure, maybe a man ain't supposed to cry,* he thought, *but sometimes ....* He looked over at Ellen with raised eyebrows. "Well, that was interesting," he said.

"So?" Jasmine asked.

Ed looked up at Jasmine, who was still standing nearby. "What?"

"Do you want to go over to Sentinel?"

"Uh, isn't the school going to be locked up at night?"

Jasmine gave them a sly smile. "If you know the right people, you can get in."

"But ..." Ed's words petered out.

"Maybe that's not such a good idea," said Ellen. She looked at Ed with suspicion, apparently still uncertain about being with him. Then she said, "I'd like to go." She placed two palms on the table like she was ready to stand and leave.

"I don't have a car," said Ed, looking back and forth between the two.

"No wheels, either," said Jasmine.

"I can drive," said Ellen. "Ralph would like to go, I'm sure."

Ralph? Who the hell is Ralph?

Chapter 12

They had just stood to leave, when a man stepped up to them. "Ellen Barnes!" He had his arms spread for a hug, but Ellen pulled back slightly, enough of a cue that the man dropped his arms to his side. "It's Lennie Berger. You remember me, Algebra 2?"

Ellen gave the man a broad smile, which Ed thought looked like one of the pasted-on variety. "Why, Lennie, of course. It's good to see you again. How are you?"

"Can we sit?" said Lennie, pulling a chair out for Ellen. He had not looked at Ed.

"Lennie, this is Eddie, I mean Ed Turner, and this is Jasmine, who's helping with refreshments tonight."

"Oh, yeah, Eddie the zombie-man," said Lennie, working to contain a chuckle, while still holding the chair out for Ellen, who gave Ed a helpless look, then sat down. Ed also took a seat, and Jasmine disappeared, probably to check on the refreshments. Lennie wore an expensive-looking, dark three-piece suit, with a white shirt and a red bow tie. His coat was open to reveal a gold chain hanging from a vest pocket, presumably attached to a pocket watch. The top of his shiny bald head was surrounded by a scant ring of gray, which he had unsuccessfully tried to comb over.

"Ellen, it's so good to see you again. You look great, I might add." He offered her a tight-lipped smile, while his dark eyes, magnified through the strong lenses of his frameless glasses, sought contact with hers.

Ellen looked back and forth between Ed and Lennie. "Yeah, so, Lennie, what have you been up to?" Then she added, "By the way, we've gotta run. We ... uh ... have to be somewhere."

Lennie rested one arm on the table and leaned slightly toward Ellen. "What have I been up to? Ha!" He looked around, then laughed. "What haven't I been up to?"

Ellen took a deep breath, then let it out slowly.

Lennie continued. "So here's the one-minute summary. I'm a psychiatrist, but then again, you probably already knew that," he said with a self-satisfied look.

"Actually, I didn't," Ellen said.

Lennie raised his eyebrows. "Yeah, medical school at UCLA, then, after residency, right into my own practice, which has kept me more than busy all these years. Of course, with writing a few professional papers and giving invited talks here and there every year, well, you can imagine that I've got my hands full." He leaned in even closer, then dropped his voice a bit, as he said, "And what about you, Ellen?"

Ellen had a peaceful smile, and looked more than able to handle guys like this. "Well, I've been busy, too. But, hey, I want to hear about you. I really do have to run pretty soon, though." She glanced at Ed, who gave her a supportive nod.

Now Lennie sat back, steepled his hands across his chest and seemed ready to launch into a long autobiography. But Ed interjected, "So what kinds of cases do you work with,

Lennie?" Ed had been digging deep into his memories, but couldn't remember Lennie from high school.

Lennie redirected his gaze toward Ed, as if he'd forgotten about his presence. "Well, all kinds, actually. But, if you'll pardon an apparent lack of modesty, I have become somewhat recognized for my work with various forms of dementia, especially dementia with Lewy bodies. Ever heard of it?"

Ed shook his head.

"It's a type of dementia that starts suddenly with fluctuations of alertness, hallucinations, maybe depression. Then it progressively worsens. Usually begins after fifty. Life expectancy, five to ten years. There's no cure, but some of my research has helped relieve some of the symptoms. I just gave a paper at the—"

Ed cut in. "How do you know if you've got it?"

"Well, that would require a professional examination. DLB, as it's called, is easily confused with Alzheimer's or Parkinson's disease, so an exhaustive series of tests of the cognitive, emotional, and motor systems is generally required."

Ed shot Ellen a self-conscious glance, then said, "I'm wondering if I have it."

Lennie raised his eyebrows, then produced a smirk. "A professional evaluation requires more than chit-chat at a party."

Ed began to describe the events of the evening, but didn't get far before Lennie cut him off.

"Have you talked to your doctor about this?"

"I don't have a doctor. I mean—"

"You don't have a doctor?" Lennie shot Ellen a concerned glance, as if wondering how she could be hanging out with such a loser.

"Not in this reality. Okay, I know that sounds crazy, and I feel weird saying it. But I'm not crazy ... at least I don't feel crazy, but maybe I wouldn't know. I guess that's what I'm hoping you could tell me." Ed realized that he was stammering, rambling. "No, I don't have a doctor. I don't have anything. No ID, no money, no home."

"Where do you live?"

"Before tonight I lived in Cloverdale, California, 913 Zinfandel Avenue. A real place."

"But you don't live there now?"

"There is no phone number for me anymore. I ... I—"

"Are you on any medications Mr. Turner?"

So it's now Mr. Turner, not Ed. Putting some distance between him and me. "No."

"No anxiety therapies?"

"No."

Lennie flashed Ellen a smile, like he was giving her a little demo of his psychiatric expertise. "Have you been ill?"

"No. Oh, I occasionally have TGAs. Are you familiar with—"

"Of course. Transient Global Amnesia. But the things you're talking about frankly don't correlate with TGAs, at least as the body of medical experience has described them. Are you in any pain right now?"

"No."

"Have you had any recent injuries to your head?"

"No."

"I think we can rule out traumatic brain injury, which in some circumstances can produce delusional behavior and a disconnect with reality." Now Lennie let out a great sigh, like he was getting ready to break the bad news. "Mr. Turner, I haven't run into very many people who seem taken with the idea of impersonating the deceased, and—"

"No, that's not what's happening here." Ed looked at Ellen in desperation.

Lennie shot Ellen a smile, as his chest heaved, like he was suppressing a laugh. His levity immediately vanished when he turned his gaze back to Ed. "Mr. Turner, like I said, a full professional evaluation would take extensive testing. So, I'm in no position to speak conclusively about this. But I'd have to say, and this is provisional, mind you, and I don't say it lightly, but I'd guess you were experiencing some kind of rare delusional, perhaps psychotic, episode."

Ed didn't know what to say.

From nowhere, Jasmine appeared. Ed saw the fury in her face. "So, you're saying he's batshit crazy."

"No, that's not—"

"Well, I can tell you that he's not crazy or psychotic or delusional." She smiled at Ed. "Yeah, he's scared, and I don't blame him. And he's looking for some help and—"

"Of course, young lady. You don't realize that—"

"No, don't blow me off. There's a lot that I don't realize, for sure. But one thing I do realize is when a good person like Ed is sincerely looking for some help. And what he doesn't need is some psycho-babble crap from some puffed-up—"

Ed cut in. "Jasmine, it's okay. He doesn't mean to—"

Jasmine turned away. Ed glanced at Ellen, who was struggling to contain her laughter. And now he wanted to laugh, too.

Chapter 13

"Jasmine, I must hand it to you," said Ellen. "You really put Lennie Berger in his place. And I'd say he had it coming." Ed and Ellen were laughing as the three of them made their way into the parking lot. But Jasmine was quiet and remote. They had slipped away, agreeing that they would return in an hour, so as not to miss too much of the festivities. And Jasmine needed to be back, too—her serving partner, Shane, had agreed to cover for her for an hour, but no more.

Jasmine shrugged. "Can we just move on? I'd rather not talk about it."

Ed stopped. "What's wrong, Jasmine?"

Jasmine kept moving. In a black turtle-neck over her black jeans, she was almost invisible in the darkness. "Let's just say I'm not a big fan of shrinks, okay? Let's just go over to Sentinel."

"I'm still not sure I don't have that early-onset dementia he was talking about. Dementia with Lewy bodies? God, that would be terrible."

Ellen turned toward him. "Okay, let's check it out. What's today?"

"What?" Okay, Ellen was checking his cognitive skills. He groaned. "Saturday, July 21."

"What state are we in?"

"Come on—"

"I'm testing you for dementia."

He sighed. "California."

She rattled off several more questions. "Who's the president?" "What's the capital of California?" "What are LA's two major league baseball teams?" and more. This was ridiculous, but the way her eyes sparkled in the cold illumination from the parking lot lights, unblinking and locked on him—he would go along.

"So, you got them all correct. I'm not sure what's going on with you, Ed, but I'd say you don't have dementia." She turned back toward the parking lot.

Ed was relieved, not only that he answered the questions correctly, but that none of the answers were different in this new world. As they walked, he said to Ellen, "Do you remember that short story? Maybe we read it in high school? Takes place far in the future, when time travel has become a real thing? There was a big game hunter—"

"And it was just after an election," Ellen interjected, "in which a moderate presidential candidate had narrowly defeated a would-be dictator?"

"Yeah, that one."

"Sure I remember it. Ray Bradbury. As I recall, the hunter paid an adventure company to join a hunting party that would travel back millions of years to kill a *tyrannosaurus rex*. Isn't that how it goes?"

"I want to hear about that," said Jasmine, suddenly more engaged.

Ed went on. "Yeah, so once they were in the prehistoric jungle, the guide warned the travelers to stay on the narrow boardwalk, so they wouldn't harm the ecosystem and possibly change the future. But when the hunter saw a T-Rex, he panicked and fled, stepping off the boardwalk. Isn't that the way it goes, Ellen?"

She nodded. "So the guide retrieved the hunter and gave him a good chewing out. When they returned to the present day, the hunter learned that things had indeed changed and that the would-be-dictator had been elected. Do you remember the closing scene?"

"Sure do. Gotta say, it still spooks me. The hunter looks down at the heel of his hunting boot and sees a crushed butterfly, whose death had apparently triggered the changes in his new alternative present. So he raised his hunting rifle and killed himself."

"The butterfly effect. So that's where that term comes from," said Jasmine.

"So why are you bringing that story up now, Ed? You think something like that's happened to you?" Ellen had now crossed her arms as she awaited his answer.

"Hell, I don't know. I'm just trying to figure out what's going on, I guess." They stood in silence for a moment. Yes, thought Ed, the reunion hotel was different in his new reality, but apparently nothing earth-shattering like a different president had occurred. He ran a hand through his hair. He had enough to worry about without digging up some depressing sci-fi story.

Moments later, Ellen announced, "Here we are," as she clicked her remote to unlock the doors of a large campervan. "Our ride to Sentinel."

"Dude, that's one awesome coach you have there, Ellen," beamed Jasmine, seeming to have regained her spunk.

"Thank you. It's my home away from home. Let me give you the tour."

Just then Jasmine's cell went off. She pulled it out of her jeans and stared at it, confused for a moment, then answered. She held the phone out to Ed. "It's for you, Ed. I think it's the guy you were talking to earlier."

Jasmine climbed into the campervan with Ellen, while Ed paced outside with the phone. "Yes?"

"This is Shipley Jameson. You the guy who called earlier?"

Again, no indication of recognition from Ship. Even so, it felt good to hear Ship's voice. It was like a connection, a lifeline, to his old life, his real life. "That's right. It's Ed Turner."

"You said something about some screwy physics."

Ed smiled. His ploy had worked. He knew that if he mentioned some bizarre physics, Ship, in spite of reservations he might have about interacting with a possible lunatic, wouldn't be able to resist. "Yes, I think there may be."

"Okay, tell me about it. It's getting late. I haven't got all night."

Succinctly as he could, Ed recounted the whole story. Arriving at the reunion hotel, passing out, then coming to and finding his possessions gone, the police having no record of his existence, and learning the reunion was at a different hotel. Then arriving at the new hotel to discover that everyone believed he had died fifty years ago.

"You say you talked to a psychiatrist? What did you learn from that?"

"Well, I guess it's possible that I have some form of dementia, such as dementia with Lewy bodies—have you heard of that?"

"Yes. Go on."

"But he couldn't be sure without tests. He suggested that I may be suffering from some kind of psychotic episode."

"The psychiatrist is probably right, but maybe there's something else going on here. Ever hear of the many-worlds interpretation of quantum mechanics?"

"Yes"—Ed had heard of it, but knew nothing about it—"but refresh me." Even in his crisis state, he didn't want to appear ignorant in front of Ship.

"First, let's back up. Think about what's involved in a decision."

"Okay."

Ship dove right in. "It's the chemistry in your brain that causes a decision to be made. You can follow that down to the electron level, where perhaps the behavior of one electron can make a difference in a decision. If so, the decision-making process now becomes a quantum mechanical phenomenon. And, if that's true, the outcome, the flow of reality, will be determined by quantum mechanical probability. We know that the properties of an electron are determined by probabilities. So, for a given decision-making problem, there are a range of decisions you may come up with."

"Okay," Ed said tentatively.

"It's like the old Schrodinger's Cat Paradox. Remember that? You said you were a physicist, right?"

"Yes, I am a physicist." Of course he remembered the Schrodinger's Cat Paradox. Something about the cat being simultaneously dead and alive, but there were underlying quantum mechanical details. Hell, he'd been teaching freshman survey courses for so many years—this was upper division stuff. "Refresh me on the details, would you, Shi... uh, Dr. Jameson?"

Ship groaned. Not only was Ship no doubt thinking this guy was crazy, but he was crazy mixed with stupid. "Okay. In a nutshell, imagine a cat placed in a sealed box, along with a radioactive atom and a vial of poison. The way the setup works is, if an electron in the atom decays, then it flips a switch that releases the poison. So, if there's a radioactive decay, then the cat dies. If not, then the cat lives. You with me?"

"Sure."

"Now the decay of the atom is determined by quantum mechanical probability, so that an electron may simultaneously be decayed and un-decayed, a superposition of states."

Ed looked over at the campervan. Instead of listening to Ship drone on about some far-fetched scenario he'd dreamed up, he wished he was there now, laughing with Ellen and Jasmine and heading to the old high school.

Ship continued. "If that were the case, then when we opened the box, we might find that the cat is both alive and dead. But, of course, we do not."

"Yes," said Ed, like he'd been studiously following along.

"And that's because, as Niels Bohr and his team concluded—the so-called Copenhagen interpretation—the electron's wavefunction collapses, so what is observed is that the cat, of course, is either alive or dead, not a superposition of both." Ship sighed, like it had been a burden to have to explain something that any first-year grad student should know.

In the background, Ed heard a voice on the phone, a female voice, but he couldn't make out what she was saying.

Oh, my God, Ship's got a woman. Ed cleared his throat. "So, yes, Dr. Jameson, but what does that have to do with my situation?"

Ship now sounded impatient. "Well, of course, probably nothing. But it could have everything to do with it. If the Copenhagen interpretation is incorrect, as some people now believe, then the cat may indeed be both alive and dead."

"Huh?"

"Don't you get it? So let's say the observer discovers an alive cat when she opens the box. But, in fact there is also a dead cat, but it belongs to a different world, a parallel universe, you might say."

A light went on in Ed's mind. *Good Lord. So, if a decision involves quantum mechanical processes, then that could explain why there is both an Eddie Turner who stayed in the car and died and an Ed Turner who dragged himself out and lived.*

"Yeah, that's far-fetched," said Ed. "But let's say it's true. Then why would the universe I was in suddenly jump to a parallel universe? That doesn't make sense. And I suspect no one's ever reported such a thing happening, right?"

"That's right, of course. Speculation has always been that contact between such parallel universes is impossible. Has to do with the decoherence of the electron wavefunctions ..." He paused, no doubt suspecting that such language was too heady for Ed, and rephrased it. "Uh ... let's just say it has to do with the mathematical properties of the probability function that describes the electron. As to why there might be an exception in this case, though, I've got to think about this some more."

Again Ed heard the woman in the background, calling to Ship. He could only make out the words, "Come to bed."

"Look, I'll call you later if I come up with anything. Please don't call me. Okay?"

Ed started to say, "Okay," but the phone clicked off before he could say it.

The night had turned cool, even though it was July in Southern California. He stared up into the dark sky. *The universe*, he thought. Just maybe not the one in which he belonged.

Chapter 14

When Ed pulled open the side door of the camper van, he was almost knocked off his feet by a huge Golden Retriever. "Ralph, come here," hollered Ellen from the rear of the van.

So this is Ralph, thought Ed, surprised at the relief he felt. Ralph immediately retreated to the interior, as Ed struggled up the step into the van.

"Do you need a hand, Ed?" asked Ellen, now by the doorway. "That's a big step."

As she leaned toward him with an extended hand, her tank top fell away just enough to reveal some cleavage. He couldn't look away. "Thanks, but I think I've got it," he said, clearing his throat.

Jasmine appeared next to Ellen.

"Damn, Ed, this thing is cool. Let me show you around." Ellen backed to the side to let Ed into the cozy space, smiling at Jasmine's enthusiasm.

"Come on, Ed," urged Jasmine. "It's called a Roadtrek. Look, here's a stove and a sink, and on the other side here, do you believe there's even a bathroom? Oh, and look at the rear." She was talking fast. "This couch folds out into a queen-sized bed. And, holy crap, even a flatscreen. Oh, and up front, the driver's and passenger's seats even swivel around, so it's almost like a living room. What do you think?"

Ed glanced at Ellen, who still wore a grin, then back at Jasmine. "Nice."

"I tell you Ed, if Ellen wanted to head out tonight to, say, Nova Scotia …" She finished her sentence with a smile.

Ellen looked comfortable, leaning against the kitchen counter, next to the stove where morning coffee could be brewed at a campground in the mountains. Her right hand stroked Ralph's head.

Then Ralph pushed his wet nose up against Ed's thigh, startling him. "Oh," gasped Ed. Then he reached down and patted Ralph's head.

Ellen laughed. "That's what he wants from you. A head rub. He'll let you do that all night. Anyway, maybe we ought to be heading out to Sentinel. You'll guide us, Jasmine? Ed and I haven't been there in a long time."

"Sure," said Jasmine, as they took their seats. As Ellen pulled the Roadtrek out of the parking lot, Jasmine turned in her seat toward Ed. "So what did the guy on the phone want? He was talking about physics, right?"

"I'm not sure about anything right now, but Ship—that's his name—was talking about a many-worlds interpretation of quantum mechanics."

"Whew, that sounds heavy, Ed," said Jasmine.

"Geez, Ed," said Ellen, "you haven't even told me what you do yet. Are you a physicist?" He suspected she'd overheard him talking to Frank Castenado earlier, while she was pretending to be fascinated with the real estate guy.

"Yes, taught at Muir College, north of San Francisco, for forty years. Just retired."

"So what does this many-worlds thing have to do with your situation, Ed?" asked Jasmine.

"Probably nothing. He was saying how when we're faced with a choice, there is a certain probability of various decisions. And here's the weird part. Quantum mechanics predicts that all of those decisions may actually get made, each one leading to a new parallel universe. It sounded pretty far-fetched."

Ellen seemed to be listening attentively, but said nothing.

"Damn, Ed," said Jasmine, "I'm guessing that no one's ever actually observed this."

"Yeah, that's the sticking point. Ship said he had to think about it some more. I suspect I won't hear from him again." Ed turned his head toward the window and watched the lights of the old neighborhood fly by.

Ten minutes later, the three of them were on the curb outside Sentinel High School. Ed and Ellen, with mouths open, scanned the old school buildings, while Jasmine watched their faces. "Well, does it look different?" she asked.

Ellen's eyes moved between Ed and Jasmine, then back to the school. "To me, it looks a lot different. The school was built, as I recall, around 1960, so when we were here, it was still pretty new. Now there are all these tall trees, and the buildings, even in the dark, look old. What do you think, Ed?"

Sentinel High School was a complex of single-story, flat-roofed buildings, with rows of windows along each side and connected by outdoor corridors. A high chain-link fence enclosed the campus. When he'd been here, there'd been no fence, and the buildings had seemed spaced farther apart. "I agree. It feels really odd being here. Yes, old, but also smaller.

Maybe that's what happens when you grow up. The things of your childhood looked bigger back then."

Ed's old house, which he hadn't seen since his family moved to Santa Rosa, was less than a mile away. *What does that look like?* He gave his head a quick shake, as if he could dispel old memories that didn't need to be revisited tonight.

"Do you want to go in?" asked Jasmine, with her hands on her hips, like a girl who didn't have all night.

"Uh, sure, I guess," Ellen said, looking at Ed. "Wouldn't we be trespassing?"

"Only if we get caught." Even in the low light, Ed could see the twinkle in Jasmine's dark eyes. "And we won't get caught."

Ellen looked at Ed with hands extended and palms up, as if saying it's up to you.

Ed shrugged, "I guess I'm game if you are."

"Follow me," said Jasmine, who then took off down the block, along the fence line. At a point where the fence cut back from the street to pass around what looked like a large utility box, Jasmine motioned for Ed and Ellen to step in behind the box. "Okay," she said softly to herself, "it's here somewhere … ah ha." She had located a patch of fence that could be lifted perhaps two feet off the ground. "I'm afraid we'll have to crawl through. Dammit, Ed, I forgot about you. Do you think you can make it?"

"I think so," he said, "if you'll help me back up." Ed could get down on his knees easily enough—he had plenty of experience in the garden—but he'd need some help getting back up. A minute later the three of them stood inside the fence.

Ed shot glances around him, like he expected security guards to be descending upon them. "So, Jasmine, how would you know about this hole in the fence?"

Jasmine flashed him an impish grin. "Maybe I read about it in Feynman?"

Ed laughed. "So, have you ever heard about Richard Feynman's days with the Manhattan Project at Los Alamos, back during World War Two?"

Jasmine turned toward him with interest.

"Feynman told the story about the security fence around the top-secret property that was claimed to be impenetrable. That was a challenge he could not resist. So he set about finding ways to sneak through the fence, and he did it, over and over again, much to the embarrassment of the security people."

"Did he get in trouble?"

"I don't think they ever caught him."

Jasmine beamed. "I knew there was a reason I liked that guy." Then she turned and motioned for them to follow. "Okay, you guys, the main part of the campus is this way."

A full moon had risen, and its yellowy, haze-filtered light shimmered off the classroom windows and shot long pale streaks down the corridors between the buildings. A few security lamps pooled light at the corners of buildings. Otherwise, it was pitch black.

"Maybe we should've brought a flashlight," said Ed.

"Not the best idea, Ed," Jasmine shot back. "There may be a few security guys wandering around. Better to just let your eyes get adjusted to the dark."

They stopped in the central commons, a black-top-surfaced square in the middle of the campus. On one edge of the space was a building that used to be the cafeteria. "Oh, man, I remember this place," said Ed.

"Yeah," said Ellen, "but I don't remember the blacktop. Didn't it used to be grass?"

"I think you're right." From the commons, wings of classrooms radiated out in all directions. Beyond one of the wings, the tall block shape of the gym dimly reflected moonlight. Just beyond the gym would be the football field.

Ellen did a slow three-sixty. "Geez, it feels really strange. So familiar, yet so alien. Almost like a dream."

"If you guys want to walk around, I'll just hang out," said Jasmine.

"Oh no," said Ellen. "You come with us." She probably wasn't ready to be alone in an isolated place with this strange person. Then she laughed. "Eddie, I mean Ed, and I might get lost." It was good to hear her laugh.

The darkness and fifty years were disorienting. "I think this is where the social studies classes were," said Ed at one point, then took it back. "Oh, wait, I think I'm turned around." He stood with an index finger pressed against his chin for a moment, then said. "No, I think this is it."

Looking beyond the social studies rooms, Ellen said, "What's that building?"

"That's the GS," said Jasmine.

Now Ed was looking, too, just beyond the end of the classroom wing, where the edge of a sleek, glass and steel structure could be seen. "Huh?"

"I should say the GSLC, but everybody calls it the GS. I suspect it's new since you were here. Come on, let's go look."

They stood in front of the ultramodern two-story building, its walls formed by dark-glass panels supported by stainless-steel columns that sparkled in the moonlight. At the entrance to a brick walkway leading to the building stood a bronze statue of a teacher—a slender woman holding an open book in one hand, while her other hand was lifted, palm up, as if she were reading an inspirational passage to her class. Ellen leaned in to read the inscription on the base. "Oh, dear Lord," she shrieked. "Ed, you've got to see this."

Ed leaned close to the inscription: *The Gladys Stewart Learning Center is dedicated to expanding imaginations, enhancing learning, and preparing students for leadership and service in the world.* Below the inscription were these words: *Constructed as part of the State of California Education-Forward Program, 2005.*

Ellen, arms raised overhead, began to dance slowly around the statue, as Ed looked on, mouth open.

"What's the big deal?" said Jasmine.

"The big deal, Jasmine, is that Gladys Stewart was our senior English teacher. She was my favorite teacher."

"Mine, too," chimed in Ellen. Then she turned to Ed. "It is so wonderful that she would be honored in this way."

He couldn't speak. There was such radiance in Ellen's face, bathed in the moonlight. Finally, he cleared his throat and said to Jasmine. "So, what goes on inside?"

"Everything, really. It's kinda the only cool place on campus. There are computer labs—I would never get to use a MacBook Pro at home. And there's a library that's really awesome. I guess not everybody appreciates that, but I do."

Ed looked at Ellen. "Remember the old library? It wasn't much, as I recall."

"All I remember is old Mrs. Lynch, the librarian, who everybody hated."

"And there's an auditorium," continued Jasmine, "where we hold our plays and concerts. It draws a lot of people from the neighborhoods."

"I'm impressed," said Ed. He turned slowly to take in the whole scene. This school was part of his life, a place that still existed in this reality. It made his presence legitimate, it anchored him in this world. Its history involved him, its history had helped shape him. He looked up at the statue of Miss Stewart, a representation of a real person, who had known Ed Turner. Taught him about Chaucer and Melville and Faulkner.

Maybe the campus hadn't meant that much to him back then—he had been unconnected to most of its activities. But it meant everything to him at this moment. Quantum many-worlds be damned. This was real, he was real. He belonged here.

"You know what else is cool?" said Ellen, now leaning in again to study the plaque. "It was built under the Education-Forward Program. That's Sandy Kaseman's program. She produced that bill when she was in the state assembly."

"Yeah, that is cool," said Ed. What he didn't say was that it was also cool that Sandy Kaseman existed in the reality he now found himself in. "She did so much for our state. My mother lives in a very clean and professionally run nursing home because of Sandy Kaseman's legislation to protect the elderly." His shoulders sagged, as he wondered if his mother was even still alive in this reality. She had lost an eighteen-year-old son, had grieved—Ellen saw that at the funeral. How had she survived that? There was no way he could dare try to contact her now, even if she were still alive.

In an instant, the new optimism that had surged through him just moments ago evaporated. Who was he kidding? The

Eddie Turner of this world only existed as a name on a weathered headstone. Sure, the silhouettes of the dark buildings were vaguely familiar, yet they were also oddly alien. Like dim memories of a life that ended long ago.

Ellen was still talking about Sandy Kaseman. "I worked on two of Sandy's campaigns. I don't know of anyone who's done more to break through the partisan gridlock in government. Frankly, I think she would have been a great president, but, of course, she wanted to stay in California, where her roots were. Can't blame her."

"Is she still alive?" Ed asked idly, his mind still filled with the image of his mother, lonely and grieving somewhere.

Ellen raised her eyebrows, like she was surprised he'd ask such a question. "Of course, she's still on the state supreme court, but she must be nearly eighty by now. Still going strong, I think."

Ed nodded like he cared. He willed himself to fight off his dark feelings. Maybe he was overthinking this. Maybe this was Eddie Turner's world, a world he left fifty years ago. A world into which he had barely fit even back then. But tonight, here he was in the moonlight at his old school with this very charming woman. Why would he want to be anywhere else?

Chapter 15

"Do you remember the football games, Ed?" Ellen said, as they stopped at the edge of the stadium bleachers.

Not really. Most Friday nights he'd be home, watching TV with his parents or lying on his bed in his darkened room, under the soft glow of the dial on his clock radio—it had been his companion on many lonely nights. On his back, with his hands behind his head, he was right there as Vin Scully called the play-by-play, as the Dodgers battled the Cards, Sandy Koufax dueling Bob Gibson.

It seemed pathetic, thinking about it now, but back then that's just how life was for him. He never recalled his dad encouraging him to get out. He did attend a few Sentinel games, and he remembered seeing Ellen there. She'd been a part of a pep group—he didn't know what they called them—not cheerleaders, but a group of girls who danced a few upbeat numbers and led some songs during the game. "Yeah," he said. "Good ol' days. Weren't you part of that dancing group, the … uh …?"

"The Sentinel Songbirds. Oh, Lord, I can't believe you'd remember that."

Then they were silent, as they gazed out onto the field. It all looked as he remembered. Other than the GS, not much had changed. The trees were taller, the facility was old. He was old.

He'd been on an emotional roller coaster all evening, bouncing wildly from terror to despair to enchantment. It would be easy to be overwhelmed by the disturbing incidents of the evening. Either he was a lunatic or he was caught up in some quantum-mechanical nightmare. But now they strolled back through the dark walkways between old classrooms, and Ellen bumped against his shoulder, intentionally, like a flirty, almost giggly high-school kid. He bumped her back—God, had he ever done that in his life?—while Jasmine smiled slyly.

"Wait," said Ellen, stopping in her tracks. "This is it, isn't it?"

Ed studied the building, then walked to one of the windows and tried to peek in. He couldn't see anything. "I think so," he said.

"This is what?" demanded an impatient Jasmine.

"Our English classroom," they almost said in unison. "The room where Gladys Stewart used to teach."

"Oh, my God," said Jasmine, "that's cool. It's still an English classroom, but I had no idea …." She trailed off.

"Lordy, how I'd love to see inside," said Ellen, now joining Ed at the windows.

"Well that can be arranged, you know."

Ed and Ellen exchanged glances with raised eyebrows. Then Ed said, "Now, that would be serious breaking and entering. I'm not sure that's—"

"So, you don't want to go in, I guess."

"I'm not saying that …What I'm saying is … I just—" Ed was aware that he was stammering.

"I'd like to go in, Jasmine," said Ellen, then turning her head toward Ed. "I mean, what's the worst thing that can happen? Seriously, a couple of old farts at their fiftieth, taking a trip down memory lane."

"Well, in fact, there is some risk," said Jasmine, "and I'd be lying if I didn't say so. There's a lot of crime around here, and a lot of folks are scared and into a lot of paranoia shit about it. I'm not sure what would happen if you got caught. Somebody might want to make an example. Personally, I'd just as soon avoid some scared guard with a taser or hell, I don't know, maybe a gun." She shrugged her shoulders. "On the other hand, if I was really old, and only had one chance, I'd want to go in."

Ed saw the questioning in Ellen's eyes. "Look, I'd like to go in, too. But this really is criminal trespassing we're talking about. This isn't just some—"

"Oh, come on, Ed," said Ellen, with a devilish smile.

"I guess what I'm saying is—"

"I can understand if you're scared, Ed," said Jasmine.

"I'm not saying I'm scared, I'm just saying …." He looked at the door to Miss Stewart's room, a portal to some of the few pleasant memories of his high school years, then at the questioning faces of his new friends. When was the last time he'd had this much fun? "I probably should have my head examined for this," he sighed, "but … what the hell … let's do it."

"Okay," said Jasmine, "but I've gotta say this—it will be a little tricky. I've got to get the door open, then I'll have about twenty seconds to find the alarm and silence it."

"And if we can't find it?" asked Ed.

Jasmine gave a deadly serious look. "Then, we run like hell. Sorry, Ed, maybe we'll have to leave you behind as a decoy." Then she burst into laughter

Ellen joined in the laughter and soon the serious Ed was laughing, too. *Screw the parallel universe. Screw dementia with Lewy bodies.* For one of the few times in his life, he was living outside the box. He had to hold in his laughter, as he pronounced, "Let's go in," with a fake authority that he hoped sounded like John Wayne leading his men into battle.

Jasmine busied herself with the lock on the door, as Ed and Ellen watched with amazement, frequently shooting glances down the moon-streaked corridor for guards headed their way with weapons drawn.

"Got it," Jasmine announced with pride. "Let's get inside and find the damned alarm."

The three of them quickly slipped inside the classroom. Immediately, Jasmine began running her hands along the edge of the dark wall, as Ed and Ellen stood by helpless. Ed couldn't help but count off the seconds in his head. *Five ... six ... seven.*

"Damn," said Jasmine, "it should have been right here." She quickly moved to another wall.

Ten ... eleven ... twelve .... Ed licked his lips and edged toward the door. This wasn't looking good. He definitely couldn't—what did Jasmine say?—run like hell. He'd have to find a place to hide. Where that might be, he had no idea. *Fifteen ... sixteen ... seventeen ....*

"Shit," Jasmine shrieked, "it's gotta be here somewhere." She was moving faster now.

Eighteen ... nineteen ... twen—

"Got it!" After a moment, she turned. "All safe now, boys and girls." She clearly felt proud.

"How did you know how to do that?" asked Ellen.

"If I told you, I'd have to kill you," Jasmine said with fake solemnity, then laughed. "Now I'm gonna wander around outside for a bit. You two can do your memory-lane thing. Have fun, lovebirds."

Lovebirds? Ed felt his face redden, and he was glad it was dark.

Jasmine slipped out the door, and they were alone in the room. Ed turned to survey the classroom, dimly illuminated by splashes of moonlight, which were sufficient for them to move around.

"I can't believe it hasn't changed that much," said Ed, keeping his voice barely above a whisper. There was still a teacher's desk facing an array of student desks. The walls were covered with bulletin boards, displaying papers, probably class assignments. There was a row of computer stations along one wall—that was one thing new since the old days. And no blackboard.

"Yeah, this really was Miss Stewart's room. I can't believe I'm standing here." Ellen sighed, then said, "I really can't believe *we're* standing here."

"I can almost see Miss Stewart at her desk. You remember what she looked like?"

"Sure. Kind of prim and proper, slender, with intelligent, kind eyes. I thought she was old, but she probably wasn't really over thirty five."

"So that would make her eighty-five today. Yeah, she could definitely still be alive."

Ellen cupped her hands around her mouth like a megaphone, then called out, but keeping her volume low,

"Miss Stewart, if you're out there somewhere, I hope you can hear us. We want you to know we love you." Then she turned to Ed. "Do you remember her vocabulary tests?"

"Are you kidding?" said Ed. "They were really hard."

"Yeah, she gave us some words I don't think I've used since then."

"Insuperable," said Ed. "Miss Stewart would be proud. Geez, I still remember that word. But I'm not sure I remember what it means."

"Insurmountable, I think. As in high school was insuperable."

"Ha," retorted Ed. "Life is insuperable."

After a moment of silence, Ellen said, "Love is insuperable."

After more silence, Ed said, "I remember once—I wonder if you remember this—Miss Stewart, for some reason, was talking about the composer Jerome Kern. Then, out of nowhere, she started reciting some of the words from 'Smoke Gets In Your Eyes.'"

Ellen hummed a bit, then sang softly, "Now, laughing friends deride tears I cannot hide ..." She looked down, then cleared her throat and added, "That's all I remember."

Ed watched Ellen in silence, feeling his eyes grow misty and swallowing what felt like a lump in his throat. Then he said, "I think you sing better than Miss Stewart." They laughed. "But what I remember most was that after she said some of the lyrics, she stopped and made a little tsk, tsk sound, like she often did. And then, and I can still see it clearly, her eyes filled with tears."

"I remember that," Ellen said. "Lordy, we were so caught up in our teenager crap, I don't think anyone thought about her as a person who fell in love, had heartbreaks and regrets …" She gave an audible sigh.

"Yeah, I'm sorry to say that too many times in my life, I've been insensitive like that."

Ellen reached out and rested a hand on his arm, then withdrew it quickly. She turned away from him to survey the room. "You know, I think these desks are laid just like they were when we were here. What do you think?"

Ed scratched his head. "Hmm … I think you're right. Good grief, I think I even remember where I sat." He made his way through the rows of student desks, leaning a hand on each desk he passed. In the dim light it would be easy to snag the cane on one of the desk legs. Then he squeezed himself into the seat of the student desk. "I think this it. But, I have to say, this desk feels a lot smaller than I remember."

Ellen walked to another desk, about halfway across the room from him. "And this was mine."

His fingers trailed across the smooth laminate surface of the desk. The room smelled of books. It felt like yesterday that he was last here. In another month, when the Fall term began, this room would be filled with kids—energetic and sleepy, rebellious and fearing rejection, curious and bored. Masses of contradictions. With a lifetime of opportunities and choices ahead of them, while at the same time feeling trapped. "It feels weird being here."

"Like a time machine," she said.

Funny, thought Ed. He'd been thinking the same thing earlier. "Yeah," he sighed.

"When we sat here, Ed, it was only a few months before your accident." Now she shifted her body toward him. "Tell me about the accident, Ed. I need to know."

Ed realized he was tightly gripping the edge of the desk. "Not much to tell, really. I was driving too fast on an icy road, lost control, went off into the woods. My legs were injured bad, but I was able to crawl out before the car burned. " He looked off toward a cork board, where class papers were mounted. There was more to say, for sure. But he was now quiet.

"It's okay, Ed. I shouldn't have asked you right now. It's just that being in this place stirs up … stirs up a lot of emotions, I guess."

Then they were quiet, and it was okay. Just soaking up the beautiful, yet somehow eerie, ambiance of the classroom was about all he could handle. But then he said, "So, why did you go to my funeral?"

She glared at him, and he could see the fury again burning in her eyes. She opened her mouth to speak, but then bit her lip instead. Then she said, "I can't believe you have to ask that question."

It felt like the air had been knocked out of him. A childhood memory flashed in his mind. He was playing hide and seek in the back yard of a neighbor's house. He'd stretched out to hide on the corrugated metal roof of a shed. When he heard the seeker crawling up the front side of the shed, he'd rolled farther toward the back edge, but he shifted too far and fell eight feet onto the dirt. Suddenly, he couldn't get air into his lungs. For minutes he thought he might be about to die. Maybe he recalled that memory because that's how he felt now.

When he looked at her, it was like he was seventeen again. It was the miniskirt era, and Ed would frequently be distracted by those long, smooth legs just a few rows away from him.

What the mind of a seventeen-year-old could do with that image. Her brown hair was now gray, but in the dim light she was that teen-age girl he'd known. It was like he had just awakened from a long, dreamless nap. And he was where he had been before, with all those old challenges, all those old possibilities. The reunion was a time machine, yes. But the machine doesn't always take you to the destination you'd expected.

He craned his head around the room, like he was taking in the classroom décor. Now he looked back toward her, reached out a hand toward her. "Ellen, I—"

A new shaft of light splashed into the room, dancing off the walls. *A flashlight.*

"Oh no," Ellen said, "somebody's coming."

"Behind the desk." He was already up and out of his chair, as he said it.

Ellen quickly joined him. Within seconds, they'd fallen to their knees behind the teacher's desk, then did their best to scrunch together into the leg opening underneath.

Ellen whispered, "If they catch us, they'll probably laugh—two senior citizens, hiding under the teacher's desk."

"Maybe, maybe not. Breaking and entering, especially at a school, isn't treated casually in this day of—" *God, that sounds like some grumpy old man.* Ellen was struggling to hold in her laughter, shimmers of moonlight dancing off her face, and he was back in high school. He didn't feel like a senior citizen. He felt like a junior citizen.

Ed risked a quick peek over the top of the desk. The silhouette of a person filled the window in the door. He couldn't be sure, but there seemed to be the outline of a gun.

Chapter 16

Pressed together under the desk, huddled in silence, they listened to the jingling of keys. Someone was searching for the correct key for the door. *Maybe it would be best to stand and offer an explanation. Isn't that what a rational, law-abiding citizen should do? But the person may have a weapon. In the dark, that person, startled, just might shoot first and ask questions later.* He scrunched down even farther into their small cave beneath the desk.

Ed felt the warmth of Ellen's breath against his cheek, even though they were struggling to keep their breathing shallow and quiet. Her body was soft against him. Her subtle perfume highlighted more than masked the warm soapy scent of her skin. He could barely breathe, and he wasn't sure if it was from terror or the nearness of her. He moved his arm around her shoulder.

Then Ellen put her hand over her mouth, as if trying to stifle a laugh.

"What?" Ed whispered with urgency.

"Sorry," she breathed.

"Sorry for what?"

"I was just picturing us sharing a jail cell."

How could she be laughing now? What could be funny about facing a confrontation that could be dangerous, at the very least humiliating? Why isn't she taking this seriously? Or maybe the question should be, why was he so wrapped up in fear?

Now the correct key clicked into the lock, and the door swung open.

They held their breath, as the person moved around the periphery of the room, the flashlight scanning the walls for the light switch. Ellen's hand squeezed Ed's shoulder, as she moved even closer to him.

Unexpectedly, Ellen began to stand—either to surrender or to confront the intruder. As Ed tried to pull her back down, she pushed him away.

Before Ellen could be seen, there was a loud noise from outside, like trashcans being overturned. The beam of the flashlight swept toward the doorway, followed by the sound of rapid footsteps. The door clicked closed.

They waited in silence a moment longer, then Ed again peeked up over the desk. "They're gone."

"I'm guessing Jasmine created a diversion. I say, let's get the hell out of here. Whoever that was will no doubt be back soon."

Ed pulled himself up from the desk. He cautiously pushed the classroom door open and peered outside into the dark corridor between the buildings. All quiet. They exchanged nods and headed out into the darkness, their speed limited by Ed's stumbling gait.

After taking one wrong turn, they finally found the route back past the social studies wing and through the commons. But then the beam of a flashlight swept across the walls of the buildings ahead of them, like the search light in an old jail-break movie.

Ed took Ellen's arm and pulled her into a row of hedge. It was *Euonymus*—Ed couldn't believe that at this moment he'd be aware of what the plant was. "You go, get back to the van," Ed urged Ellen, but she wouldn't leave him.

"Maybe we should surrender, I mean explain," Ellen whispered.

Ed said nothing. Now they could see a person approaching, with a flashlight sweeping a wide arc. There was something in the person's other hand. A gun? Ed felt his heart in his mouth.

Then a voice from behind the person hollered, "Hey, asshole!" A shadowy figure appeared at the far end of the corridor. Jasmine.

The person turned, shook a fist and took off after her.

"We can't let him catch Jasmine," said Ed, trying to stand and almost falling over on the cane. "Over here," he called out, waving wildly, but the guard was long gone.

"We'll never catch them." Ellen stood, upset. "Let's get back to the Roadtrek, maybe we can intercept her."

"You run ahead, I'll come as fast as I can," said Ed. Ellen touched his arm, then took off. She moved surprisingly fast for a woman her age and quickly disappeared around the corner of the building.

Ed galumphed his way toward the hole in the fence, unable to contain a smile. *Running from the cops, driving the getaway car with a good-looking woman. Good Lord.* He was alive.

At the next intersection of sidewalks between buildings, Ed paused, uncertain which way to go. He headed right. Moments later he arrived at the opening in the fence, where Ellen was just now crawling through. When she saw him, she hollered, "Sorry, Ed, I made a wrong turn back there."

Jasmine was waiting by the campervan. In her black turtleneck and jeans, she looked like a cat burglar. Hugging herself, she said, "Dammit, guys, open this sucker up. It's freezing out here."

Inside, Ellen asked, "How'd you get away from the cop?"

"Seriously?" Jasmine said with raised eyebrows. "I run fast. For that poor cop, it was sort of ...." She patted Ralph on the head, then added, "Sort of like ol' Ralph jumping into the lake, hoping to catch a trout."

Chapter 17

Ellen pulled the Roadtrek into the lot at the Golden Foothills Inn and turned off the ignition. She glanced at her watch, then looked over at Jasmine, in the passenger seat next to her. "Sorry, Jasmine, that we got you back late."

Jasmine generated a smirk that turned into a smile. "Guess old Shane will just have to handle it by himself. Anyway, the refreshments business is winding down for the evening."

Ed pushed open the side door, but pulled it closed again when Ellen stayed seated. She moved a hand to a lever at the side of her captain's-chair seat, then slowly swung the seat around to face Ed, sitting directly behind Jasmine.

"Cool," said Jasmine, who then spun her chair around, also. Now they faced each other in a small circle.

"It's time to hear your story, Ed." Ellen reached into a drawer and brought out a battery-powered candle, flicked it on and set it on the counter top next to them. Then she sat back, with arms folded, ready to listen. "You can run on in, if you need to, Jasmine."

"And miss this? No freaking way. I want to hear about the quantum mechanics shit." Jasmine leaned forward with her elbows on her knees.

Ed shook his head slowly, then began. He'd already told this story several times this evening. He went through his arrival at Villa Solana, his going unconscious, the loss of his car and ID, then learning that everyone at the reunion believed he had died fifty years ago. Then he recounted the sequence of events of the accident. "So, here I am," he concluded, "completely clueless about how this could be true. I mean, there is the dementia possibility, and—"

"I'm pretty sure you don't have dementia, Ed," interjected Ellen.

"Tell her about the screwy physics, Ed, the many-worlds stuff."

"So ... um ... you heard me mention that earlier, I think. That's a theory my physicist friend—well, he doesn't acknowledge knowing me tonight, so there's that little piece of data. Shit." He shook his head, then recounted the idea of decision-making being a quantum mechanical process, about the decision that day in the wrecked car—to stay with the car or climb out. "Anyway, he's conjecturing, and I do mean conjecturing, that somehow I may have entered a parallel universe, where Eddie Turner died in that accident. He can't explain it, says it has to do with one way that a quantum-physics theory gets interpreted."

Ellen's eyebrows were raised. "And ... are you buying into that? I mean, the parallel universe thing ... okay, this is getting kind of creepy for me."

"I'm not gonna lie," said Jasmine, "I think this many-worlds thing sounds cool. Much better than my mutual induction or imaginary numbers theories."

Ellen looked at Jasmine open-mouthed, like she was thinking, *Who is this person?* Then she turned back toward Ed.

"But who are you now, Ed? I mean, over the past fifty years?"

"Well, like I said, I've been a physics prof at this small college up north. Did that for nearly forty years. Then retired. And here I am." He shrugged. What more was there to say? His life had been monotonously simple. He didn't need to mention Carmen, good grief.

"That's it?" Ellen said, making a disappointed hiss. "I mean, Ed, a lot has happened over fifty years. Seriously, if you can say nothing more than that you worked for forty years and retired, then I have a hard time believing you are who you say you are."

Ed opened his mouth, but no words came out. *Nothing more than that you worked for forty years and retired?* He bristled at this. Of course there was more, much more about him. He started to speak again, as Ellen sighed and sat back in her chair. But then he closed his mouth and reached down and rubbed Ralph's head.

Ellen cleared her throat, ready to move on, then began. "I went to UC Riverside, intending to major in English literature. Wanted to write poetry. But I got pregnant by the end of my freshman year, so I dropped out to marry this fellow student. Had a miscarriage. By twenty I was divorced. I was a wreck. Moved back in with my parents for four years. Got some therapy. That's when I started drawing—it was part of the therapy. Learned I was good at it. It brought me out of the dark night."

Jasmine now pulled her legs up onto the seat, brought her knees up under her chin and surrounded them with her arms.

Ed was already realizing how superficial his story had been. Ellen continued. "Got married again when I was thirty. Phil, that was my husband. I got a job as an illustrator for children's books. Turned out I was pretty successful."

Ed manufactured a laugh. "So you were a professional artist? No wonder that map of Uruguay turned out so well."

"One of my books was a runner-up for a Newbery. That's a children's lit award. Anyway, I had a son, Jeffrey, who now lives in Oregon and has two small children—they're my treasures.

"Phil died ten years ago. For a while I didn't know what to do. Then I ran into Gloria Marquez-Herrera—do you remember her? She was Gloria Marquez back in high school."

"Of course. One of the brainy ones, as I recall."

"That's right. So I ran into her at our fortieth reunion. I thought she'd be here tonight—you'd love her. Anyway, Gloria started out as a lawyer, but then she became a priest—can you believe that? Episcopal—got me going back to church, showed me a lot about how much I'd been missing. Gave me the confidence to get the Roadtrek and hit the road. Good Lord, I'd lived in Southern California my whole life, had never traveled much, but now I've been all over. Yes, I get lonely—even with Ralph." She reached down and rubbed his head. "But I've seen so much and learned so much about life and who I am."

"So, what do you do on your travels?"

"Oh, everything. Would you believe I've even gotten into birding?"

"Geez, so you can identify all the kinds of birds?"

"Hardly," she laughed. "I'm still a rookie. Do you know that there are over fifty species of sparrows in North America alone?"

Ed shook his head slowly as he smiled.

"But the main thing I'm excited about is that my church connected me with advocacy groups working to end poverty, especially among children. That's how I got involved with some of Sandy Kaseman's causes, too.

"Anyway, I've used my Roadtrek to travel on mission trips to work at schools and orphanages in disadvantaged areas—Appalachia and among the Lakota in North Dakota. I've also used my illustrator skills to do posters and even create picture books for some of the children." She gazed out through the driver's side window into the darkness. Then she looked back at Ed and Jasmine. "Someone, I think it was Maya Angelou, said, 'You're only free when you realize you belong no place—you belong every place.' It's taken me my whole life to learn that. I guess the Roadtrek is a symbol of that."

Belong no place? Ed grimaced. *I must be the freest person there is.* It didn't feel good.

"These past ten years began as a tragedy and have since turned out to be, in some ways, the most enriching years of my life." There was a catchlight in her eyes that exuded confidence mixed with mischief.

Ellen clasped her hands together in her lap. "Yeah, I'm almost sixty-eight. Some would say I'm old. But I still have dreams and I want more. Oh, and late in life I've started writing poetry again. Still trying to get up the nerve to submit it. We'll see."

Ed ran his fingers along the edge of the smooth kitchen countertop next to him, studied the flickering candle. "So, it looks like you're all set, Ellen. You've got everything you need."

Ellen looked down.

After some silence, Jasmine spoke up. "Okay, since we're suddenly getting all honest and everything, I've gotta say this. I said I hate shrinks. Yeah, I'm not gonna lie about that. But here's what … hell …" Jasmine stopped midsentence and shook her head. She stared down at the floor of the van, avoiding eye contact. "My mom and dad got divorced when I was twelve. It was ugly. My dad used some shrink to get my mom declared mentally incompetent. It was a total crock, but that's what he did. The court said she was some kind of psycho, and I was forbidden to see her. So, I had to live with him. I mean, she was an emotional person, sure, but she was just fine. I … I loved her." Now, Jasmine covered her face with her hands and her body began to convulse with sobs. Ellen reached over and softly stroked her shoulder.

Jasmine let out a laugh through her tears. "Geez, has anybody got a Kleenex?"

Ellen handed her a box of tissues.

Jasmine blew her nose, then continued, still looking down. "So, like I said, I couldn't see her." She shot them a quick glance. "At fourteen, I would have been legally able to decide who I would live with, and it would have been my mom, for sure. Every night I prayed to God that I would get to be fourteen so I could go live with her. But then, before I ever got the chance, my mom OD'd on some kind of bad shit, I don't know what. Had gotten depressed after the divorce, not seeing me. God, I don't like talking about it. Don't usually. But tonight …"

Ed felt his eyes growing misty, but said nothing.

Ellen leaned toward Jasmine. "Oh, God, Jasmine, I'm so sorry."

"It's okay," said Jasmine, not looking up.

"Are you still with your dad?" asked Ellen.

"Yes. He's okay, I mean, he doesn't mistreat me or anything, just pretty much lets me do whatever I want. Next year I'll go to college, I hope." A twinkle returned to her black eyes. "Me and Richard Feynman," she said.

There was silence for what seemed like a long time, and it was okay. Ed laid his hands out on his knees, palms up, and they were trembling. Ralph now stood and rested his golden head on Ed's knee, his huge sad eyes bathing him, as if giving him permission to speak.

Ed kept his eyes on Ralph, as he stroked the top of his head. "So, hell," he began. "Here I am at sixty-eight, and it feels like I've missed everything."

He looked up at Ellen and again noted the flicker of the candle in her eyes. Jasmine now leaned in closer, giving him her full attention. "Maybe for me, life is too scary to look straight in the eye."

Ed shook his head and turned his eyes toward the ceiling of the campervan. "I guess my dad wasn't the greatest in the world, either." He rubbed the bridge of his nose with a forefinger. "Crap, I remember him saying to me one night—he was always doing this, saying some insulting thing, usually in the context of joke. Sometimes he'd say it to my mom, with me in earshot, then laugh, like it was a joke. Anyway, I'd told my mom about some girl I liked, I think it was the eighth grade, and he said, 'You seriously think some sexy chick is going to have anything to do with you?'"

Ellen gasped. "God, that's awful."

"Yeah, it is. But I couldn't see it then. I just thought that was my dad making, I guess, an honest assessment of me. I remember him saying things like—and I can't believe I remember it like it was yesterday—'The good lookers are only after some wild-ass punk with greasy hair on a motorcycle, with no job, no education. If not that, then some limp-wristed beatnik, spouting bad poetry, while he shoots up with heroin. Hate to break the news to you, sonny boy'—he called me 'sonny boy' when he was putting me down—'but they're not gonna be looking your way ....' I can't believe I still remember that."

"God, he must have hated women," said Ellen.

Jasmine chimed in. "Sounds like he wasn't such a big fan of himself, either."

"What did your mother do when he said things like that?" Ellen asked.

Ed chewed his lip, then rubbed Ralph's head. "She didn't speak up, other than saying something like, 'Now, Carl ...,' then later she'd say to me, 'You know your father loves you very much; he just doesn't know how to say it.'"

"Did your dad ever say he loved you?" Ellen said.

Ed gave out a self-deprecating chuckle. "On his death bed. He died of cancer while I was in grad school, and he said it then." He removed his glasses and cleaned the lenses on his shirt, replaced them, then said, "I don't know why I'm talking about all this now." He felt his eyes swollen and for a moment he feared he might be about to cry. "Yeah, my dad was a strange character. Wouldn't let me play in Little League because he said it was about a bunch of loud-mouthed parents showing off their kids. Wouldn't let me take driver's ed in high school because the government had no right taking over the responsibility of the parents. Geez, why am I digging up all this crap now?" He breathed out a loud sigh. "He wouldn't even let me go to the public swimming pool because he claimed they put dangerous chemicals in the water." Now he laughed. "So, I guess it's no wonder I'm a little messed up, huh?"

"Did you ever get married, Ed?" Jasmine asked.

"Yeah. That's another story. After the accident, I couldn't walk. I was in bed at my parents' house for months. I was very depressed. At times, I wished I hadn't crawled out of that car—dying in that car fire would have been preferable to what I'd become. And I also thought about how I should have jumped out when the door popped open, but I didn't—I chose the worst path." He smirked and blew out an audible grunt of disgust.

He shot them a quick glance, then returned his eyes to Ralph, whose warm eyes oozed sympathy. "Eventually, I started coming out of my funk, the doctors ordered more aggressive physical therapy, and I started working really hard to get back up on my feet."

"What did your dad say about all that?" asked Ellen.

"I think the accident knocked the wind out of his sails. He sort of went silent after the accident. Wouldn't talk much."

"So the physical therapy helped?"

"Yes, a lot. Got me into a regimen that I've followed most of my life, and I progressively got better. It's where I met Diane."

"That was your wife?" Ellen asked.

"Yes. She was my PT. That was a disaster from the beginning. I was still depressed and self-absorbed. I was a terrible husband, mainly feeling sorry for myself. And Diane, I think she saw me as her project, a helpless creature for her to nurture and care for. After two years of that crap, she left me … I can't blame her."

There was another period of silence, then Jasmine asked, "Did you have any children?" Then she looked down toward Ed's legs and quickly added, "Oh, I'm sorry, maybe I shouldn't have—"

"Oh, no, that's okay. I'm all right in that department." Now he felt himself blushing. "I mean ..." He didn't continue. They all shared a much-needed laugh.

"But, no, I never had any children. I think in many ways my students became my children."

"You were a professor, Ed. And you were a physicist." Ellen was obviously trying to lift his spirits.

"That is true. Know why I went into physics?" He pursed his lips. "To impress Dad. In my screwed up way, I thought if I could please him, then ... anyway, I went to Sonoma State and majored in physics. I wasn't in love with it, but I discovered that I had some aptitude for it. Good enough to get me into grad school at Davis, into the Ph.D. program. But it became clear that I wasn't going to make it, no way was I going to pass the qualifiers. So, when—"

"How did you know you weren't going to pass?" asked Jasmine.

"Oh, I could tell by the way I was doing in my class work, but, yeah, sometimes I've wondered if I'd stuck it out, maybe I could've made it through." He scrunched his lips like there was a bad taste in his mouth. "So, anyway, when the job opportunity at Muir came along, I pounced on it. The Davis folks were generous enough to let me go with a master's, and I've been teaching the freshman survey courses ever since." He looked up at them and shrugged. Their eyes were locked on him. "But, you know what? I learned that I loved teaching because I loved the kids. I could have been teaching music or geography or Spanish, it wouldn't have made any difference."

God, he'd been rambling on, he thought. "You must think I'm a real loser."

Ellen leaned forward and took both of his hands in hers. "Anything but that, Ed. Anything but that."

Then they were silent, until Jasmine said, "Like I said, if you guys were ready to head out tonight, maybe to Canada, and wanted me along, I wouldn't say no."

Chapter 18

"Oh, good, you came back," hollered Dottie Arnold, hurrying toward them with outstretched arms, from across the room. They had just entered the Grand Ballroom, and Jasmine had disappeared, apparently to find and mollify Shane.

While Ed was crafting some apologetic excuse for their disappearance, Ellen said, "We went to see the old school."

Dottie gave them a devilish smile, like they were naughty kids, cutting class. "How was it?"

Dottie seemed to feel responsible for everyone at the reunion. Nurturing, protecting, like a mother waiting up until her kids are safely home. Her eyes glowed with a homey warmth that made you feel appreciated. Ed couldn't imagine anyone else heading up this reunion. He looked at Ellen, then back at Dottie. "It was good to be back. I hadn't seen it since graduation." Dottie would have no doubt enjoyed the story of their break-in of the English classroom, but Ed decided against sharing it, in case it might get Jasmine into trouble.

Ed scanned the room. Things were hopping—Cream was pounding out "Sunshine of Your Love," and the volume of chatter was high and animated. Denny Jones, the perfect co-host, was making his way from table to table, patting shoulders and laughing and listening attentively to stories. Chuck Barlow still sipped his cola cup with a group of guys off in one corner, probably plastered by now. "It's a great reunion, Dottie. I'm glad I came." He said this because he knew Dottie would love hearing it, but also because it was true. *Dammit*, he thought, *it really is true.*

While the three of them stood in silence, taking it all in, voices on the far side of the room rose above the rest. It sounded contentious. It sounded like an argument was brewing.

Dottie took a step forward. "Oh, my, what could that be?"

As Ed turned his attention toward the ruckus, Jasmine materialized beside him, holding her phone up toward him. "I think it's the many-worlds guy again," she said.

Ed shot Dottie and Ellen a quick glance and said, "I've got to take this," then retreated to the corner of the room, where it was only slightly quieter. He pushed open a door and stepped out into what appeared to be a service hallway.

"Put it on speaker." It was Jasmine, who had quietly followed him. "Please," she added. "I want to hear about the many-worlds quantum mechanics."

"Sorry, Jasmine," he whispered, "this is—" Her expectant eyes caused him to stop mid-sentence. "Okay. But you're just listening, got it?"

Jasmine nodded, as Ed spoke into the phone. "Dr. Jameson, this is Ed Turner."

"So, Turner, I'm still thinking about the screwy physics."

"I'm listening."

"So, if the Copenhagen interpretation is wrong," he began, "then an explanation opens up, as we said before."

"Yes, the many-worlds idea. Look, Dr. Jameson, as fascinating as that theory is, it's hard for me to digest. I mean, I'm a real person, I'm here in a real world, where—"

"Gell-Mann," interrupted Ship.

"Huh?" Ed shot Jasmine a glance, but her eyes were glued to the phone, like she could see into some deeper truth that was somehow eluding Ed.

"Gell-Mann's Principle. Gell-Mann's damned Principle."

Ed knew that Murray Gell-Mann was the famed Nobel-laureate who developed the theory of quarks. But he didn't know about a Gell-Mann Principle. "Sorry, Dr. Jameson, but I don't—"

Ship cut him off. "Didn't figure you would. Gell-Mann's Totalitarian Principle states: 'Everything not forbidden is compulsory.'"

"What does that have to do—"

"You said you were a physicist, right?"

"Of course," Ed said sheepishly, looking down at Jasmine.

"Let me spell it out for you." Ed heard Ship sigh. "If the mathematics of quantum theory does not forbid the many-worlds interpretation—and it doesn't, as far as I can tell—then a many-worlds interpretation is compulsory, Gell-Mann would say." He paused for a moment to let this sink in. "I might add that the Principle is not just a willy-nilly hunch. It's actually been applied to predictions in particle physics that eventually were verified."

"Okay, so what does this have to do—"

"In the many worlds interpretation of quantum mechanics, this means that every possibility of every interaction—like perhaps the decision-making process in your brain—which is not forbidden by some physical law, will actually happen with some finite probability."

Ed felt his irritation rise. He was lost in some new reality, struggling to understand what had happened to him, and Ship was reveling in the excitement of being at the cutting edge of some new physics discovery. He took a deep breath and willed himself to remain calm. This was, after all, perhaps his only chance to be saved from being stuck here forever.

Ship went on. "This possibility has always been there in the equations, but physicists dismissed the predictions largely because their predictions didn't jive with what was observed—the cat was always either alive or dead. Reminds me of something Weinberg once wrote: 'The problem with physicists is not that they trusted their equations too much, but that they didn't trust them enough.'"

Steven Weinberg, Ed knew, was yet another Nobel laureate that Ship was fond of quoting. Shipley Jameson was brilliant enough to have been a part of that community of the physics rock stars, but instead—because of that unrevealed secret—had wound up at Muir. "So why hasn't this been observed before?" Ed asked. "I mean, to use your example from before, how come we haven't ever found a cat that was both alive and dead?"

Jasmine gave Ed a confused look. Then Ship said, "Maybe that's what we're finding tonight."

A chill shot through Ed.

Ship continued, "Or maybe, we're just dealing with a highly delusional person, who—"

"Ed's not crazy," Jasmine blurted, then gave Ed an apologetic look.

"Oh?" Ship sounded suspicious.

"She's a … um … a friend. A physics student, actually. Jasmine."

"Look, Turner, I'm not—"

Jasmine cut in. "I've been reading Feynman. You ever heard of him, professor?" She gave Ed a wink. "Anyway, I was just reading his lecture series—I'm only in volume one—but I found this quote. I was re-reading this section after Ed told me about your quantum mechanics explanation. Here, listen." Jasmine produced the volume of Feynman and began reading: "*'… there is nothing that living things do that cannot be understood from the point of view that they are made of atoms acting according to the laws of physics.'*" Jasmine put the book down, then said, "So is that what we're dealing with here, Dr. Jameson?"

There was silence on the other end, then Ship said, "Yes, that's exactly what we're dealing with here. I mean, what we *may* be dealing with."

Ed gave Jasmine a thumbs-up, which made her smile, then said, "Look, Dr. Jameson, we can quote Gell-Mann and Feynman all night, but the truth is, there hasn't been a recorded case of this ever happening before. Is this not true?"

"Recorded may be the key word in that statement, Mr. Turner. Maybe what you're really saying is that all this talk of a parallel universe may seem too far-fetched to be true, that it just doesn't mesh with what we know as reality. Is that correct?"

Ed didn't want to sound unimaginative, but, in fact, that pretty much was correct. What he said was, "Well, I wouldn't word it quite like—"

"Listen, Turner, I'm going to tell you something you must already know. And you, too, Jasmine. We find ourselves in a bewildering world—that's a direct quote from Hawking, by the way. If we're brandishing around all those other big names, we may as well throw a little Hawking in, too." Then Ship laughed. It was the first time this evening that Ed had heard Ship laugh, and it felt good. He continued. "We live in a universe where 96% of the matter and energy is unaccounted for, the so-called dark matter and dark energy. Where is that missing matter, Turner? Tell me, if you know."

Jasmine looked at Ed, as if expecting a learned response, but he was at a loss for words.

Ship continued. "And we live in a universe, where—if string theory is correct, and at present, it seems that it may be—instead of the usual three spatial dimensions plus time, the fourth, there are actually eleven dimensions. Where are those extra dimensions, Turner? Tell me if you know."

Ed felt a bead of sweat forming on his forehead. He licked his lips that had suddenly gone dry. He looked down at Jasmine, whose eyes were now locked on him. "All of this talk about the universe is amazing, Ship, I mean Dr. Jameson. But we're talking about my life, my fragile, precarious, scary life. We can spout physics theories all night, but meanwhile I'm stuck here, and I'm really scared. I don't know how I got here, and I don't know how to get back."

Ship started to speak, but then there was a female voice from the background, the one Ed had heard before. He couldn't make out what the woman said, but he heard Ship's response. Tenderly, he said, "I know it's really late, Leyla. I'm coming to bed soon, my darling." Then he returned to Ed. "Look, Turner, I've got to go. I know you must be scared. Sorry I can't help much with that right now. But let's keep thinking about it." The phone clicked off.

Ed looked at Jasmine, expecting some sympathy. Instead, she said, "Eleven freaking dimensions? Holy crap."

Chapter 19

Dottie and Ellen stood where Ed had left them, looking out into the room. Many of the guests were now standing around the tables. Only a few, such as Chuck Barlow and his drinking buddies, were still seated.

A woman Ed didn't recognize had just stepped up to the microphone and had begun to speak. "So, our graduation year began with Martin Luther King still alive. In case you've forgotten, and it sounds like some of us have, let me refresh your memory about his message to us. Here's what he said in his last speech, in April of 1968." She looked down at her phone and scrolled for a moment. "He wrote this. '... *the world is all messed up. The nation is sick. Trouble is in the land; confusion all around. That's a strange statement. But I know, somehow, that only when it is dark enough can you see the stars.*'"

Now she looked up from her phone. "The next day this man, who dreamed dreams of freedom and justice and unity, stepped out onto the balcony of his motel room into the cool of the evening. A thirty-ought-six bullet ripped into his brain, and he died." She paused for a moment, and there was silence in the room. Then she said, "'Seeing the stars in the darkness. But maybe we weren't ready to see those stars in the darkness.

Maybe we preferred the darkness. By November of that year, we had elected Richard Nixon."

"At least I love America," yelled one man. Ed couldn't see who it was.

"I do, too," another voice, a woman's, cried. "But sometimes love has to acknowledge that things have to change, that wrongs have been done, even by people we respect and love."

"I don't buy that crap, not for one minute," hollered another man. Now he approached the microphone.

Ed now felt both of Dottie's hands gripping his forearm, like someone being swept away in a flood clinging to a tree branch. Denny Jones had been going from person to person, obviously trying to calm the anger that seemed to be growing by the moment. But now he came over to where Dottie stood with Ed and Ellen. He shook his head, as he raised his hands, palms up, in an expression of hopelessness. "I don't know what to do. I had no idea there was such pent-up anger."

"Good God, it was fifty years ago," said Dottie, still clinging to Ed. Her eyes were wide and watery, effusing a mixture of disappointment and fear. "Can't they let it go?"

"I'm not sure this is really about what happened fifty years ago," said Denny. "I think it's about now."

Dottie was on the verge of tears. "Our reunion, it's been ruined," she shrieked. "I don't understand why there is such anger in the world."

Ed looked down at Dottie next to him, then up at Denny—the perky cheerleader-grandmother and the veteran firefighter. Too bad, he thought, there were not more Dottie Arnolds and Denny Joneses around—that was the answer to all the anger.

Now another man—Ed didn't recognize him—spoke into the microphone, his voice shaking, either with rage or fear. "Our country was built on hard work, on standing up for our beliefs—not being some chicken shit who runs away to Canada, who burns our flags, who's living a Woodstock life of drugs and sex or at least wants to, while our brave soldiers were dying in all those terrible places for all of us." There was a burst of applause and several cries of *U-S-A, U-S-A,* as the man fiddled with the buttons of his sport coat.

Across the room, Jerry paced back and forth, looking frantic. He tapped in a new song, Johnny Cash's "Folsom Prison Blues," and turned up the volume.

The man continued, now speaking louder to be heard above the music. "The sixties was the first time that people began to question our country. I grew up, like a lot of you, believing that America was the best, most generous, principled country in the world. Our people were the most free. I still believe that." He was interrupted by more applause. "But then it became fashionable to question our leaders. To question our values. Our morals. Our purpose. Our military had not lost a war until Vietnam, and if you ask me, it wasn't because our military lacked the power or the will or the courage. It was because a generation of soft people had suddenly forgotten that it's been our military might and our will to fight and stand up for freedom that has made this country great. That sorry time was just the beginning. Then it was Iraq. Then Afghanistan. Because we've gotten so soft, weak, apologetic about our greatness—we've lost our will, we've lost our way, and we've become the laughing stock of the world." Now there was more applause, another outbreak of the chant, now louder, of *U-S-A, U-S-A.* "Okay, I'm not going to talk all night, because we've already done too much of that. It's time to act, my friends, it's time to take our country back."

As the emotional temperature of the room continued to rise, Ed remembered reading that the hit version of "Folsom Prison Blues" had actually been recorded before a live audience of inmates at Folsom Prison and how the men had cheered when Cash sang about killing a man just to watch him die. *Maybe not the best song choice, Jerry.*

What the hell was going on here, Ed wondered. It seemed bizarre to see a bunch of senior citizens going at it like this. Shaking a fist while leaning on their walker with the other hand. Ready to march when they could barely walk. Wasn't this a time in life to be more mellow, a time in life when wisdom and tolerance and understanding have replaced the easily stirred passions of youth? Or maybe it was the nature of the evening—the time machine—that was rekindling old fires and old memories. Or maybe it was the signature of a world gone mad, where people of any age had lost the ability to listen, to forgive, to tolerate.

Now Vivian Thomas, who'd spoken earlier, approached the microphone, which the man reluctantly surrendered to her. She cleared her throat, then said, "During 1968—when most of us were thinking about dates, acne, football games and passing finals—up to 300 body bags were being shipped home every week. Young men and women. Good people. Kids from the farm belt, kids from the inner city, kids from the coasts, kids from places like Sentinel High School. Brave, yes. Our best." She was interrupted by applause.

Vivian Thomas licked her lips, then continued. "I think everyone supported them. But supporting our troops did not mean sending them into an ill-conceived war, begun and fostered by politicians who were either worried more about re-election than about human lives, or maybe they just didn't grasp what was really going on. From their comfortable leather chairs in their paneled offices, wearing their blue business suits and knowing that after this meeting, they'd all be gathering for martinis at some local watering hole—from that vantage point, maybe they couldn't grasp what was going on in the sweltering jungles, where young people were blowing each other's heads off." There was more applause and a few cheers, mixed with boos.

"You know what pisses me off?" she asked. "People who say we don't support our troops because we don't approve of every military adventure concocted by some old man who probably never himself served in the military, who never got shot at, who never saw his best friends blown up by artillery fire or IEDs." More applause and boos. "I'm not saying all our uses of military force are politically motivated—yes, we need to protect ourselves and we need to stand up for our friends, but what we don't need to do is give a blank check to our leaders, under the guise of supporting our troops."

Vivian stepped away from the microphone, as a few loud voices cried out jeers. "Sit down, commie," and "We don't need fuzzy-headed do-gooders, we need leaders." One woman called out, "I'd rather trust our elected leaders than a VW bus packed with six naked, unwashed hippies smoking mushrooms." This brought laughter and another round of U-S-A, U-S-A.

Ed wondered what their grandkids would think if they could see their grandpas and grandmas now? Was there some principle for which they were standing up? Or were they just acting up? Would little Kyle put a restraining hand on his grandma's arm and whisper, "Let's just calm down, Nana."

Ed could see where this was headed, and it was scary.
Two large groups had begun to move toward the middle of the
room, now separated by only twenty feet or so, and it didn't
require a lot of imagination to fear that the evening might
devolve into something dangerous. Shouting at each other
over Vietnam and the country's military policies was probably
only the beginning—government spending, healthcare, the
environment: there were a lot of topics that could ignite these
sparks into a full-fledged conflagration.

Maybe for the people here, it felt good to get the old
juices flowing again, like a dose of emotional Viagra. Or maybe
the evening was pulling scabs away from wounds that had
never healed.

Now yet another man stepped up to the microphone and
began to speak, then tapped it when no sound was produced.
Someone had apparently cut the power to the mic. *Probably a
good move*, thought Ed. But the man was not thwarted by this.
He stepped to the center of the room, and raised his voice.
"That's the problem with you libs, you're just standing on the
sidelines wringing your hands, shedding your crocodile tears,
while the future of this great nation is at stake. Yeah, this has
been going on for a long time. Too long, I say. I, for one, am
not going to stand for it anymore." He thrust a clenched fist
into the air.

Now several other people stepped out and joined arms
with the man.

Denny shook his head. "I'm not sure if I should laugh or
cry. A bunch of people pushing seventy getting ready for a
gang fight."

Yeah, maybe this was silly, thought Ed. Maybe we should
be laughing at this embarrassing, almost comical, scene. But

maybe it wasn't silly. Maybe it was a grasping for relevance. As old as everyone here was, as out of touch as they might seem to be, they were all as young as the two most recent presidential candidates, as young as many of our political leaders. Maybe their passions weren't so irrelevant after all.

Ed looked at Ellen, then to Dottie and Denny. Their faces reflected what was in his own heart and mind: despair and fear.

Chapter 20

Ed Turner had taught Physics 101 for decades. This entailed speaking to a hundred students who didn't really want to hear from him, getting their attention and then telling them what they needed to know. Often, they were glued to their phones or chatting with friends or dozing off, and the last thing they wanted was a lecture on, say, mutual induction.

It was funny. Ed could speak easily to a large crowd, down front in a huge auditorium—confident, self-assured and in charge. Yet, in one-on-one interactions, even with acquaintances, he struggled to make conversation. It was a problem that had plagued him since high school. It was worse with girls. He'd try making relaxed small talk, cracking jokes, laughing—but he was always too aware that he was talking with a woman, and he'd choke up.

The Schrader Lecture Hall at Muir College was a conventional teaching auditorium like those found on many college campuses. With a seating capacity of about 200, it sloped from the back down to the lecture area, so that the teacher stood a good thirty feet below the students in the back, top row. The rows were slightly curved around the lecture area, providing a theatre-in-the-round effect. The auditorium always reminded Ed of a Roman coliseum, where citizens would gather to watch the Christians being fed to the lions. The similarity could be no accident.

Ed had learned how to stay calm and focused and how to project his voice with authority. Still, he remembered how on the first day of class each semester he'd stand at the door, before entering the big auditorium, his hands shaking, his heart in his mouth.

Dottie Arnold was visibly agitated, as the arguing had now reached even higher decibel levels. The Grand Ballroom had separated into two large groups, facing off, the large space between them shrinking. Ed took Dottie Arnold's hands in his, then nodded at Ellen and Denny. "Wish me well," he said. Then he let go of Dottie's hands and stepped out into the room alone, between the converging groups.

"Quiet," he bellowed. It was not an angry voice, but it was loud and carried authority. It was commanding. The room immediately went quiet. Ed recalled the advice a fellow teacher had given him when he began at Muir: *the first rule of swimming with sharks is, if bitten, don't bleed.* He was not going to bleed.

He glanced at Ellen, Dottie and Denny—each bore looks of uncertainty, no doubt wondering what he was preparing to do. Somehow, this gave him confidence.

Then he began. "Some people here," he said, "have put a lot of work into this reunion. It was more than work. They put their hearts into it. They did it out of ...." He looked over at Dottie and Denny again. "They did it out of love, thinking of you, each of you, as they put this thing together, knowing it might be the last time some of us might see each other."

Now Ed looked down, not in shyness or because he didn't know what to say next. He understood that timing is everything. Then he looked up. "You know, I almost didn't come tonight. I thought it wasn't that important, I mean, what difference would it make if I'm not here?" He paused again. "You know what? I was wrong."

He looked over at Ellen now, who was beaming. "We've come down long paths in our lives, the world leading us in many different directions. But we started out here at Sentinel, together. We started out into the world at a time of great turmoil, thrust into it unprepared. I wasn't ready, for sure. It challenged us all, even those of us who tried to ignore it. Surrounded by conflict and uncertainty, you can't help but be affected.

"We've got our opinions about the world, strong opinions. I've got mine, too. But at the bottom of everything, it's just us. Just us. Just kids from Sentinel High. Drawing Social Security now, but still feeling like kids inside. Still trying to figure out what we want to be when we grow up." This drew a few chuckles.

"If our arguments tear us apart, if we come to hate each other, if we get to where we can't listen to each other, can't respect each other, then what have we gained? I can't see that we've gained anything, but oh, we will have lost everything." He turned slowly, carefully planting his quad cane for balance, so that he could face each sector of the room. "This could be the last few hours that we have together. I urge you to think very carefully about what you want to do with those hours."

Now one man, who Ed did not recognize, spoke up. "Nice words, Eddie, but it's all crap. There are issues that go above laughs with old high school friends. There are—"

"That's crazy," Ed shouted, cutting him off with that authoritative voice, just as effectively as he would deal with a smart-ass, out-of-line student at Muir. "Completely crazy!" Then he lowered his voice to a gentler, more pastoral tone, but kept the volume up just high enough that everyone could hear. "Look, we don't have to agree with each other. We never have, we don't now. But what we can do now is accept each other. Otherwise, what are we doing here?

"Look at us," he said. "We can't even talk to each other. This isn't a reunion. It's a disunion. If we can't care for each other as we are, then what hope is there?

"You thought Eddie Turner was dead. And you were wrong. But maybe the truth is: maybe we're all dead." He was silent again, measuring out in his mind how long the silence should be. "Maybe, just maybe, it's time to start living.

"You know, I don't see two sides here. I see one group of human beings, one group of 68-year-old people, people who know about challenges of all kinds ... but also have beautiful grandchildren, great stories, stretching back decades—tears and tragedies, laughter and joys—who all live in one country. A country that is so wonderful because we are one group of people.

"Maybe what we can give the world, what we can give each other, even at this late date, is hope that diverse people can live together, can love each other, can listen to each other, can forgive each other. Can see that what unites us is greater than what divides us. That we can have deeply held opinions, that we can work together to change, to improve the world. That we can do that without marginalizing, alienating, hating those who don't see it our way. Maybe that's what we can do. Yes, I think that's exactly what we can do. What we must do."

Then Ed was silent. He continued to turn slowly, leaning heavily on his cane, making eye contact with as many people as he could. Many of them looked down. Some nodded. A few were in tears.

Ed said to himself, *Class dismissed.* He was suddenly self-conscious, as the whole room remained quiet. He had talked too long.

Then Jerry, who had been watching the whole thing quietly, his mouth open and his face red with anxiety, bent down and fiddled with a box behind him. Then he stood up straight and brought the trumpet to his lips. He began playing the school alma mater—Ed hadn't heard it in years. Jerry played it slow, like he was playing taps. Many in the room began singing the old school song.

"Oh Sentinel, oh Sentinel, we pledge our love to thee. Though years may go, we'll ever show unending loyalty."

When it ended, there was a long period of awkward silence. Then, Sherrie Blanton, who'd been part of the initial polarizing words of the evening, stepped across the space between the groups and put her arms around Vivian Thomas.

As Ed made his way back toward the edge of the room, Jasmine came up to him. "That was pretty cool, Ed," she said, "but I gotta admit, there at the end I was getting worried I might have to watch a bunch of old farts singing Kumbaya."

Chapter 21

Denny raised a hand for a high five, and this brought a smile to Ed's solemn face. He slapped Denny's hand, putting some muscle behind it. Ed hadn't played football like Denny, but they were on the same team now. It was good. Dottie bounced toward him, and it was easy to imagine her waving a pom-pom. "Way to go, Ed!" she gushed.

Ellen stood to the side with a shy smile. When he turned toward her, she placed a hand on his arm, then pulled it away like a child caught in the act of reaching for a forbidden piece of candy. "Ed, I don't know what to say. You saved the reunion."

"Well, I—"

"Oh wait," Ellen interrupted, as she now looked over Ed's shoulder toward the entrance. "There she is. I'll be right back. I want her to meet you."

Ed turned and recognized Gloria Marquez entering the room. *Didn't Ellen say her name was now Marquez-Herrera?* She was arm-in-arm with a slender, distinguished looking man with wavy white hair. Gloria was just like he remembered her from high school. Petite, except now with gray hair instead of black, olive skin—he was too far away to see any wrinkles—an intense face, like she was concentrating on a hard problem.

She had been a quiet, brainy student, pretty but not super popular. It was easy to believe she had become a lawyer, but, good grief, a priest? She wore gray slacks and a long red cardigan, open around a high-neckline white blouse. Ed had little experience with clergy, but his image of a priest was an old man in a heavy cloak—the hood shadowing his eyes—processing slowly with a candle, while chants were being sung off in the darkness.

As Ed watched Ellen greet Gloria and her companion, Jasmine came up to him again. "What was it like living through Vietnam? Nobody my age ever talks about it."

As Ed pondered her question, Jerry bellowed, "Okay, Titans, it's time for feelin' good. So here's a little something to get the old juices flowing again. Let's have a good time!" He'd apparently regained his upbeat DJ mojo. Soon the Stones were belting out "Jumpin' Jack Flash." A few couples headed for the center of the floor.

Ed turned toward Jasmine, then took a few more seconds, while he studied the curiosity in her dark eyes. "Well, everyone was suffering back then. Week after week we heard the reports of 100, 200, 300 body bags coming home."

Jasmine shook her head, her eyes narrowing like she was struggling to comprehend this.

"Everyone wanted it to be over," he said. "The protesters said just get out, but I think the politicians didn't want to admit defeat on their watch. And maybe it wasn't that simple, I don't know. Others said we had to hang in there, maybe we were just one more push away from winning. The political leaders clung to an idea called the domino theory, that if we let South Vietnam fall to the communists, then all of southeast Asia would also fall. Like a row of dominos."

He stopped to look out across the room, where more people were rocking to the Rolling Stones, at least as much as senior citizens can rock. Mick Jagger was singing about how he'd been drowned and left for dead and got a spike driven through his head. But it was all right now. Sure—the Stones seemed to suggest—just laugh, dance and forge your way through the pain and ugliness, getting high along the way.

Jasmine's eyes were glued to him, as he continued. "Yeah, we had technology and brave soldiers, but North Vietnam had an endless number of people. Even women and children were fighting. I understand they also had a good supply of weapons from China and Russia. Our young people were trampling through swamps and jungles that were full of land mines. It was almost impossible for them, I guess."

"How many people died?"

"Well over fifty-thousand Americans."

"How many Vietnamese?"

"I'm not sure anyone knows exactly. I've heard over a million."

"God." She said it in a way that sounded more like a prayer than a curse.

Out on the floor, people were dancing like they'd miraculously shed fifty years, laughing with arms in the air, apparently oblivious to the dark words of the song.

"It happened gradually, over years. Our leaders kept thinking, or at least saying, that the end was coming soon, that victory was just around the corner. We had started with just a few troops in Vietnam—they called them advisors—but before it ended we had a half-million soldiers there." Ed shook his head slowly. "Many brave soldiers. But some of the political leaders we were supporting in South Vietnam were corrupt and that didn't help. Some people began to consider it an unjust war, an unwinnable war.

"There were lots of demonstrations against the war, and some of them were unruly. Some people left for Canada to avoid the draft. Some saw the demonstrators as heroes. Others saw them as un-American—deserters, cowards, traitors. A deep rift began to form in the country. I'm no political scientist, but it seems to me that that time may have planted the seeds that have caused the great polarization that's in our country today."

Jasmine licked her lip, taking all this in. "But there've been lots of wars. Why was this one so different?"

Now Dottie joined them, listening to their conversation, but not speaking. Her pep rally demeanor was gone, replaced by a serious, focused look.

Ed nodded to Dottie, then scratched his head. "When I was a kid, my parents told me two things about war. One, America always fought on the right side, the side of honor and good. And second, America never lost a war. I guess Vietnam challenged all that. Hell, we were just innocent kids, and we came out into this world to flag-draped coffins, pictures of naked children running from napalm, college students being shot by the National Guard, slaughters in Vietnamese villages, drugs, chaos, Americans turning against each other.

"And here we are today." He started to say more but pursed his lips instead.

Jasmine looked stunned, like a patient who'd just received a bad diagnosis. "Holy crap, do you all hate each other?"

"No, not at all." Ed paused to look around the room, like he might be reconsidering his answer. "I mean, it's complicated."

"It sure seemed like you hate each other. Geez, screaming and accusing. I thought there'd be a fight for sure."

After some silence, Dottie said, "My older brother, Jack, joined the Marines in '67. We were so proud of him. He'd graduated from Sentinel three years before me, he was my hero." She looked out to the room, where more couples were now dancing, nodded her head in beat to the Stones. Now she looked back at them.

Ed bit his lip, sensing that something disturbing was about to be revealed.

"May 11, 1969, a Saturday." Dottie shook her head. "I was home for the weekend. I remember the doorbell ringing and my mom getting it. Two soldiers were standing there." Her lower lip now puffed out and trembled. It seemed like she might be about to cry. But then she pursed her lips like she'd claimed a sudden resolve and wiped an eye with the back of her hand.

Ed tried to offer some words, but could only whisper, "I'm sorry."

Dottie continued. "An ambush. That's all we ever learned." She shook her head again. "It changed me. I had been a big supporter of the war, of our military, because of my brother. But after that I changed. I couldn't watch TV any more. The news was everywhere." More silence.

Dottie breathed out a sad groan, a far cry from the cheery persona she had displayed all evening. "But that was a long time ago. Now … now … I just don't know. I try not to think about it." Then she pasted on a smile. "I try to think about the good times.

"When I saw all that anger out there tonight, it just brought it all back. So I really appreciate what you did, Ed. Not just for the reunion … but also for me." More silence.

Then Dottie said, "I'd better get back out there. Life of the party, you know." She looked from face to face, then laid a hand on each of their forearms. "Hey, don't mean to get you guys down. I just gotta let it out once in a while." Then she launched herself back into the crowd, seeming as bubbly as ever.

After Dottie left, Ed and Jasmine exchanged troubled looks. "Dear God, that is so sad," Jasmine said. Then she added, "Did you fight in the war, Ed?"

"No." Ed looked at the ceiling, then back at Jasmine. "I probably would have been drafted, if I hadn't been injured in the accident. Got a low draft number when the lottery came out the year after we graduated."

"Lottery?"

"Yeah, lots of people were being drafted, so to make it more fair, the government set up a lottery by randomly assigning a number for each day of the year. So, you looked up the number assigned to your birthday, and that was the order in which you'd be drafted."

"And you got a low number?"

"33. Would've been drafted for sure, but I couldn't even walk by then. So I was unfit to go." He looked down. He had once been afraid of being drafted, but he still carried shame about not having served. He glanced toward the far wall, where the poster display with pictures of all the deceased students stood in the shadows. No one was looking at it.

Now they were quiet, as the Stones wrapped up. Ed didn't know what Jagger and Richards had in mind when they wrote "Jumpin' Jack Flash," but maybe they were writing about his generation. The worst had happened to them— violence, betrayal, broken trust. They'd been brought to their knees. But it was all right now, they screamed. Was it all right now because they had transcended the brokenness of the age, or was it all right now because of complete denial? He wasn't sure which was the correct answer.

Chapter 22

As soon as Ed was alone, the terror returned. Jasmine had disappeared to tend to her hospitality duties, Denny and Dottie were moving among the crowd, and Ellen was still laughing with Gloria Marquez-Herrera by the entrance. He chastised himself about his terror, reminding himself of Dottie's brave brother.

Yes, he'd been distracted by the events of the reunion. As long as he could bask in the conversation and laughter and intrigue of these people, he was okay. Maybe sometimes important things that are too astounding to grasp do not command our attention like lesser, more ordinary things that are right before our eyes.

Ed paced near his chair, too rattled to sit. There were immediate practicalities that he would soon have to confront. He had no money, no identity. He had no place to go after the party tonight. Sure, Cody had said they had rooms available at the Villa Solana, but Ed had no credit card, no cash. He literally did not know where his next meal would come from.

As important as having food and shelter are, it was the growing realization that he was in a different universe that overwhelmed him. It wasn't like the world he had left was that great, but at least he had an identity there, a place to live, an income.

The muscles in his jaw involuntarily clenched, biting down on bleak thoughts, terror that only served to disable him further. He forced his attention to the room around him, determined to purge his panic with thoughts about more mundane things.

The Grand Ballroom. It was such a vanilla space, he thought—plain and square with a bland peachy-beige finish. Calling it the Grand Ballroom was like calling a Corvair a Cadillac. Except for the gaudy chandeliers, it could have been a warehouse.

The boring venue did little justice to the rich soup of life represented here. Here was a collection of lives, the culmination of over sixty years of history, complexities beyond description—formed by joy and loss, hope and disappointment, a hundred people who had not only weathered Vietnam in various ways, and apparently were still weathering it, but had seen so many other things.

Everyone here, he thought, had been shaped by Y2K and 9-11, Watergate and Monica Lewinsky, had struggled to adjust to the explosions in technology. Just when they'd finally learned how to program their VCRs, those disappeared, and then so did CD players. These people, who grew up writing letters, now struggled to grasp Instagram and Snapchat. They had smoked dope and experimented with LSD, suffered through broken hearts and saw parents die. They grew up lusting for muscle cars—maybe an Olds 442, with its huge 455 V-8, four-barrel carb, dual exhausts and four-on-the-floor— only to live through gas rationing and coming to terms with the ideas of electric and self-driving cars. They had searched for meaning, had tried to hold onto meaning. They understood what it means to see youth fade, knees weaken, wounds heal more slowly, to check for the label that says 'relaxed fit.' They knew what a Do Not Resuscitate order means. Learned about statins and colonoscopies and CPAP machines.

But the people gathered here didn't seem impaired by these changes. Maybe it was because they had each other. In spite of their conflicts, like the shouting match that had just subsided, they had each other. And ultimately, maybe that's all they needed. He grasped the cane even harder, suddenly staggered by the long years he had been alone. You don't ever get used to loneliness, you just learn ways to deal with it. Music or baseball games playing in the background 24-7, hobbies that keep you busy, like gardening. Diversions that are just the glaze of marmalade that keeps you from noticing how stale the bread is.

Shit, here they came again—those unwelcomed memories of the early months after the accident. Each morning he'd wake up with sunlight streaming in the windows of the hospital and begin to think about his day and then it would hit him: he would never walk again. Only eighteen and unable to walk for the rest of his life. There would be panic attacks—he couldn't breathe, he would scream, cry and thrash in his bed, but nothing was changed. Doctors, therapists, and social workers visited every day, but that made little difference. His parents came, too, his mother offering empty words of comfort—"Oh, Eddie, I know you're going to be just fine"— and his dad standing silent, head cast down.

It was Mrs. Benson, the unlikely visitor from the gardening club, who brought him the distraction he needed to survive. She was a member of the Master Gardeners in Santa Rosa, and a part of her gardening work included visiting sick people in the hospital. She brought fresh-picked flowers from her garden—even though it was early winter, she had orchids and gloxinias from her greenhouse. They were beautiful. Then she'd launch into long stories about how she'd raised these plants, about what was required for their care, about the emotional attachments she'd developed toward them. At first, Ed had dreaded her weekly visits, with her interminable discourses on pruning, protecting from frost, dealing with aphids and mildew and whatever.

But as the weeks continued, Ed found her talks to be a needed distraction from his self-pity. And then, slowly, he became actively interested. When she wasn't there, he would sometimes crane his neck to better view the hospital gardens through his window, study the peonies and petunias and speculate on the problems they were facing—clearly the hospital did not have the same commitment to gardening that Mrs. Benson had.

When he was finally discharged from the hospital, and even before he returned to Sonoma State, he signed up for a Master Gardener class in Santa Rosa. He'd been an oddity in the class, this nineteen-year-old in a wheelchair among a dozen mostly-elderly women.

His plants gave him purpose. They were, after all, living things, although he sometimes strayed too far in anthropomorphizing them. They all depended upon him. Who would care for them if he left? Plants were an answer to the awful question, assiduously avoided, raised by the person who is alone: what difference would it make if I didn't exist? Their care needed discipline, commitment, study. In some ways it was as complex as raising a child. He rolled his eyes—what a crock comparing raising plants to raising kids. Yet, studying plant food compositions, watering cycles, sunlight placements, pruning schedules, pesticide attributes and cautions, nonetheless, made his responsibilities seem more considerable. Made him more needed.

He pictured his garden back home. *Back home, dear God.* Apparently there was no longer a "back home" for him.

He was trembling again. *Damn.* He closed his eyes and forced the image of a camellia blossom into his mind, with its complex and intricate layering of soft petals, its mélange of subtle colors smeared across the spectrum from near white to intense pink. Yet, for all its beauty, the camellia was ultimately simple, predictable. If you cared for it in the correct way, you'd get the correct result. But something more complex, like Ellen's face, though beautiful as well, was full of danger. There were so many uncertainties there. Mysteries. Behind the soft features of her skin, more lovely than any camellia, there was a brain, churning with analysis and emotion, shaped by her history and heredity, that produced responses that he couldn't predict—moving in a world rich with travel and children and art, writing poetry, serving on mission trips, and pondering the fifty species of sparrows—a life filled with activity and purpose.

Shaking his head, he turned and there she was, almost startling him. He forced a shallow laugh, but couldn't speak.

For a moment Ellen's eyes were locked on his, but then she looked down. Speaking fast, she said, "Gloria will be over in a bit. I want you to meet her. She and Martin, that's her husband, are saying hi to some other friends." Then she was quiet, apparently feeling awkward with him.

Dusty Springfield began to sing "The Look of Love," and this didn't help Ed find words. The song was romantic, erotic, nostalgic. The look of love surpassed time, ignored time, made time irrelevant. Here was this woman he'd only been with a couple of hours, or had he been with her his whole life? Was this their destiny, even when they sat on the carpeted floor of their sixth-grade classroom, hands gooey with papier-mache, fashioning the map of Uruguay? Were they fashioning something else now? Something that even the grave could only interrupt, postpone, but not destroy? A look that time could not erase, the song said. Someone said the eyes were the windows to the soul, yet through these windows he could barely handle what he was seeing. He needed to look away but he couldn't look away—here was everything he ever wanted, everything he'd dreamed about, but it was too real, too intimate, too risky: this chaotic, incendiary, zesty mix of terror and ecstasy. He could hardly breathe, much less speak—maybe Dusty was speaking for him. He needed to flee, even though this may be the destination he had been seeking his whole life.

As the song continued, they stood looking at each other, silent. A few couples now snuggled close on the dance floor. They used to call such dances "belly rubbers"—*did Chuck Barlow say that?* The silence lasted just a few seconds. Or was it an hour? Or was it fifty years?

Ellen finally said, "Why don't we find a place to sit?"

Unable to speak, Ed nodded in compliance and together they walked without words toward an empty table.

He sat next to her, turned toward her. With her hands folded in her lap, she said, "What you did out there, Ed, took a lot of courage."

Ellen, 67 going on 18, brushed a wisp of silvery hair away from her eyes. He imagined trailing his fingertips along the side of her face. He cleared his throat. "It was just something I knew how to do from all my lecturing experience," he said. "Actually, I've been pretty short on courage for most of my life." He was aware that confessing his lack of courage to this engaging woman was in fact a rather courageous thing to do. Ed had been taught that when you swim with sharks, you must not bleed, and he had applied this rule to much of his life. But sometimes, perhaps right now, it may be best to risk the bleeding.

Ellen tilted her head to one side, narrowed her eyes, and smiled. "I find that hard to believe, Ed."

Then she took his hands and cradled them in hers, like she was holding a baby chick.

Chapter 23

Maybe he could swim with sharks, but it was swimming with mermaids that was his undoing. Good God, how he'd fantasized about a moment such as this—back in high school and here tonight, after a fifty-year interlude, as if time had not changed anything. Now, Jerry put on Credence Clearwater Revival singing "Suzie Q," and John Fogerty was having no problem at all saying, plain and simple, what he thought about the sexy Suzie Q. Instead of giving Ed confidence, the primal erotic beat only made him more nervous. No way he could speak to her now plain and simple. But finally he gathered himself and began. "Ellen, I—"

"There you are," said the upbeat voice from behind him. They both turned. It was Gloria Marquez-Herrera.

Ellen stood. "Oh, good, Gloria. Ed, this is Gloria. You said you remembered her."

Ed began to struggle to his feet. "Oh, don't get up, Eddie—I mean Ed," said Gloria, extending a hand, as she took a seat on the other side of Ellen. "It's good to see you. Again, sorry to be late. Like I told Ellen, I had to visit a parishioner in the hospital."

"Where's Martin? I want Ed to meet him."

Gloria scanned the room. "Oh, he's visiting. I suspect he'll be over in a bit."

Shane appeared at their table with a tray of snacks and set small plates in front of each of them. Crème puffs, circled by scoops of whipped crème.

"Thanks, Shane," said Ed, as he took a bite of one of the crème puffs.

Ellen considered the desserts, then looked at Gloria. "God, these do look good, but ..." She pushed her plate away.

Gloria grimaced, pulled her cardigan a little tighter around herself, then pushed her plate away, also. They shared knowing smiles.

Ed finished chewing, then gave them a guilty grin, as he also pushed his plate away toward the center of the table.

Gloria said, "So, what have I missed?"

Ellen laughed. "Oh, about everything. We just averted World War Three, thanks mainly to Ed."

Gloria looked at Ed with inquisitive eyes. They were large and brown and gave her a gentle look. But they also had an intensity that suggested she was listening carefully to what you were saying. She wore little makeup, but her olive skin was smooth, except for wrinkles around her eyes and mouth that were shaped in a way that indicated that she had spent a lot of time smiling. "Oh?"

Ed shrugged. "I think it was just the remnant of the divisions that have been there since Vietnam. Maybe looking back to '68 tapped into those old feelings. All I did was remind people to look past all that." He shrugged again.

"Okay, so Ed, Ellen told me at the door that you were here, and I asked how could that be, and she said I should ask you. So, if it's okay, I guess I'm asking." She folded her arms in front of her and focused those gentle eyes on him, waiting for his answer.

Ed looked at Ellen with a sudden panic.

"You can talk to Gloria," said Ellen. Then she placed a hand on Ed's arm. "But if you'd rather not talk now, it's—"

Ed shook his head. Gloria's face glowed with peace and patience. He needed to talk. He had nothing to lose. He told his story again, starting with his arrival at the wrong hotel, not leaving out any of the speculation that Ship had offered. Gloria's attention never wavered during the story, nor did her face betray feelings of judgment or even surprise. When he was finished, he looked at Ellen, then back at Gloria, and smirked. "So, that's it. Like I said to Ellen, maybe I'm crazy or have some kind of weird dementia, or ..." He exhaled a loud breath. "Or maybe the quantum physics explanation is correct. I'm guessing a priest might find that appalling."

"I don't find anything you said appalling, Ed. Surprising, yes, I'll say that." She gave him a little smile. "You said you're a physicist. So tell me: I'm guessing no one's ever observed this—what did you call it?—many-worlds phenomenon before?"

"Not as far as I know." He shook his head. "So, what do you say about this?"

"Well, I'm getting pretty old, you know." They all shared a needed laugh. "So I've seen a lot of things. I've learned that just because I don't understand something doesn't mean it isn't true. You've come here from a parallel universe? I'm not sure I believe that. But I'm open to mystery. After all, I'm a person who believes a man rose from the dead." She laid her palms flat on the table, looking relaxed.

Ed shot Ellen a smile, who returned a nod that said, *I knew you'd like her.*

Then Gloria said, "Here, listen to this." She hoisted a colorful handbag up onto the table and fished through it before pulling out a small red book. She paged through the book, then found what she was looking for. "This is from the bible, from the Psalms." She shot him a quick smile before she began to read. 'How deep I find your thoughts, O God! How great is the sum of them! If I were to count them, they would be more in number than the sand; to count them all, my life span would need to be like yours.'" She closed the book and set it on the table in front of her. "So, of course I'm surprised by what you've told me. But maybe that's only because of my limited vision. That's what I have to say about what you told me."

Ed looked down at Gloria's book—a bible, he thought. He'd never gone to church. But he remembered once attending a classical music concert held in a church. It had dragged on for three hours, and, out of boredom, he'd picked up a bible in the pew rack and read all of Genesis. What struck him was the violence and deceit in the text. Cain killing his brother Abel. Jacob deceiving his brother Esau and lying to his father. Brothers leaving Joseph to die. Injustice everywhere. But in the midst of all the family betrayals, there was one line by Joseph, who said something like, "Even though you intended to do harm to me, God intended it for good." That had stuck with him. Joseph had decided to make the best of a sorry situation. Ed knew something about sorry situations.

After that evening at the concert, Ed had decided to read the bible. He knew that Christians most valued the New Testament, but he would start at the beginning. You would never study physics by starting at the back of the book. He only made it to Leviticus, then got bogged down in the seemingly cruel and strange laws. And so he'd quit. He smiled at Gloria. "That makes me feel a little better," he said. "I guess," he added, causing them all to laugh.

Then Gloria leaned closer toward him. "Ed, you must be pretty shaken by all this."

Ed's laughter dissolved. "That's an understatement." He ran a hand through his hair. "I'm not sure what to do next."

"I can only imagine, Ed," Gloria said, now sitting up straighter. "But, you've got this going for you. You're here tonight among people who care about you." She shot a quick glance at Ellen. "We'll look out for you."

Ed looked at Gloria, then at Ellen. What he saw made his jaw drop: people caring for him. Ed hardly knew Gloria, but her words came across as sincere and authentic. He had doubts about the book she'd been reading, but any doubts he may have had about her had vanished.

Chapter 24

"A lot of people would say I was crazy," Ed said.

Gloria reached across Ellen and rested a hand briefly on Ed's. "I'm not ruling out that possibility yet," she said, and they all laughed. "But I'm a pretty good judge of people, Ed, and you strike me as rational and serious." Now she looked at Ellen. "And I've learned to trust Ellen's judgment, too."

Ed pressed an index finger against his chin and pursed his lips. "I mean, think about all the stories about parallel universes. There must be a million of them."

"Hmm … *Through the Looking Glass*," said Ellen, "and maybe *Gulliver's Travels*."

"And the scene in *It's a Wonderful Life*, where Jimmy Stewart comes back to Pottersville," added Gloria. "And maybe Scrooge's dream worlds in *A Christmas Carol*."

"Not to mention a ton of sci-fi stories," Ed added. "But the truth is, all of those stories rely upon angels or ghosts or magic rabbit holes or machines created by mad scientists. There never has been any actual recorded proof of a parallel universe, and I suspect that's because the laws of physics won't allow it." He was silent for a moment, then said, "Although I confess I don't know the relevant laws of physics well enough to be sure about that." He shook his head slowly, suddenly struck again by his dire situation. "My friend, Shipley Jameson—he's the smartest guy I know—" He shook his head. "That is, he used to be my friend. I'm counting on him to explain this."

As if on cue, Jasmine appeared beside him, holding out the phone again. "We've got another call from Ship."

We? And she's now calling him Ship? "That's him now," he said to Ellen and Gloria. "I'll be right back."

Ed took the phone and, with Jasmine right behind him, stepped out into the service hallway where he'd taken the last call. "Put it on speaker," Jasmine urged.

Ed rolled his eyes, as he tapped the speaker button, then said, "Dr. Jameson, Ed Turner here."

Ship skipped over any greeting. "Tell me more about your TGAs, Turner. I think that may be critical."

Ed described again how the TGAs would leave him without any memory of pertinent personal data—address and phone number, names of other people or his location—for a short period of time.

"Yes," said Ship, when Ed was done, "that's what I picked up off the internet. Here's what I think. It's not the complete answer for the mechanism we're looking for, but it may be a start. Here's the deal. The cognitive data we have in our brains—our names, our birth date, address, age, location and so on, a long list of data—keep us on track in our lives, keep us, you might say, locked into reality. Those data set the conditions that prevent a drifting from one reality to another. We know who we are, where we are and so on. It's the brain's way of keeping us where we belong."

Ed and Jasmine exchanged looks, as Ship continued.

"But in a TGA, much of that information is lost, at least temporarily. The brain has become a blank slate for a time, onto which new conditions could be written. I think it's important to note that in a TGA, we're not talking about brain damage, in which case a new reality could not be written, at least in a realistic or healthy way. So, the TGA may open the brain up to new programming, a new quantum mechanical configuration of the electron system, if you want to look at it from a physics point of view.

"So, I think we may be making some headway, but there are some real technical physics issues here, Turner, that I won't bore you with."

Ed winced. *I'm a physicist, I can talk about technical issues.* But he didn't object.

"Things like time-reversal symmetry of the wavefunctions and the second law of thermodynamics. Spelled out simply"— Ed winced again at the idea of Ship simplifying things for him—"you can't just roll back to some point in the past, like the night of your accident, when the initial decision was made. Physical systems, like our brains, cannot easily do this. I'm not sure we can get around this, frankly. That's why I'm dubious about this whole idea, Turner."

Ed felt the hair on the back of his neck stand up. "You may be dubious, Dr. Jameson, but meanwhile, I'm trapped in a place where I have no identity, no money, no job, no place to stay, no—"

"That's a sad situation, Turner, I agree, but frankly there are a lot of refugees, immigrants and poor people in this world who are in the same boat. Here's what I suggest. You're in the reality you are in. I suggest you get used to it, get some help and do something about it. To pretend or long for anything else—now that's bordering on delusional." Then a click indicated that Ship had hung up.

Jasmine's intense dark eyes searched Ed's face. "I'm sorry about your situation, all those things you said you don't have. But you do have me and Ellen and all those people." She gestured toward the room. "Isn't that better than nothing?"

Ed's mouth fell open. Images flashed through his mind. Ellen cradling his hands in hers, Jasmine sharing her passion for Feynman, high fives with Denny Jones, Gloria's confidence, Dottie's bouncy warmth. These were things he'd seldom had in his real life. Or maybe this was now his real life. No ID, home or money—ultimately, those were secondary, really. What he had here wasn't so bad. Not so bad at all.

Chapter 25

"Did your friend have any new insights?" asked Ellen. She sat alone at the table, as Gloria was now across the room with her husband, talking to other people.

Ed shook his head slowly, as he took the seat next to her. "He thinks my temporary amnesia spells may be a factor, but the laws of physics still seem to stand in the way of really understanding what's going on. Unless, of course ..." He offered a self-deprecating smirk. "Unless I'm crazy."

Ellen seemed to be considering this. "I don't know what's going on here, Ed, but I'd rather us focus on the good things." She leaned toward him and laid a hand on his. "And I think there are a lot of good things going on."

Ed felt his body relax. "I think there are, too," he said. He laid his other hand over hers.

Jerry put on "Since You've Been Gone," and, as Aretha Franklin began singing, several more couples headed for the hardwood space between the tables.

Ellen said, "Do you want to dance, Ed?"

Panic surged through him. "I'm afraid I might make a fool out of myself."

Ellen gave his hand a tug toward the dance floor. "I can't imagine you being afraid of anything."

Uncertain how this was going to work, Ed followed her toward the space where other couples now danced, one hand in hers, the other holding tight to the quad cane. At the edge of the hardwood area, she turned toward him and smiled. "You just hold onto me."

Ed placed his left hand in hers, but held onto the cane with his right hand. They didn't really move across the floor, but more or less swayed in place. She whispered into his ear, "I've got you, Ed."

He wasn't sure how to take this, but then he let go of the cane—left it standing on the floor—and moved his right arm around her shoulders. Aretha sang breathlessly, with urgency, about the loss of her lover—her sweet baby, baby—and how she's got to get him back somehow. Her voice was raw and full of need. Just like him. Ellen moved closer, her body pressed against his. Her head rested against his shoulder, and his cheek pressed into her hair, as he was soaked in the scent of a field of flowers in the sunshine. Her right hand squeezed his left hand tight, and his right palm was flat against her back—he could feel the muscles and bones of her shoulders beneath the soft material of her cardigan. He wanted to hold her all night, to pull her even closer, to let this moment flow into the rest of his life.

When the music stopped, she pulled away just a few inches. Her eyes were full of life and questions. Her lips parted slightly and waited for him. Maybe to kiss her? He wanted to, God, he wanted to. But instead, he said, "Thank you, Ellen, I enjoyed that," and immediately hated himself for missing the moment. She smiled as she backed away, then took his hand as he took hold of his cane, and they made their way back to the table.

For a while they sat in silence. Her eyes were locked on him. He was able to hold her gaze, but he could hardly breathe. *What a chicken shit*, he thought. Finally, he said, "God, Ellen, I don't know what to say." He looked away for a moment, to catch his breath, then returned his eyes to her. "I'm not very good with words sometimes."

"Seriously, Ed. I saw what you did out there tonight. I don't think anyone else in this room could have pulled that off."

"But this is different," he said. He licked his lips. "This is you."

She seemed pleased with this. "Oh, Ed, I'm still just the girl who made the map of Uruguay."

"But …but …." He couldn't finish the thought. Instead, he reached out and touched her cheek, gently, as if checking to verify that she was real.

She didn't move. She opened her mouth like she needed more air, but said nothing.

"I don't know, Ellen, tonight has been so strange. I don't know what's going on." He placed his forefingers against his chin, like he was in deep thought, then took them away. "But more than anything, I never thought I'd be here with you … like this." He wanted to say more, but this was all he could manage. Jerry had just put on "I'll Be Your Baby Tonight," and Dylan was saying what Ed wished he could say. He wondered if she was hearing the words like he was hearing the words. She had said, "I've got you." He shouldn't read too much into comments like that, should he? Or maybe he should. Maybe a lifetime of missed opportunities was about to finally turn around.

His life had been one of going slow, maybe not going at all. Measured responses. Caution. Not sticking his neck out. But tonight with Ellen, he wanted to break through all that crap, overcome his reticence, his shyness, his fear. To be where age didn't matter, where his regrets didn't matter, where his missed opportunities didn't matter. What he wanted was … hell, he wanted to be her baby tonight.

Ellen seemed suddenly shy. With a schoolgirl smile, she picked up one of the colorful pens from the table—it had a tiny hula dancer on the top, which swayed as she wrote. She took his hand and drew a little heart with an arrow through it. She giggled. "Remember when we did silly things like this in school?"

Ed had never had a girl write anything on his hand in school, although he would have liked that. But that was so long ago. And tonight, right now, everything seemed new, literally everything.

Ellen continued to write on the palm of his hand, laughing, then on his wrist. Then she set the pen aside and looked up at him. "Ed, I guess some things never really change. Back in high school, we never went out or anything, but you know, I really—"

"Why, if it isn't Ellen Barnes," said the voice behind him. Ellen dropped Ed's hand and went pale. Ed recognized the voice behind him. It was a very familiar voice. It was his voice.

Chapter 26

He didn't want to turn and look—he couldn't—he was instantly paralyzed. The terror that was filling Ellen's face was quickly overwhelming him.

"Ellen Barnes, right? Don't you remember me? Edward Turner."

It took everything he had for Ed to turn and look at the man standing behind him. *My God. It's me.* He had to grab the edge of the table to keep from falling out of the chair. He could not speak, and Ellen was silent.

The man's jaw dropped. "What the ..." He looked at Ellen, then back at Ed. "What the hell is going on? Who is this?"

Ed understood immediately what was happening. If he had come from a parallel universe tonight, what was keeping some other version of himself from visiting also? He should have expected it, in fact. Ed glanced at Ellen, whose face was drained of all color. Her hands were across her chest like she was either in prayer or experiencing the symptoms of a heart attack. He wanted to say something to her, reassure her, but he couldn't speak.

The man took a step back, then seemed to brace himself, like a fight might be about to break out. "Okay, if this is some damn joke, I get it, but you just scared the holy crap out of me."

All Ed could say, meekly, was, "This isn't a joke. I'm Ed Turner."

The man took a step toward Ed, moving without a cane. *His parallel reality must have split off before the accident.* "Don't mess with me, asshole. I didn't come here to be messed with." He looked at Ellen again, who still sat motionless. "Laughs are great. Ha ha." He pulled out a chair and sat, then leaned forward with his arms on the table. "Now I'll say it again. Don't screw around with me."

This Edward Turner was not some flickering hologram or shadowy ghost. His folding chair squeaked when he leaned forward—he had mass. His breath had a scent of booze and mouthwash—he had a respiratory system. His forehead was wrinkled—he was subjected to aging. He was not an illusion or a nightmare or a hallucination. He was a real person.

Edward was well dressed, business casual was what they called it. A sleek gray sport coat over a pale blue dress shirt, open at the collar. He was more tan than Ed, and more slender, but his hair, gray and combed over, was identical. He didn't wear glasses. *And he goes by Edward.* These were all the superficial differences. But Ed could see deeper. There was no question about it. This man was him. "Yes, you deserve an explanation, Edward." He was amazed how calm his voice sounded. "And I'm glad you're sitting down. It will take a few minutes to explain, and you'll find it hard to believe, in fact, you'll—"

Ellen stood suddenly, and Ed spun toward her. "God, I can't take any more of this. It's too … it's too … it's …." She looked around the room in panic, probably searching for Gloria. She stepped back from the table. "I've got to get out of here." With that, she strode quickly toward the door.

"No, Ellen," cried Ed to her back. "Don't go. Please." But she was already half-way to the door. He grabbed his cane and followed, leaving the newly arrived Edward Turner sitting there with his mouth open.

Ed stepped out into the cool night and scanned the parking lot for Ellen's Roadtrek. Down to the right a few spaces, she was backing out. He staggered toward the campervan, waving with his free hand. "Ellen, please," he cried at the top of his voice. The backup lights dimmed, and the van moved forward toward the highway. "Ellen," he cried again, waving frantically, "Don't go." The Roadtrek paused at the parking lot entrance, and Ed thought for a moment that she might be about to back up. But then it pulled out into the late-night traffic, and soon its taillights disappeared into the sea of red. He watched the driveway for a long time, breathing heavily through his mouth, hoping she might return. Then he turned and slowly made his way back toward the entrance.

Gloria stood by the entry doors, looking concerned. "What happened, Ed?"

"She's gone," he said, choking up. He thought he was about to cry. "You must have her number. I need to call her."

"I'm sorry, Ed. You know I can't give you her number. If she wants to get away, we've got to honor that. Do you want to tell me what happened?" She gestured toward a wooden bench beside the entry doors.

Ed sat with both hands atop his cane, feeling suddenly weak and defeated. Gloria sat beside him, turned toward him, her hands folded in her lap, waiting for him to speak.

Ed looked down at the concrete pavers. "Things were going so well. I mean, with Ellen and me. I thought …" but then he trailed off.

There was more silence, Gloria obviously willing to wait him out.

"I never told her how I …." Again he trailed off, and now he hung his head, fighting back tears. "God," he shrieked suddenly, "why did this have to happen to me?"

Gloria put a gentle hand on his shoulder, but remained silent.

Now Ed turned toward her. "Did you see him come in?"

"See who, Ed?"

Ed shook his head. "You're not going to believe this. I can't believe it. It's why Ellen ran away." Gloria seemed unmoved, her eyes patiently watching him. "God, I don't even know how to say this. Another version of me just showed up."

"What do you mean, Ed?"

"Edward Turner just came into the reunion. From another reality, apparently." Now he chuckled, a lifeless chuckle of self-deprecating misery. "Now there are three of us. One dead and two very much alive." He was quiet for a moment, then searching Gloria's face, said, "What am I going to do?"

Gloria's hand remained on Ed's shoulder. She closed her eyes for a moment. "You say there's another Ed Turner back in the meeting room?"

Ed nodded.

"God, dear God." Now she pressed her index finger against her lips, like she was searching for an answer. Then she sighed and began. "As far as Ellen's concerned, I can understand why she needed to get away, and I'm sure you can, too. What's happened here tonight is crazy. I've got to say this challenges everything I thought was possible." Gloria stood and paced for a moment, then turned toward Ed. "Look, I'll call her tomorrow, unless she calls me first. I'll tell her you want to see her. She's going to need some time to get a hold on all this. And you need some time, too. In the morning, things will look better, I am convinced, and we can figure out what to do next."

Ed shook his head. "I can't look as far as tomorrow. I don't even have any place to go tonight. No home, no car, no money, no ID." He felt the terror rising in him again. "So saying things will be better in the morning is sort of like telling me I need swim across the ocean."

"You can stay with Martin and me tonight, Ed. We have a comfortable guest room. You'll be fine there."

"And what do I do with that Mr. Turner, who's back in the meeting room right now?"

"I guess we need to go talk to him. I'll go with you, if you like."

"Yes, I would like that." He looked back out at the dark parking lot, just in case a Roadtrek was pulling in. He wanted to leave also, to run away. But he knew he had to go back in and face Edward Turner. He wasn't ready for this. One moment a flirtatious Ellen had been scribbling hearts on his wrist. The next moment she was gone and he was left to confront the most terrifying person he'd ever met. Himself.

Chapter 27

Just inside the door of the Grand Ballroom, Jasmine was waiting. "What the hell's going on, Ed?" She pointed toward Edward Turner, who was now chatting with Chuck Barlow. "There's another you. Freaking amazing, Ed. If that's what I think it is, shouldn't we call Ship?"

Ed shook his head. "Maybe. At some point, yes. But first I've got to understand a little more about what's going on."

Ed and Gloria made their way over to Edward, Jasmine trailing behind, but not so far back that she couldn't hear what was being said.

"So, you picked up any chicks yet, Ed?" Chuck Barlow said to Edward. Before Edward could respond, Chuck turned and saw Ed. His mouth fell open, as his plastic cola cup fell to the floor with a loud, wet splatter. He stared at the puddle of lost booze, no doubt wondering what the hell was in this stuff. He looked at Edward, then back at Ed. "Uh ... I need a drink," he said, backing away until he disappeared into the gathering.

"Edward, this is Gloria Marquez-Herrera. I know you remember her."

"Gloria, sure," said Edward.

"Gloria's a priest now."

"A priest?" Edward had a confident smile that looked like he liked you, but couldn't care less what you thought of him.

"Hello, Edward," said Gloria, extending her hand to shake.

"A priest?" he repeated. "A woman priest?"

"That's right," said Gloria, not wincing, as maybe she should have.

"Edward, there's something you need to see. Come with me," Ed said.

"No. Hell, no. I've got to get this shit straight. Who the hell are you?"

"Just come with me." He led the way toward the poster of Fallen Titans, Gloria and Jasmine following behind.

At the poster, Ed stood silently as Edward perused the photographs. "Shit, this is depressing. God, there's Danny Rogers. Used to play wiffle ball in his front yard."

"I know," said Ed.

"Oh, God, there's Evelyn Holiday. She was so hot."

"Here, look at this one, Edward." He pointed toward the photo of young Eddie Turner.

"What? What the—" He spun toward Ed. "Okay, time to tell me what's going on."

Ed was aware of the clamminess under his collar. "So, I'm guessing you passed out tonight when you arrived at the reunion."

Edward's mouth fell open. He took an aggressive step toward Ed. "So what do you know about that? Some asshole got my wallet and my phone and my Rolex. Got my car, too. If I get my hands on the slimy son of a—"

"And I'm guessing that you have had periods of temporary amnesia in your life."

"So? Yeah, I get these spells sometimes, it's no big deal. Now, are you going to tell me what—"

"They're called TGAs, Edward, transient global amnesia. And tonight, when you suffered your spell, as you call it, you somehow entered into a parallel reality. So did I. We are both Eddie Turner." Ed turned toward the photo on the poster. "And we entered into this Eddie Turner's reality, and he's dead."

Edward looked at the photo, then back at Ed.

Then he glanced at Gloria and Jasmine. "What are you staring at?" he barked, causing each of them to take a step back. Edward's eyes tended to dart from one person to the other, Ed noted, like he was suspicious. *An odd difference from me*, thought Ed, who had a tendency to stare, to focus, perhaps too much, if he could look a person in the eye at all. He'd always attributed that to his physics training, which required single-minded concentration.

Now looking back at Ed, Edward said, "Okay, Candid Camera time, huh?" He produced a nervous laugh. "Where's the camera? You assholes are pretty funny, but I'm not stupid." He leaned over and peeked behind the poster display, as if a camera might be hidden there.

"Yeah, we watched that show, didn't we, Edward? While others were meeting up for pizza at Octavio's, doing homework together, or on the phone with friends planning the weekend's activities, we were at home with mom and dad, weren't we? Watching Candid Camera or Bonanza, The Beverly Hillbillies or one of dad's other favorite programs. Then we'd go to the darkness of our bedroom and that soft, yellow glow of the dial on our clock radio, checking in with our best friends: Chick Hearn calling the play by play for the Lakers, Vin Scully calling the Dodgers and Buddy Blattner calling for the Angels. That's what we did, didn't we, Edward?"

Edward's face scrunched up like some awful truth had just been revealed, which it had. "I need to sit down," he said, now breathing through his mouth in gulps. His aggressive tone had diminished to a near-whisper. He flailed with one hand, like a blind man searching for something to hold on to. Jasmine set a folding chair next to him, then got one for Ed.

When they were seated, Ed said, "I'm just as scared as you are, Edward. I've just had a few more hours to get used to it."

Edward squinted his eyes and puckered his lips, looking around with quick, erratic glances, as if somebody might be watching. Then he looked back at Ed. "How can you explain this?"

Ed began by telling the story of his own arrival at the reunion, then tried his best to explain the quantum many-worlds theory that Ship was proposing. Throughout Ed's explanation, Edward shook his head, as if in denial of Ed's words or indicating his struggle to understand. When Ed had finished, Edward said, "Okay, I don't believe this shit for a minute, not one damned minute." He looked up at Gloria and Jasmine, who were still standing nearby. "Stop leering at me."

"They're my friends," said Ed.

Edward ran both hands through his hair, then said, "So you're saying that you and I are both the same person?" He nodded toward the posters. "And so is he?"

"Yes."

"Your science crap sounds just like that. Crap." Clearly, this version of Ed had not studied physics. "But I have to admit, you look like me, you sound like me. But I still don't understand. You could be some kind of impersonator, like a double in a movie. Yeah, that's it, isn't it? Some asshole put you up to this, didn't he?" He leaned toward Ed with a penetrating look.

"Look, Edward, I want you to believe me because I'm trying to figure this out, too. I'm stuck here in this place, like you, with no ID, no home, no money, no—"

"Wait a second. Yeah, the losers got my wallet and my phone and my car, but what do you mean I have no home, no identity?"

"Just what I said, Edward. In this world, we died fifty years ago. Go ahead, call your phone. Check it out."

As if on cue, Jasmine stepped forward and offered her phone to Edward, who shot her a suspicious look. "No, I don't want to make the call."

Ed bit his lip. "So, Edward, tell me, I must have been thirteen or so. It was late, mom and dad had gone to bed. I stayed up listening in bed to the radio station in San Francisco, KSFO, if I recall, listening to the Giants playing the Braves. The station was far away and the signal kept coming in and going out. Juan Marichal and Warren Spahn pitched a scoreless game into the sixteenth inning. Do you remember that, Edward?"

Edward's jaw dropped.

"And dad took me to see an Angels game, also when I was around 13. I remember it well, because it was the only game he ever took me to. The Yankees were in town. Mantle and Maris were in the lineup, Whitey Ford was on the mound. Do you remember that, Edward?"

"Of course," Edward said quietly.

Ed shot a glance toward Gloria and Jasmine. Their eyes were locked on him. Gloria gave him a supportive nod.

"And when I was very little, we had a cat. Burgess. A big gray tiger. Got run over out on Catalina Street. I cried for days. Do you remember that, Edward?"

Edward's face had reddened.

"And I remember when I got my tonsils out when I was around five. They put me out with ether. It hurt like hell when I woke up. Mom brought me ice cream and a baseball cap. Do you remember that, Edward?"

"It was a Brooklyn Dodgers cap," Edward said.

"Yes. I loved that cap."

Now they both were silent. Ed didn't know what else to say. He shifted his gaze toward the entrance, still harboring a hope that Ellen might have returned. "So, why do you go by Edward instead of Eddie?"

Edward shook his head. "It was after I got back from Nam. I thought Edward sounded more distinguished than Eddie." He gave out a little chuckle. "So, how come you go by Ed?"

"I didn't like Eddie either." They shared a brief laugh, which was weird, because their laughs sounded identical. "I thought Ed was simple and unassuming. I guess I didn't want to stand out." After a moment, he added, "You were in Vietnam?"

"Of course. Low lottery number."

"33," said Ed.

Edward opened his mouth, like he was surprised, but then narrowed his eyes, like he'd found a flaw in Ed's argument about them being the same person. "You weren't drafted?"

"I was injured in a car accident. Couldn't walk."

"Yeah, I wondered about your gimp."

"Guess you missed that."

"I was in a car accident, too, right before getting drafted. Up on US 50. That the one you're talking about?" When Ed nodded, he continued. "But I got out with no major injuries. Guess I was lucky, huh? If you can call going to Nam lucky."

So, there he was. The Ed Turner he had never been. The slender, tanned, well-dressed Ed Turner. The Ed Turner who could walk. The Ed Turner who had served his country in Vietnam. The Ed Turner who had a Rolex. He shot Gloria and Jasmine a helpless look. He was now glad that Ellen had left. Left before she could witness firsthand just how far Ed Turner had fallen short in life.

Chapter 28

Edward stood and pronounced, "Sorry, Ed or whoever the hell you are, but I've had enough of this crap for a while. I came to have fun, not be a part of some freak show." As he passed Jasmine, he gave her a disapproving look. "What's a teenie Goth chick doing here?"

Jasmine winced, then shrugged.

"Boolin?" said Edward, then walked off before Jasmine could answer.

She turned to Ed, her pale face reddened. "Boolin? Huh? Some kids talk like that—the cool ones or the wanna-be cool ones." She shot a quick glance over her shoulder in the direction Edward had headed. "In case you hadn't noticed, I'm not like cool. And I'm hardly a"—she gave out a little smirk—"what'd he say, a teenie Goth chick? Hell, I read Richard Feynman!"

Ed managed a weak smile.

Then Jasmine said, "Okay, so the new improved Ed Turner has showed up, I guess that's the big news. But, hell, Ed, why'd Ellen stomp out in such a huff? I was startin' to have some hope for you two."

"She just couldn't handle two or three Ed Turners, I guess. I don't blame her. It really is creepy."

"How are you holding up, Ed?" Gloria asked.

"I don't know. I think I'd like to be alone now. I've got a lot to think about."

Gloria didn't look convinced. "I'll check back in a while."

"You don't need to bother," he said. He didn't need some priest hovering over him.

"Whatever," she said, then left.

Ed made his way back to the chair at the edge of the room, the out-of-the-way place where he'd begun the evening. This was where he belonged, on the sidelines watching as others lived. It felt like a dark curtain had fallen over his heart. He sagged into the chair, leaning forward with elbows on his knees, cradling a plastic cup of water in his hands.

Not only was his future bleak, but he had just had his face rubbed in the stark reality of how bleak his past had been. Maybe a reunion was a place and time when you are brought face to face with your whole life: who you are and who you've been and who you didn't turn out to be. For a while this evening, he'd begun to think that there was something between Ellen and him. But now he could see clearly that tonight he had merely rekindled the memory of the Eddie Turner she'd known in high school, the one who died. Not the Ed Turner who had mangled his legs and his whole life on that icy day in the mountains. Edward Turner demonstrated how a healthy version of himself might have turned out—hell, *did* turn out. Not the Ed Turner who was a stumbling introvert, who was most comfortable dropping down onto his kneeling pad, working plant food into the soil around his dahlias. The three Ed Turners were present at the reunion tonight, and this one, himself, he thought, was the worst of the lot.

Ed looked up as Gloria pulled up a chair and sat down next to him, turning her chair so that they both looked out into the room. He didn't acknowledge her presence. A nice little pep talk was the last thing he needed now.

But Gloria said nothing, just watched the room with him.

Finally, Ed turned to her and said, "You don't need to sit here, you know." When she didn't reply, he added, "I don't need to be some do-gooder project for you."

Gloria said nothing.

He looked out at the room again. "Shouldn't you be visiting with your old classmates?"

"I am visiting with them. You don't need to worry about me."

"Maybe you don't need to worry about me either."

"Well, I'm not the one lost in an alternate universe."

He shook his head as he let out a nervous laugh. "Look, I know you mean well. It's just that I don't see how talking about this is going to help with anything."

"So you'd rather go through this by yourself?"

"I guess I'm not saying I'd rather go through it by myself."

"Then don't."

Another five minutes passed. Ed turned to her again. "Sometimes I wish I could start over."

Gloria continued to face the room, but said, "Why don't you?"

Ed grimaced. "As you know, Gloria, I'm 68. Kind of late for me, don't you think?"

Gloria now looked at him. Her brown eyes were full of warmth. "I don't know. Apparently, that was pretty amazing what you did to calm that ruckus earlier. Maybe you're starting over tonight. Perhaps you don't realize how much potential you have."

Ed bristled. "I don't need somebody telling me I have untapped potential."

The warmth in Gloria's eyes now turned to fire. "I agree. You don't need somebody telling you that. What you need is to actually realize it is true."

He opened his mouth to respond, but took a sip of water instead. After a while he said, "I have nothing to look forward to. I should have died on that highway fifty years ago."

Gloria smiled like she understood, but was way ahead of him. "Maybe you don't see much to look forward to tonight, Ed. But I suspect that you may be on the verge of having everything to look forward to." She was silent for a moment, then said, "So, you taught for how long? Forty years?"

He didn't want to be in this conversation. "Something like that."

"So, you've taught how many students, Ed? I'm guessing thousands."

"Probably," he said, almost in a whisper.

"I'll bet there are a lot of them who are glad you didn't die fifty years ago."

Ed started to say, "I don't care." But the truth was: he did care. For years, he had checked the online teaching evaluations, *Rate My Professors,* almost weekly, chastising himself each time he did. After all, why should he let the opinions of a few students affect him? In any case, the students who post ratings online, aren't they often the ones with a beef? The unhappy ones? But he couldn't *not* look. It was like trying to turn your eyes away from a house fire.

He cared what the students thought of him, and his ratings were generally high. By some measures he was a poor teacher, as he did little to modernize the content of his lectures. His textbook needed to be upgraded—there were better ones now available, he'd been told by colleagues in the department. And he often recycled the same PowerPoint visuals from his lectures over and over. Hey, he rationalized, it's mainly classical physics. How much has really changed in the last hundred years?

Though he cared little about the content, he did care about the students, and that's where he had put his energy. He had the most generous office hours of anyone on the faculty. He would patiently work through the details of the ideal-gas law with a clueless student, when other professors probably would have lost patience. And in the classroom, what he lacked in intellectual rigor he made up for with personality. Such an introvert in his personal life, he came alive before a crowd, and that had been on display again earlier this evening.

He'd never had children of his own, but he would have been a good parent. Students and teachers alike had told him that. And though he'd always dismissed such compliments, he never grew tired of hearing them. The bottom line: he genuinely cared for the students. He said to Gloria, "Yes, maybe that's true."

Now Gloria shifted her body to face him. "Look, Ed, we are born, but that's not the end of it. Things happen to us in our lives—bad things and good things—but that's not the end of it, either. We are in a continual state of birth. Just like the universe. I don't believe that God just snapped his fingers fourteen billion years ago, then walked away. The universe is still being created. That should give us hope." She leaned toward him. "Ed, that should give you hope."

Gloria was right. Maybe he didn't have a Rolex and a cool sport coat. Maybe he didn't fight in Vietnam. Maybe he couldn't walk without considerable assistance. Maybe he didn't have love. He looked over toward the entrance again and sighed. But he did have some things going for him. He looked back at Gloria and managed a smile. "Thank you, Gloria."

He was about to say more, but noticed Dottie coming toward them, fast. He was sure it was about the sudden appearance of Edward Turner. He didn't know what he was going to say.

"What in God's name is going on, Ed?" Dottie shrieked, stopping right in front of him. She started to say more, but threw her hands into the air instead and turned to look out into the room toward Edward Turner. Now she turned back toward Ed, and it seemed there were tears in her eyes. "God, Ed, something's really wrong here, isn't it?"

Ed opened his mouth, but no words came out. He was becoming used to being caught speechless. He shot a desperate glance toward Gloria.

"Dottie, we've got a complicated situation here," said Gloria. She looked at Ed, as if asking for his permission to tell Dottie the story, or at least some version of it. When Ed nodded, she said, "And Ed's struggling with the situation just as much as you or anyone else." She took a deep breath and released it slowly. "Something very strange has happened. I presume that Ed told you about the car accident all those years ago?"

"He said he was injured, when we all thought that he'd been killed. We believed him. But … but … now this. I mean …" Her voice started to rise. But then she stopped.

"What Ed told you is true," said Gloria. Ed nodded to support Gloria's words, relieved that someone else was having to go through this story again. "He did survive that accident. But, Dottie, here's the part that we don't understand. You know me, Dottie, and you know I won't tell you anything that isn't true." She paused and waited for Dottie to nod, which she did. "One Eddie survived the accident, but Eddie Turner also died that day. And out there is yet another Eddie Turner who wasn't even injured in the accident."

Dottie was pale. "You mean ... you mean there are three Eddie Turners?"

"Ed can explain this better than me—he's the physicist. But, no, there's only one Ed Turner, at least in the universe we know. But apparently there are other universes ... dear God, I know this sounds insane ... other universes that exist alongside our own universe. In our universe, Eddie Turner was killed in that car wreck fifty years ago. But in another universe, parallel somehow to ours, Eddie was only injured, and in yet another universe, Eddie wasn't injured at all. And somehow ..." Gloria glanced at Ed for reassurance, and seemed buoyed by his smile. "Somehow, all three of them are here tonight. It's because of some weird wrinkle in the laws of physics, started apparently by some brief amnesia episode—heck, I don't know. It's way beyond me, Dottie, but it seems to be true."

"This is crazy, Gloria," said Dottie. "How can I believe that?"

"I assure you, Dottie, it seems crazy to me, too, and it's got Ed here just as upset as anyone else. Even more so, because, after all, it's his life that's being messed with tonight."

This seemed to soften Dottie. She turned and shot another glance toward the room, then turned back to Gloria and Ed. "I still don't get it."

"I know. I don't get it either. Neither does Ed. But it seems true." She paused, then said, "You believe in God, don't you, Dottie?"

Dottie's eyes seemed to mist up. "Yes."

"Then here's what we've got to keep in mind. God knows how all this weird science stuff works, even if we don't. You probably remember the line in the Bible where it says that God's ways are higher than our ways?"

Dottie nodded, entranced by what Gloria was saying.

"This strange scene tonight is all a part of God's creation, even if we don't understand. Okay?"

"Okay. I guess."

"And here's the part that we do understand, the part God wants us to understand." Now she looked at Ed. "Here is a good man. I think you know that by now. I heard about what he did tonight to save the reunion. And you know why he did it, too, don't you? He did it out of love for all of us."

Dottie seemed to melt. "Oh, Ed," she gushed. Then she stepped toward Ed and wrapped her arms around him. "Oh, God, Ed, I'm so sorry you're having to go through this." Then she stood up straight, wiping tears from her eyes. "This still scares the crap out of me, though," she said, her words breaking into a laugh. They all laughed.

Ed looked at Gloria with gratitude, then up at Dottie. "It scares the crap out of me, too," he said.

"So, that's it, Dottie," said Gloria. "There's a lot we don't understand, but we're all God's children, and we need to stick together, look out for each other."

Dottie rested a hand on Ed's shoulder. "Okay, I'm on board. I'll stick with you, my friend."

Ed laid a hand atop Dottie's hand. "Thank you," he said softly. What he was thinking was that Gloria must have been a hell of a lawyer, and it was clear she was a pretty good pastor, too. What he was hoping was that Gloria would give the same moving speech to Ellen.

Chapter 29

Invigorated by his talk with Gloria, Ed was ready to face Edward again. He wanted to call Ship, but he needed to learn more first.

Ed worked his cane toward the center of the room, where Edward stood in a small circle of laughing people. He apparently had developed social skills that Ed still lacked. The only one Ed recognized was Lila Panovsky, from the Shutterbugs. When he stepped into the circle next to Edward, the laughter and words came to a sudden halt. Ed wanted to laugh—he was becoming accustomed to this craziness. People stared at the two of them, mouths falling open. One person finally said, "Edward, I didn't know you had a twin."

Edward fumbled for words. At first, it seemed like he might seize upon the twin explanation. That would be the easiest way out of this, wouldn't it? But he probably considered it only for a moment, realizing that any person who'd known him in high school would know he didn't have a twin. Lila Panovsky would, for sure. Ed suspected he knew how Edward would think about things, even though they'd lived different lives for the past fifty years—after all, they were the same person. Edward muttered, "I don't have a twin." Then he focused angry eyes on Ed.

The small group began to disperse, people uncomfortably backing away. "Well, better go mingle a little more, don't want to miss anyone" was pretty much the theme of the excuses, as one after the other moved off toward other parts of the room.

Lila Panovsky, probably realizing something unusual was happening, pulled out her iPhone. "Let me get a shot of you two," she said, offering a pearly-toothed smile.

As Lila framed her shot, Edward stepped away from Ed, arms out with palms up like stop signs. "No way, Lila."

"Why not?" She lowered the phone. "What's going on here?"

"It's a long story, Lila," said Ed.

"So, if you're not twins," she said, "then what the hell is …?" She shook her head and left.

When they were alone, Edward turned toward Ed, full of rage. "Thanks for screwing up my evening, asshole. Why are you following me around?" Edward apparently had decided to deal with their situation with complete denial.

Looking at Edward, Ed felt a sloshing mixture of terror and fascination. Maybe it was the same way he'd always felt about his own life in moments of introspection. He had to remind himself that in some dimension of reality, this was his own life. He was Ed, and this Edward was also him. Was his resentment mixed with envy toward Edward akin to his own periodic bouts of self-loathing, with which he was so familiar? "Let's get a seat," Ed said. "I need to know about you."

Edward looked around, as if searching for a better offer. Then he shrugged and said, "Whatever."

They found a table where they were alone. After a time of awkward silence, Ed said, "I need to know about your life. I need to know everything. Why weren't you hurt in the crash?"

Edward was silent.

Finally, Ed said, "When we were playing wiffle ball one day, I dove for a line drive that Danny drilled down the line, just inside of the hedges. I missed the ball, but collided with the water faucet next to the hedges. My arm scraped against the water-faucet handle and it ripped me up pretty good. I ran home. My mom put some bandages on it and wanted to take me to the ER, but dad wouldn't let her. Didn't trust doctors. Remember that?"

Edward sat silent, mouth open.

"And it left a terrible scar, right here on my right arm. I've still got a trace of it, Edward." He pulled the sleeve of his corduroy sport coat halfway up his right arm and held it out for Edward's inspection.

Edward leaned close to look, then sat back. "Oh, God," he breathed. He pulled up the right arm of his sleek gray coat and held his arm out to display his identical scar. He breathed heavily, like he was hyperventilating. "Okay," he said, "I guess I'm convinced. Now what?"

Ed felt like he was hyperventilating, too. But he needed to stay focused. "The day of the accident. The car went into a skid, remember that?"

Edward nodded.

"Take it from there," Ed said. He was shaking inside, bordering on panic, but his voice projected with remarkable calm.

"I'd rather not." Edward looked down at his watch, then back up after he realized his watch was missing.

The damned Rolex, thought Ed. "Well, then I'll tell you my version. Can you handle that?"

Edward looked around the room again. He pushed back from the table, and for a moment Ed thought he was about to leave. But then he scratched his chin, sighed, and scooted his chair back up to the table. "Talk about whatever you want. I don't give a shit."

"You don't care?" *What the hell's going on with this guy? I should be able to understand him—for God's sake, he's me.*

Edward leaned in toward Ed, his lip raised in a sneer. "Somehow, you need to go over all the crap of the past. I don't get it. That wasn't part of my life that I want to remember. I don't know about you, but that time sucked. And, by the fact that you're a crip, and that happened in the accident, I'm guessing it wasn't the best time of your life, either. So, why the hell would you want a little stroll down memory lane, when the lane is strewn with shit?"

Why wouldn't Edward be eager to learn more about this universe-hopping doppelganger before him? Was the past too painful for him to talk about? He wasn't the one who was crippled for life. "Okay," Ed said. "Then tell me about Vietnam."

"For God's sake, aren't you little miss sunshine? Why don't we talk instead about hot chicks we've made it with? Or something not so damned depressing."

Hot chicks we've made it with? Good God, that's me talking. Is that who I really am? Maybe so. We've got the same brain. But perhaps that isn't true. Surely the brain is changed by education and problem solving and life experience. Just like the differences in our bodies. Yes, he's me. But maybe he's not me. And why is he so angry and contentious? What the hell is he after? I'm not his enemy. I'm him. "Did you see action?"

"You don't give up, do you?" He sat with both hands on the table, fists clenching and unclenching.

"Would you give up right now if you were me? Since you are me, I suspect not."

Edward shook his head, then looked off into the room, his lips pulled tight in the shape of sadness or perhaps disgust. "God, this is really weird. I'm guessing I'm going to wake up any minute now."

"I was thinking that, too. But not anymore."

Edward unclenched his teeth. "Yeah, I saw a lot of action."

Ed waited for Edward to continue.

Edward scratched the side of his neck. "Oddly, when the action came, it wasn't that scary. Adrenalin pumping like some massive video game with rock music turned up loud. It was, how can I say? A turn on."

Ed said nothing.

"The terror came in between—the waiting, anticipation, and the reflection after a battle—after the adrenaline rush had left. Thinking about your buddy who you saw killed."

"Did you kill anyone?"

"Yes," he said with a crispness that indicated he wouldn't say any more about it. Then he was quiet.

"That's awful."

"You deal with it." Edward leaned forward. "So you missed Nam. I'd say you were the lucky one."

"Lucky one? I was unable to stand upright for many months. Only after a lot of PT and after I got through my depression was I able to start improving. But even after all these years, I can only walk with these damn crutches."

"Did you go back to Sonoma?"

"Yeah, after a year or so."

"You finished?"

"Yeah."

Edward shook his head. "I never went back. Thought about it. Planned to. But I never did." Now Edward leaned back and studied Ed. "So what do you do?"

"I taught physics at a little college all these years. Forty years. Retired now."

"So that's why you spout all that science bullshit."

"Well, it's not my theory. And it's definitely not—"

"Whatever. Total bullshit. Get a handle, sonny boy."

Oh God, that's what his dad used to call him. "Sonny boy?"

"You remember that."

"Of course. So, what happened to Dad in your life?"

"Got the Big C. The miserable SOB died a couple years after I got back. And you?"

"Pretty much the same. And Mom?"

"She's still alive. In a nursing home up north."

"Same with me. Do you ever see her?"

Edward managed a laugh. "Hardly ever. She lives in a run-down dump. Place smells like urine and shit, dirty, people crying. I can't stand the place." He looked down for a moment. "But it's all she could afford. Dad left her with almost nothing."

Ed scrunched his mouth and squinted in disgust. "My mom—er, our mom—er, whatever, lives in a nice place, called Sycamore. I see her probably every week."

"So you want some kind of a medal? Thanks for the guilt trip, asshole."

"Look, she couldn't afford it either, and I wasn't able to help much, but the State of California has a system that's made Sycamore possible—ElderHealth, I think they call it ."

Edward's eyes narrowed for a moment. "Never heard of it." He said it in such a way that it was clear he didn't want to hear any more about it, either.

Ed raised his eyebrows, then leaned back and crossed his arms. "So, what do you do, Edward?"

Edward rubbed the underside of his chin with a forefinger, like he was pondering his answer. "I've done a lot of things. Sales. Real estate. Some, let's say, entrepreneurial activities. You name it."

"Are you retired?"

"Hell, no, I'll never retire."

"So, what are you doing now?"

"I'm, uh … in between things right now. Got some irons in the fire, though. Looking at some new opportunities."

Ed fiddled with one of the noisemakers on the table centerpiece, wondering how he could steer the conversation back to the accident. That's where the universes separated, he was convinced. The accident probably held the key to understanding why he and Edward had burst into this different reality. But he was at a loss for words. "I see," he said.

Now Edward looked up at the ceiling. "Those freaking chandeliers are pretty hokey, really. Place looks like a warehouse."

Ed smiled. He'd been thinking the same thing earlier.

"That day." Edward shook his head, like he was trying to rid himself of something awful. "That damned day." Now he looked off to the left and waved at someone, then turned back. "They said I was going too fast."

"Yeah. Maybe we were."

Edward ignored the comment. "Hit some ice, but I guess you know that."

"Went into a skid," said Ed, hoping to keep Edward going.

"Lost control. Tried to turn in the direction of the skid, like I'd heard."

"That's right."

"Crossed the center line and clipped the damn guard rail on the far side of the road. The door popped open. Saw my chance—there was only a second—and I bailed. Wound up with a broken ankle and lots of scrapes. But I was okay." He looked hard at Ed. "At least physically."

Ed, of course, remembered the moment. He'd relived it many times. Remembered how he could have jumped, should have jumped. And now he knew what he had always wondered about. He would have come away with minimal injuries. But he hadn't jumped. There was that other car. He had to try to steer away from it. But maybe it hadn't mattered.

Edward now studied Ed. "So why didn't you jump?"

"You know why. Up to that moment, we were the same person."

He swallowed hard. "You tried to avoid the other car."

"But I couldn't control the car very well, it went off the road, right into the forest. Smashed into some trees, I was knocked unconscious."

"Shit," breathed Edward.

"When I came to, there was the smell of gas. I had to get out, but my legs were crushed under the collapsed dashboard and the broken windshield."

"Okay, I get it now. You crawled out, and that poor bastard over there"—he tipped his head toward the posters—"didn't crawl out, and the damned car blew."

"Yeah, that's pretty much it."

They were silent for a moment, then Ed said, "So, it looks like you made the right decision."

"And, just how the hell would you know if I made the right decision?" Edward's face had suddenly reddened and his eyes seemed filled with hate. He pushed away from the table and stood. "Screw you."

What just happened? Ed struggled to his feet and reached toward Edward. "Wait. Please." But he had already disappeared into the crowd.

Chapter 30

The Grand Ballroom had become suddenly claustrophobic. *God, I need to get out of here. Anywhere but here.* He worked his way as quickly as he could toward the entrance, out past the reunion sign-in table, where he'd first learned about the dead Eddie Turner, and on into the lobby—now nearly deserted—where the gurgling fountain and Spanish tiles still provided their fake-hacienda ambiance. He stopped at the curb outside the hotel entrance, where he'd watched the taillights of Ellen's van disappear into the night. There was nowhere to go from here. No car, no money, no ID. Everyone who knew him in this world was back there in the Grand Ballroom.

With a sigh of resignation, he turned and began to make his way back toward the reunion. But instead of returning to the Grand Ballroom, he headed toward the rear of the lobby and out into a large patio. It was dark, except for the aqua shimmer from the surface of a large swimming pool.

Ed pushed open a gate and stepped to the edge of the pool. He expected that there would be people gathered here on a July Saturday night, even this late, but perhaps the weather turning cool had kept them inside.

He stood alone in silence, staring at the underwater pool lights and the undulations of the surface, stirred by a soft breeze. There is something about moving water that's almost hypnotic. A waterfall, a river, waves breaking on the shore. Even a hotel swimming pool with a faint odor of chlorine. It creates peace.

But peace was the last thing that Ed experienced now.

Why had Edward exploded? If anything, Ed thought, he'd been gracious toward Edward, had tried to explain their situation to him. They were both in the same mess now, probably for the rest of their lives. Edward should be able to see that. It would be necessary for them to find some level of trust in their relationship. There was so much to be learned from each other.

He paced along the edge of the pool, unable to get a handle on much of anything. There seemed to be no kindness, no gentleness in Edward. Was it due to PTSD from Vietnam? He'd seen friends killed. Ed couldn't imagine what that would be like. Had it caused him to devalue life? Including his own?

What troubled Ed most was that this person was him. Did Edward reveal a darker, uglier side to his own life? The way he saw Edward: was this how others saw him?

Hell, what really troubled Ed most was that he was jealous. Edward was the mobile, confident, worldly man he'd never been, but could've been. Should've been. Why wasn't he? Was it because the bold Eddie jumped out of the car on that icy highway, while the two spineless versions were too petrified to act?

While Edward had moved confidently through life, making it with hot chicks and obviously not giving a damn what anyone else thought, Ed had lived his predictable, quiet life, tending his garden.

The morning breakfasts with Ship were about all the social life he could handle, and that wasn't so hard, as most of the time he just had to sit and nod as Ship pontificated about some new paper in *Nature* about the latest experiments at the Large Hadron Collider or the current thinking on gravitational waves. That was about the entirety of Ed's interaction with the rest of the world, unless you counted his weekly visits to his mother at Sycamore—twenty miles away, down in Santa Rosa—usually followed by a trip to the nearby Costco.

Ed seldom went out to eat, preferring to cook at home. The vegetables from his garden usually provided the basis for most meals. But occasionally, he'd splurge and grab a foot-long polish dog and a Diet Coke during one of his expeditions to Costco. He cringed now, as he thought of Ellen traversing the whole continent in her, what did she call it? A Roadtrek?

This is pathetic. He's trapped in some bizarre alternate reality—the troubling interactions with Edward being just the latest chapter in this unfolding nightmare. And here he is reflecting on trips to Costco. Even in his inconsequential life, trips to Costco would be considered mundane. And yet, at this moment, thoughts about something as mundane as chomping into a foot-long seemed to be just what his frazzled nerves needed.

There were few practical reasons for him to go to Costco. After all, how could a guy living by himself use a twelve-pack of paper towels or a gallon of salsa? He knew that some people shared their purchases with others, but Ship had shown little interest in this idea, and there was no one else to share with. But he would occasionally buy clothes there from the vast displays of bargain-priced duds—mainly socks, T-shirts and undies. He seldom replaced his other articles of clothing. He ran a finger over the worn sleeve of his sport coat and thought of Edward's expensive sport coat.

Mostly, Ed enjoyed being among other people who were stocking up: people in the midst of life, piling 6-packs of ribeyes into their cart for the weekend barbecue, or two gallons of milk for the four kids, fancy bottles of single-malt Scotch for special celebrations. For the time he was in the store, he was part of that community.

And he didn't mind standing in the long lines to get his foot-long and Diet Coke for a buck and a half. He and all the others were going through this together.

Yes, this is pathetic. He imagined Edward boasting about the hot chicks he'd met this week, then asking, "How's your week been, Ed?" And Ed would say, "Let me tell you about my trip to Costco."

He took a step forward, almost tripping over the feet of the quad cane. *You bumbling cripple,* he thought. His personal slide-show of despair, one he was skilled at replaying, flashed through his mind, with a few new entries tonight. *Don't go there,* he thought. But despite Gloria's pep talk just a while ago, the images flashed before him, bright, unrelenting, ugly.

The usual, familiar images in the slideshow included his handicap, his life of limited accomplishment, his solitude. Ah, solitude. It was funny how solitude was something that busy, fulfilled people pursued in order to meditate, rest, gain perspective. But for lonely people like Ed, solitude was something you worked hard to avoid.

The new entries to the slideshow tonight were killers. Lost in a new world. That was the biggie, the overwhelming biggie. At least, it should be the biggie. But at this moment he was more troubled by two other new entries to the slideshow. Ellen's face and the taillights of her van disappearing into the late-night traffic. Edward's healthy body.

Ed looked down at the water again. Edward probably knew how to swim, but he'd never learned how. The marking on the edge of the pool said nine feet. It would be so easy. Just take a step forward. Someone would find his body floating in the pool tomorrow. Would anyone actually care? Hell, he didn't exist anyway. Even in his real world, he had barely existed.

He wondered what it was like to drown. Is there a moment after the initial panic when there is peace? He'd never considered suicide, even in those early days after the accident. Was this an indicator that he was strong or just a chicken shit?

As Ed eased his cane forward a step, the voice startled him. "Hey Eddie." A person stood on the far side of the pool, blue rippling shadows washing across his face. It took a moment for Ed to recognize Jerry. A soft orange glow came from a cigar. Ed looked back down at the water.

The last thing Ed wanted right now was a conversation, especially with some upbeat guy like Jerry. When Jerry didn't move, Ed let out a big sigh, then began his slow gait around the perimeter of the pool to where Jerry stood. As Ed came up alongside him, Jerry didn't look up, but kept his eyes on the blue water, like he was in some kind if trance.

"Finally getting a break, Jerry? You've been busy tonight."

"Yeah." He showed no signs of being the jovial DJ.

Ed took the cue, and turned his attention to the water, too.

After a time of silence, Jerry said, "That was a pretty amazing move you made in there tonight, saving the reunion." He made no mention of Edward—it was hard to believe he hadn't noticed him. Maybe Dottie had spoken with him about it.

Ed shrugged. "And that was pretty amazing when you played the alma mater. Had me tearing up." That was a lie, but he knew it should have had him tearing up.

"I don't know why the world is so difficult sometimes." Ed heard Jerry exhale a heavy breath that implied that it was his world that was difficult.

"Well, if everybody had the great attitude you've got, Jerry, then—"

"That's a crock."

Ed nodded in the darkness, but kept quiet.

"Hell, I was a high roller. Investment broker with a big S&L downtown, had been there for years, worked my way up through the ranks. I was ass-deep in the big bucks. Ridin' high. Jenny and I had this great home in the hills behind Laguna Beach."

"Sounds pretty good."

Jerry let out a self-pitying laugh and now turned toward Ed. His face was full and round, surprisingly wrinkle-free, and his head was bald. The pool lights sparkled in his large eyes. With a white beard, he'd have made a great Santa.

"It was pretty good, but then the recession came along." After a pause, he said, "Geez, I don't know why I'm digging up that crap tonight. You've got better things to do than listen to my bitching." He turned back toward the water and was quiet.

Ed said nothing.

Jerry turned toward him again. "So, anyway … the S&L folded, I was out of a job and for a while I was facing jail time for my work on the subprimes." Even in the dim light, Ed could make out a look of … of what? Pleading? "Eddie, I'm no crook."

"I'm sorry," was all Ed could say.

"Looking back, I can't believe I bought into all that crap. Thought I was hot stuff, making big deals left and right. Then, suddenly I couldn't even get a job. Everybody hated me." Ed thought Jerry might let out a sob. "But I suffered, too. We had a fat 401k and a bundle tied up in the stock market. Giant mortgage on the house. Overnight, I lost almost everything.

"Here I was, pushing sixty, broke and with a dark shadow hanging over me, having to start over." He let out a little smirk of self-pity. Now he held up his cigar and looked at it. "Sure as hell ought to give up these things, but crap, I've got to have some pleasures." He shook his head, then put the cigar out in a pedestal ash tray between two webbed chaises. Then he returned his stare to the water. The undulating blue light on his face was like a slow-motion strobe.

"You know, I'd always seen my career—my life, they were the same thing to me—as a path leading up a mountain. I started out at the bottom. But if I worked hard and plugged away, I'd make my way up to the top. And dammit, I did. But now I'm right back where I started, at the bottom." Jerry gave his head a slow, fatalistic shake.

Ed looked up at the night sky. Through the haze, he could make out perhaps a dozen stars, which in Southern California qualifies as a clear night.

Jerry laid a beefy hand on Ed's shoulder and squeezed. Then he grinned, while he shook his head. "Hey, thanks for listening, Eddie. I still can't get over what you said out there in front of everybody tonight. Got me thinking, that's for sure." His grin widened. "Wish I'd known you back in high school. I missed out."

Ed wished that, too, but all he could do was nod.

Jerry checked his watch. "Uh oh, I'd better get back in there. Dottie's gonna rip me a new one." He laughed, the jovial Jerry re-emerging, then left.

Ed stayed by the pool. He wondered if there was a parallel universe in which he and Ellen and Jasmine actually had headed off into the night in the Roadtrek. They'd be a couple hours north by now, up over Cajon Pass, looking for a place to camp. Jasmine would bed down up front in one of the captain's chairs that fold down into a single bed. They'd probably hang a sheet or blanket to give her some privacy. Ralph, of course, would be curled up on the floor. That would leave that queen-size bed in the rear. Decisions would have to be made, and there'd be another parallel universe in which she came into his arms. He could be there now.

But instead, he had ended up here. Ellen was gone, and most likely he would never see her again.

There was that moment tonight when the music had ended and she had pulled away, but only slightly. He closed his eyes and imagined her in his arms again. Oh God, he should have kissed her then. Kissed her hard. Let her know how he really felt, let her know who Ed Turner really was.

But he hadn't, and now she was gone.

Chapter 31

"There you are. I've been looking all over for you." Ed had barely gotten back in the door when Jasmine brought him the phone again. "It's Ship," she said.

"Oh? I wasn't sure he'd call again."

"Actually, I called him." She gave him a cheesy smile. "I told him about Edward."

"You …?"

"Sorry, but I mainly wanted to try out my mutual induction analogy."

"Jasmine, you shouldn't have—"

She pushed the phone toward him.

Ed cleared his throat. "Yes, Dr. Jameson. First, let me apologize for—"

"Turner," Ship said, "Jasmine told me about the other person who appeared. Is that right?"

Ed should have called Ship about Edward's appearance, and he would have, eventually. But he needed to learn a little more on his own first. He shook his head, as he shot Jasmine a glance of disapproval. "That's true."

"And you're sure about this?"

"I'm sure."

"Do you know when the two of you split from each other?"

"The day of the accident."

"I figured. Have you learned anything from him?"

Ed licked his lips. "Well, he's not the most communicative—"

"Look, Turner, I want to hear what you learn from him, but maybe hold it until the morning. It's getting late."

"Understood, Dr. Jameson. Again, I'm sorry that Jasmine—"

"I think your protégé may be on to something."

"I'm sorry that … what?"

"She mentioned mutual induction. You know what that is, right?"

Ed rolled his eyes and shook his head. "Of course. It's when—"

"So, you said this happened as you neared the entrance to the reunion, right?"

Ed ran a hand through his hair and gave Jasmine a look that was a mixture of annoyance and embarrassment. "That's correct. I was just on the other side of the door from the people."

"So, here's the deal, Turner. You said you may have had some brief amnesia episode, right?"

"Yes. It's called a—"

"TGA, I know. So, if that's true, your brain had, at least temporarily, lost much of its short-term memory and perhaps information about your identity. Is that correct?"

"Yes, that's—"

"Do you know if the other version of you also experienced this?"

"Yes, as a matter of—"

"That's what I thought. So, listen. Here's your brain, temporarily a blank slate, more or less, adjacent to a large group of people whose minds are focused on the year, what was it, 1968?"

Ed took a deep breath and let it out slowly. "Yes," he said, meekly.

"Here's where the mutual induction idea comes in. We're not, of course, talking specifically about mutual induction, as in the way an electric motor works."

"Of course."

"So, somehow, this combined focus of the attendees may have been able to write onto your blank slate and transfer you, mentally, back to 1968. Following me, Turner?"

"Yes, certainly." Jasmine was watching him intently, and he was trying to avoid her stare.

"And if your mind were to be restructured, let us say, to be back in 1968, then the electron configuration in your brain may have returned to what it was at that time. So, that fateful decision may have been made again. And, somehow, this time, the cat was alive instead of dead." Now Ship laughed like he had scored a great victory.

Ed didn't know what to say.

"Now, there's a lot I don't know about this collective phenomenon of many minds focused on one thing—say, the year 1968—imprinting an identity onto another mind. Might need to talk to a psychiatrist about this."

Ed stayed silent.

"The beauty of this idea, which I admit was all Jasmine's, is that it does not require a roll-back in time to that initial moment, fifty years ago. This is not time travel. And so, the issues I was worried about—time-reversal symmetry of the wavefunctions and the second law of thermodynamics—those concerns are removed, because we are not talking about a shift in time at all, but rather a re-programming in the present by which the initial conditions of that event fifty years ago might be re-experienced. Following me, Turner?"

"Yes, of course, Dr. Jameson. I just want to—"

"Anyway, that's all—"

Ship was interrupted again by the woman in the background. Ed couldn't quite make out the name she called him. It sounded like "Ya Hayati."

"Yes, Leyla, my darling, I'll be right there."

Ship came back on the phone. "Okay, Turner, I've got to wrap this up, if I want to keep my marriage." He let out a brief laugh. "Anyway, I need to get a more complete account of the events of your evening. This could be very important."

"So, Dr. Jameson, maybe we should meet to discuss this further." A chance to reconnect face to face.

"Uh … I don't think we're at that point, Turner." Still harboring suspicions that he was possibly a lunatic? Ed slouched. "What I would like is for you to write down for me the exact chronology of the events of the evening, with as much detail as possible, including everything you observe about your duplicate, and send it to me. Okay?"

"Okay."

"Might the duplicate be willing to speak with me at some point?"

"I don't think so, at least not yet," said Ed.

Ship gave Ed his email address, which, of course, Ed already knew.

After Ship hung up, Jasmine told him about her conversation with Ship. "I hope it was okay that I called him. After all, he is your friend."

"It was fine, Jasmine." It was better to have the Edward development out in the open, he guessed. "In fact, it would seem, your mutual induction analogy may have been the missing ingredient. Nice going."

Jasmine glowed. "Yeah, I can't believe it. He said it was brilliant, although, like you said, it was hardly an earth-shattering idea."

Ed cringed, embarrassed by his earlier rejection of Jasmine's idea.

"Anyway," said Jasmine, "Ship said that tomorrow he was calling some guy at Stanford. Jergen Shimsky, I think. Ever heard of him?

Holy shit, Jergen Shimsky? Shimsky was a big gun at Stanford, seemed to be in the running for the Nobel the past few years, according to Ship, for his theoretical work in atomic physics. He was one of the few big-name physicists Ship still interacted with. He'd apparently known him when they both worked at the University of Chicago. "Certainly, I've heard of him. He's a very well-known physicist."

"So Ship said he was going to talk to this Jergen Shimsky guy about me going to Stanford. Can you imagine that?"

Ed certainly could imagine that. One supporting word from a luminary like Shimsky would almost guarantee admission, probably with a full-ride scholarship.

"Good grief," Jasmine gushed, "Me at Stanford? I mean, I thought I'd be at the local JC or at best a state college for sure."

Of course he could see Jasmine at Stanford. He shook his head slowly, and a smile came across his face. His time in this alternate reality had accomplished at least one good thing.

Chapter 32

"So, did the Cubs win the World Series two years ago?" Edward's voice startled him.

It was after ten. Jasmine had left to serve the last round of snacks, and Ed was pacing along the rear of the ballroom again. Edward had removed his sport coat and rolled up the sleeves of his pale-blue shirt a few inches above the wrists. He held a plastic cup in one hand. *Some of Doug Barlow's special cola?* He had a sly grin on his face. Ed was cautious. "Not sure about this universe, but where I came from, they did."

"Cool. And how about the Angels in 2002?"

Ed had always been a die-hard Angels fan, and their 2002 World Series win had been a glorious end to forty years of despair. He still followed them, and the games were a key ingredient in filling his empty life. "Yes, they did. Do you still follow them?"

"Not as much as I used to. Sports doesn't hold the appeal it once did." He said it in a way that implied he had more important things to care about.

Well, sports still held an appeal for Ed, and Edward's words seemed to demand a response from him. He wouldn't say it directly to Edward, but his mind whirled for a few moments, crafting a justification.

For Ed, sports was full of numbers and statistics and analysis that kept him busy, figuring out complex but ultimately irrelevant details, like whether Mike Trout was as good as Mantle or Ruth.

But it was more than the statistics—it was also about relationships. The true fan, like Ed, cared about the players—people he'd never meet, people who weren't aware of his existence, had no interest in learning about him. Guys making millions, living in mansions, forty or more years younger. It made no sense at all. Yet, he'd follow their performance, their salary negotiations, their off-field lives. It was just plain stupid escapism, really, and that's the first thing a non-sports-fan would tell you. But for Ed, following sports was a way to belong, to have a challenge, a goal to fight for.

"I still love sports," he said.

Edward shrugged, now clearly bored with the topic. "So, we scared old Ellen off."

The images from Ed's slideshow of despair threatened to again switch on in his mind. Maybe he could swing the conversation back to sports.

Edward's eyes twinkled with devilish pleasure. "Kinda had a thing for her in high school. But I guess you know that." He gave out a big laugh that didn't sound authentic. "Shit, I was such a limp wrist back then. Never made a move."

Ed thought about telling Edward that Ellen had gone to Eddie's funeral, but decided against it.

"If I'd known what I know now, I'd have been all over that."

Ed tried to produce a smile. He was relieved that Edward wouldn't have a shot at her tonight.

"Hell, she still looks pretty good, don't you think? I mean, for an old broad. I can see why you were moving in on her."

Ed looked away. 'Moving in on her' was hardly the way Ed would describe his approach to Ellen.

"So, are you married? Or ever been married?" Edward looked at Ed like he would be surprised if the answer were yes.

Ed briefly recounted the story of Diane, his PT. "Yeah," he concluded, "that was a long time ago."

"And nothing since?"

Ed wasn't sure what Edward meant by 'nothing,' so he shrugged.

Edward laughed. "So, I'm guessing you probably weren't going to jump old Ellen's bones tonight."

Ed bristled. He didn't like talking about Ellen this way. And he didn't like Edward's insinuation that he had no romantic intentions toward Ellen. After all, he had to admit, those bones were rather appealing. "So, what about you, Edward? You married?"

"Not married, although that could always change." He gazed out across the room, like he was sizing up opportunities. "So, yes, I have been married. But I'm not going to say how many times." He gave Ed a wink. "At some point, you start to lose count. Got any kids?"

Ed shook his head. "You?"

"Hell, no. What a pain in the ass that would have been."

You've got to be kidding. This guy is me? Ed managed an uncomfortable smile.

"Anyway, looking out for myself is about all I can handle. One thing I learned in Nam is to take care of myself. I don't let people push me around anymore. I was such a wimp in high school. Afraid of my freaking shadow. Afraid to ask a girl out. Afraid of my old man. But, when you've got an M-16 in your hands and assholes are spraying you with gunfire, and you see a buddy take one in the head, then you get over that fast."

I guess I still am a wimp. Another failing exposed by Edward.

"That's really why I switched to 'Edward.' It was dignity. Eddie's the name of some squishy sissy with thick glasses and bad breath." Ed had to laugh. "Do you know there have been kings named Edward?" Of course Ed knew this. Everybody knew this. "No king ever named Eddie." Edward laughed, as he took a slurp from his cup.

"So, I had to come over and check this out." It was Denny Jones, and Ed was glad to see him. The big hulk of Denny stood back from them and eyed each of them from head to toe. "Good God, so you're not twins or anything?"

Ed shook his head. He thought about how twins were the closest two people could be in this world. How they often had the same thoughts, selected the same kinds of clothes, even if they lived far apart. Closer than siblings. He'd never had a sibling, so he really didn't know much about this. Nor had he yet come to terms with the reality that standing before him was someone much closer than a twin could ever be. Someone with his DNA, the same body, same history before age 18, but now different. Shaped by fifty years of life. "No, we're not twins, Denny."

"And who are you?" asked Edward, his voice tinged with wariness.

"Oh, sorry, Denny Jones." He stretched out a hand to shake. "Dottie filled me in. Had to see for myself." He shook his head. "Gotta say, I don't understand it. Not at all."

"Neither do I, I mean we." Ed shot Edward a helpless glance.

"But I've learned one thing," said Denny. "You've got to accept things as they really are. Guess you learn that as a fireman. It's possible to over-analyze things. If there's a fire, you can't stand around scratching your ass. You've got a fire to put out." He looked at Edward. "So, how'd you slip in without any of us noticing?"

"Came in late. Guess there was nobody out front. Truth? If I'd known about this shit, I'd just as soon gone to the worst movie in town and called it a night."

They all laughed.

Denny looked from face to face. "So, why did you both show up tonight?"

"Beats the hell outta me," said Edward.

"Well, there's a theory," said Ed. No point trying to go through the many-worlds explanation now. "But maybe you said it best, Denny. Got to accept things as they are." Ed heard his mouth say these words, and although his brain had now accepted his new reality, down at the gut level he was far from accepting things as they really were.

Denny turned to Ed. "Dottie says you went to check out the old school tonight. So, how was that?"

"Hadn't been back in fifty years. It was good to be there, but it also felt weird."

Edward chimed in. "No way I'd go back to that dung hole."

Denny focused a serious look on him. "Hmm." That's all he said for a moment. "I just live over in Orange County, so not far away. Still, I always like to get back to the old neighborhood when I can. The old house where I lived—can you believe it's still there?"

Edward hissed. "Maybe life was better for a big guy like you. Probably played football, made it with all the cheerleaders, felt like a hero. Of course, you'd want to go back."

Denny apparently chose to ignore Edward's nasty comment. "So you've never been curious enough to go back and see the old homestead?"

"I've never been back," said Ed. "Not sure I want to see it, either."

"Okay," said Denny, with a shrug. "But, if it were me, I think it'd be good to see it. Hell, I'd take you both over there, if you wanted. Couldn't be far away."

Ed surveyed the room. It was getting late. Sherrie Blanton hadn't made any more announcements since the Vietnam shouting match. No one seemed to care. Jerry was still playing 1968's greatest. But Ellen wasn't there. The place seemed empty. He had no place to go and no way to get there if he did. "Guess it wouldn't be so bad to get a little fresh air," he said, looking at Edward.

Edward threw his hands in the air. "Whatever. It's not like this place is boiling over with thrills."

Out in the parking lot, Ed gave Denny the address, and they all piled into Denny's pristine Crown Victoria, maybe a '98. Edward rode shotgun, while Ed sat in the back.

It was only a ten-minute drive over to the old house. Much had changed along Rincon Boulevard. Where Ruth's Flowers once sat, there was now a seedy-looking payday-loan store. The White Front discount store where he'd gotten his clock radio when he was a kid was long gone. The lot, surrounded by a high fence, was now a parking area for RVs. Some places were still there. Trujillo's Mexican Foods—Becky Trujillo had gone to Sentinel and was a grade ahead of Ed—

still looked open and flourishing. Ed's mom used to buy homemade tortillas there.

When Ed was born in 1950, the population of the LA metro area was perhaps four million—a teeming metropolis even back then. But, today it was pushing twenty million. Greater than many nations.

When he was a kid, the region was a collection of small cities with unique identities. He could remember miles of orange groves. He wondered if there were any left. Today, as best he could tell, LA was a continuous smear of suburbs, strip malls and freeways stretching for fifty miles in every direction from the civic center. On his drive down this afternoon, he'd seen the downtown skyline. He remembered when the LA City Hall was the tallest building in downtown. Now it was a small historical relic, off to the side of a cluster of steel and glass skyscrapers twice its height.

This familiar-yet-unfamiliar place was his home town.

Chapter 33

"This isn't the best neighborhood," Denny said. Ed and Edward leaned against the chain-link fence—barbs were up—looking into the yard of their old house, while Denny paced around behind them, looking up and down the street. "Snooping around a place like this is a good way to get shot."

But Ed and Edward were focused on the house. "It looks empty," said Edward. The house was dark, and there appeared to be no window coverings. Steel security bars on the windows were a testament to the truth of Denny's words. The whole street was deathly quiet.

The house was even smaller than Ed remembered. A simple frame box, two bedrooms and a bathroom. He could remember the inside of the house like it was yesterday—his small bedroom across the hall from Mom and Dad's, the kitchen with its scarred laminate counter-tops and the outdated O'Keefe and Merritt range with burners that had to be lit with a match. He'd had to take a tub bath, because the shower fixture leaked, and his dad had never gotten it fixed. In the square living room that you stepped into through the front door—even his low-end condo had a foyer—he knew which corner the 17-inch black-and-white Zenith had sat in.

The chain links dug into his fingers—he'd been grasping them tight. He pulled his hands away.

What had once been a lawn was now gravel. "I remember mowing the lawn and wishing I didn't have to do it," said Ed.

"Yeah, it seemed so big then. Plus, the cheap bastard only had a push mower, never sprang for one of the power models. That would've made it a little more tolerable."

"They didn't have much money," said Ed. Of course, Edward knew this, but some explanation seemed needed.

There were no plants around the house. Ed couldn't help but think that if he lived here he'd plant something hardy, maybe some short junipers around the edge of the structure. Maybe colorful annuals or bulbs fronting them. Zinnias, maybe, or marigolds or, yes, that's it, ranunculus. He'd add some shrubs just inside the fence to offset the prison-yard motif that the chain link created. And some low hedge plants, maybe Texas privet. And, he'd get that gravel scraped off and put a lawn back. Even if he had to mow it with a push mower.

"Dang, I never realized you lived over here," said Denny, still out on the curb. "Not sure I'd have suggested we come over, if I'd known this was your neighborhood. No offense intended, but everyone used to call this area Pittsville, because it was so poor."

Edward produced a cynical grunt. "Hell, if they called it Pittsville back then, they must call it Shitsville now." It was true, the neighborhood had taken a nosedive.

Ed had never heard his neighborhood called Pittsville, nor had he been aware that his home was inferior to others in the area. But it was true that his dad was reluctant to allow other kids to come to the house. He never gave an explanation that Ed could remember. Maybe he was ashamed. Ed turned and looked across the street. Where there had been houses, there was now a row of rental storage units. "Larry Gregg used to live over there," he said to Edward.

Edward turned and looked across the street, too. "Yeah, he was always organizing the over-the-line games on Saturday over at the Sentinel baseball field."

"I remember that, too," said Denny.

Ed scratched his head. "Geez, do you think anyone still plays over the line?"

Edward shrugged. "I do remember how shitty I was."

"Yeah, me too. Uh, I mean, Lord, this is really weird."

They stared at the storage units for a while, not that there was much to see, then turned back toward the house. "Remember the leaks in the roof?" said Ed.

"What do you think, Einstein?" Edward laughed. It was good to hear him laugh.

"Buckets everywhere and dad didn't have the money or something to get it fixed."

"The something that dad didn't have was a concern for his family. He was a mean ass, and if you want to use modern words, I'd say the bastard was abusive. Wish I'd had the balls back then to stand up to him."

Ed knew it was true, but he needed to say something to justify his dad's behavior. An explanation, isn't that what physicists sought? Something to make a bad situation a little more tolerable? Maybe that's why Ed needed to hear the speculations from Ship and Edward didn't. "I know, but he must have had it tough. I mean, he was pretty much a common laborer. We must have been the poorest people in the neighborhood."

"Don't go making apologies for that SOB. Maybe that makes you feel better, but it doesn't change anything."

"But he wasn't always terrible. He did take me fishing and to that one Angels game."

"But it was because he wanted to go. It wasn't for me."

"And he didn't stand in the way of me going to Sonoma State."

"But he didn't encourage it, either."

"He never went to college, so maybe he didn't understand."

"Whatever."

"And he let me use the Valiant." The Plymouth Valiant. Yes he did do that. He started to say more, but went quiet instead.

Edward grunted.

"Dad must have been unhappy."

"But he didn't have to take it out on me and Mom."

"He never hit her. At least I don't remember—"

"But there was a lot of shouting. I remember some of those nights."

"Yeah," conceded Ed. When Edward spoke, it was like he, Ed, was thinking out loud. He realized that, in truth, he was having a conversation with himself. Wrestling with his contradictory memories, he looked down. *God, this is depressing.*

They both returned their eyes to the house. Edward said, "Remember the workbench I helped dad build?" The garage was made for two cars, but Dad and Mom only had the Valiant. That left Dad room to set up a small workshop in the back corner. There he had built a sturdy workbench, which supported a bench grinder and several other power tools. Off to the side was a wood lathe. Ed remembered helping build the workbench, cutting and sanding the plywood sheets and measuring and cutting the supporting four-by-fours. It had been a disaster. Half-way through trying to cut a piece of plywood, his dad stepped in and took the hand saw, and said, "Oh, hell, let me do that. You're going to take all day, sonny boy." He'd have done better, he justified to himself now, if his dad hadn't been watching him like a hawk, judging him. Later, Dad had said to Mom, in earshot of Ed, "I swear, Bess, that boy couldn't pour piss out of a boot if the directions were on the heel." His mom made her usual ineffectual protest.

Ed looked away, then said to Edward, "Yeah, I remember." He needed to lighten the mood. "But there were some good times. Remember when we'd go deep-sea fishing?"

"The half-day party boats out of Pierpoint Landing. Huntington Flats and the Horseshoe Kelp, isn't that where they'd go?"

"If you don't remember, then you know I probably don't, either." They both laughed. "But, yeah, I think those were the places." The Horseshoe Kelp and Huntington Flats were nearby fishing holes in the Pacific, not far off shore. You could see the mainland from there, Ed recalled. Dad could never afford one of the all-day boats that went all the way to Catalina Island, to find the big Yellowtail and White Sea Bass.

"We'd catch bonito, barracuda and halibut—but on a lot of those days we didn't catch anything," reminisced Edward.

Denny looked back and forth between Ed and Edward, grinning and shaking his head.

"Remember—Geez, of course you do—how Mom would fillet the barracudas and soak them in salt water to take out the fishy taste?"

"Hell, yes," said Edward, "then broil the filets, I think. Damned good."

"Remember the big halibut I caught?"

"Twenty-eight pounds. But correction, butt-head," Edward laughed, "I'm the one who caught it." He gave Ed a friendly punch to the shoulder.

Ed retorted, "I've never known anyone like you." More laughter.

"What kind of fishing tackle were we using? I remember, at least I think I do. Penn Jigmaster with, um, fifteen-pound monofilament line. Live anchovy for bait."

"What kind of rod?"

"Hmm. I don't remember. Do you?"

"Nope."

Edward tapped Ed's chest with his forefinger. "Well, it looks like our brain cells are dying off at about the same rate."

"Remember Spud?" Spud was the mutt that came along after Burgess the cat died.

"He slept at the foot on my bed."

They were quiet for a bit, then Edward said, "So, the day I took the Valiant up toward the mountains. Did Dad ever chew your ass about that?"

"You mean because I wrecked the car or because I had lied to him when I said I was going to stay in our area?"

"He'd have never let me go if I'd said I wanted to go to Tahoe."

"Well, it's fifty years later, and I still haven't ever made it up to Tahoe," said Ed.

Edward shrugged like it was no big deal. "The place is overrated."

"But there are mountains up there. I wanted to see the mountains."

"Yeah."

"Remember the San Gabriels?" Ed turned toward the street, the direction where the high mountains ringed the LA basin. In daylight, you could see them, even through the smog, from his front yard.

"I always wanted to climb them," said Edward. "But I … we … never did."

"Remember when I checked out the John Muir book from Mrs. Lynch, the librarian?"

"Oh my God, Mrs. Lynch, that mean old broad. Haven't thought about her in years."

Ed only remembered because Ellen had mentioned her when they were at Sentinel. "*The Mountains of California*," he said.

"Climb the mountains and get their good tidings." Edward was quoting from the book.

Ed continued. "Nature's peace will flow into you as sunshine flows into trees."

Edward turned to Ed. "The winds will blow their own freshness into you, and the storms their energy, while cares will drop away from you like the leaves of Autumn."

Ed shook his head slowly. "Can't believe I still remember that whole passage."

Denny looked on in amazement.

Ed cast his gaze back into the yard, down at the gravel. "I never climbed a mountain. Did you?"

"Not the kind John Muir was talking about."

Then there was silence.

Edward turned toward Ed. "So, why the hell are we here?"

"You mean, like is there some purpose or something?"

"You know what I mean."

"Yeah." Nervous laughter. "I guess all I have is the physics theory I told you about." He knew Edward didn't buy any of it.

Edward was quick to snap at the comment. "That's some crap idea. Personally, sonny boy"—there it was again—"I've seen some shit that you, in your ivory-tower, don't-get-your-hands-dirty life, haven't. And I'm tired of know-it-all elitists like your professor friend, sitting back with his feet up on the desk, telling me why my life's so screwed up. Get the drift?"

Ed felt his stomach clench. It was amazing how quickly Edward's mood could change, as if his rage was just below the surface. "Got a better idea?" he said.

Edward licked his lips, then turned back toward the house. After a while, he said, "Are we stuck here forever?"

Chapter 34

Ed knew the trip to the old house would be depressing, but it had been a way to connect with Edward. *God that's weird. Connect? We're talking about me.*

On the short drive back to the reunion, Edward again sat in the front seat with Denny, who did most of the talking, telling Edward about his high school days, his long career at the fire department and what he was up to these days. He seemed unconcerned with the bizarre fact that he had two versions of the same person riding in his car.

So, why would Ed even want to connect with Edward? Ed feared him, was jealous of him, found him unpleasant. But he also was drawn to him. There was a deep bond that he couldn't explain, like what it must be like to have a twin, only probably deeper. Despite the different lives they'd led over the past fifty years, Edward understood things about him that no one else could. The troubled relationship with their father was just one of those things.

But Ed also needed to understand more about why Edward was here, how he got here. He'd report back to Ship about it. Perhaps there was a clue that would help them both return to their native realities.

Ed again turned his attention to the scenes from his old neighborhood, flickering by his window like frames fast-forwarded in a familiar old movie.

Back inside the Grand Ballroom, Ed found himself standing alone with Denny. Edward had darted off into the throng of laughing people.

"So, how was it, going to your old home tonight?" Denny asked.

"Pretty emotional. I mean, thanks, Denny, for taking us, but I'm not sure it was really the best idea. Brought back some pretty painful stuff."

Denny, several inches taller than Ed, looked down at him with concern. He brushed an itch on his nose with the back of his hand and said, "Sorry to hear that, Ed."

"Not your fault. I guess those days were pretty rough for me. Maybe a guy like you, who had a lot of great memories, can't understand that."

Denny chewed his lip. "Yeah, I do have some good memories. I know Edward made those nasty remarks about making it with all the cheerleaders. I did date some of those girls and guess what? They were just scared, ordinary humans like everyone else. If I was confident then, it was because I was stupid—so full of myself that I couldn't see straight. Yes, it was great playing football. Maybe it was the best time of my life. But it seems to me that the best time of your life can be at any age."

Ed's brow furrowed. "At any age? No offense, Denny, but maybe you're saying that because we're both old."

Denny laughed. "Maybe. But here's what I'm getting at. Running down some field with a football, under the lights at a high school, winning the game, a game that matters in the long run about as much as a cup of spit—is that really more important than what I'm doing now? Maybe this sounds strange to you, Ed, but when I'm helping some gal figure out how to connect up her new ceiling fan, or I'm helping some old guy select the right piece of plywood—maybe that doesn't sound like much, maybe it's not what the world calls success, but I think it is success. I've come to realize that success is when you can help someone else with a problem. Does that make sense?"

Hell, yes, it made sense. Ed thought about those C-minus students who sat in his office for hours trying desperately to understand Newton's Laws. None of them was going to be the next Stephen Hawking, but they were people, people who mattered, and helping them pass a course was important. "Yes, it makes a lot of sense."

"You know, I can't get my head around what's going on with you and Edward. And ..." He nodded toward the posters across the room. "... and Eddie. Dottie tried to explain it to me, but maybe she didn't really understand it, either. I just thought that going back to your old home tonight might help you guys out a bit. Maybe not, huh?"

Ed leaned toward Denny, with both hands on the cane. "When I think about it—maybe this won't make any sense to you—I'm not sure I've ever really had a home." *Maybe heading up over Cajon Pass with Ellen in her Roadtrek ...* He shook his head, as if that sudden thought could be flung away. "I guess what I'm trying to say is, maybe I've never had a place where I felt really accepted for who I was, where it was okay to be just me and not some improved version of me."

"God, Ed, I know exactly what you're saying. Two divorces. Hell, I certainly know what it feels like to not have a home. I don't mean because I lost my houses in the divorce settlements—well, actually I did and that sure hurt." His eyes sparkled as he laughed. "But what I mean is, I know what it's like to not have a place where they love you, even if you don't measure up."

Ed nodded in agreement.

Denny squeezed his chin between his thumb and a forefinger, like some new insight was about to emerge. "So maybe home is where you don't have to earn your way or deserve to be there. It's where you belong because, well, just because you're you."

Ed pursed his lips. "Just because there is a place where you've always been, where you've always stayed—like my old house—that doesn't mean that's your home." He looked up at Denny for affirmation. Denny nodded knowingly. "Home may be a place you've never been."

Denny gave Ed a penetrating look, like this old fireman was staring into a house ablaze. Then he laid a hand on Ed's shoulder. "Just because you don't live here, Ed, doesn't mean you don't belong here. Maybe you've been heading for home all your life, and now you've finally arrived."

Ed's mouth fell open. It was like someone had just pulled open the curtains to let sunlight pour into a darkened room. All he could say was, "Thanks, Denny." He laid a hand atop Denny's hand on his shoulder.

As soon as Denny left, Edward approached him, shooting a glance over at Denny, who was now chatting with Dottie. "So, it looks like you and ol' Denny are striking up a bromance."

Ed winced.

"Shit, that poor bastard. Big football stud, told me he now helps out at Home Depot. All those swooning cheerleaders would probably have second thoughts if they could see him now, helping old geezers pick out nails."

Ed opened his mouth, wanted to say something, but no words came out.

Edward wasn't finished. "You know how to pick 'em, Ed. Take your buddy, Gloria. Hell, I remember her as this shy, brainy type. Now she's miss know-it-all, come-let-me-introduce-you-to-Jesus, goody two-shoes—but dontcha know it's an act? Woman priest? Come on, sonny boy. Dontcha think she's just as scared as the rest of us? She doesn't have any more answers than you, but she wants you to think so. She's gonna do that fake listening, I-feel-your-pain crap, but she's not really listening to you. Couldn't give a good crap about what you really think. I've had it to here with preachers. Saw plenty of them in Nam. That was enough for me. My advice, sonny boy: stay away for your own good."

Ed felt his face redden. "I've had enough of this …," he blustered, then tried to find more words. He couldn't, so he walked away.

But Edward caught up to him. "Don't walk away from me, you jerk. Okay, maybe I was a little hard on your friends. But I've seen stuff you haven't. I haven't had the soft life you've had. You haven't—"

"Shut up, Edward, just shut up. I don't want to hear any more of your crap. One fact: you walked away from the accident unhurt. Sure, you went to Vietnam. Got to be the big hero with your M-whatever. Mr. Tough Guy. I was rotting away, unable to walk. My legs weren't the only thing that was crushed. My soul was crushed." He licked his lips that were suddenly dry. "Yes, I also got 33 in the lottery. But I was, what did you call me? A crip? Yes, that's what I was. Damn you, Edward, that's what I still am." Ed's voice was shaking. He didn't want Edward to see him lose it, but that's what he was on the verge of doing.

Edward was seething. He turned and looked off into the room for a moment, then back at Ed. "But you got an education, which I never got. You became some professional ivory-tower bull-shit artist, spouting your physics theories about this and that. Probably used to having people listen to you. Had the same job for forty years, never had to worry about where your next meal was coming from. And you look down on me because—"

"I don't look down on you, Edward. How could I? You're what I might have become. Healthy. Confident." His voice cracked on the last words. *God, he's what I did become, just in a different universe. How do I get my mind around this?*

Edward ran a shaky hand through his hair, then said, "Okay, we need to talk."

They made their way to one of the empty tables and sat. Edward took a deep breath and began. "So, yeah, I was able to jump free from the car. Sure, I only had a broken ankle. Hurt like hell, but in a few weeks I was good as new. But here's the part I didn't tell you." Edward's eyes were hard to read. No longer darting around, they were wide and unblinking; they seemed defocused. "First, I need to ask, what happened to the driver of the other car?"

Ed squinted. *What the hell is this about?* He rubbed his chin with a hand, then said, "I was told later that they were uninjured. I never saw who was in the car, don't even know how many there were or who they were. After I crawled out of the Valiant, I do remember there being someone else there next to me, saying something like we'll get help and you'll be okay. Never found out who it was. Next thing I remembered was being in the Placerville hospital. I was told the other driver had called for help, probably had to drive ten miles to find a phone."

"There were two in the car."

Ed was now breathing hard.

"I saw it all. After I jumped, the Valiant careened off the guard rail and back into traffic, right into their path. It was a terrible collision."

"And?" That was all Ed could say.

"They were both killed."

Ed couldn't speak.

"It took a long time for help to come. I heard them dying, Ed. You want to feast on that image for a while? But my ankle was broken, I couldn't move. I couldn't do anything about it. The screams. The God-awful screams. Still think I got the better end of the deal, sonny boy?"

Ed gripped the edge of the table, feeling suddenly light-headed.

"I was arrested and charged with vehicular manslaughter. I was eighteen, so I would be tried as an adult. You should have heard Dad, that SOB. 'I should've never let you use the Valiant,' he said. 'You just couldn't handle it, sonny boy.' Meanwhile I was in jail. Dad wouldn't or couldn't post bail, so I rotted there. How do you think that felt? You're me, asshole, you certainly know how it would have felt."

Ed shook his head slowly.

"I was in there for two weeks, then the charges were dropped. Police finally determined that the road conditions had been just too bad. It was just an unfortunate accident."

But I was going too fast, recalled Ed.

"I had been destroyed. Some shit-for-brains doctor said it was depression—that was crap. But I sat around home for months. No way I could go back to Sonoma State. Dad screamed at me constantly, and that only made things worse."

"God, I ... I ... I'm sorry. That was horrible."

"Then the draft lottery came along, and lucky me, got number 33. Freaking number 33. Prime draft bait." Edward let out a grunt. "Only time I was ever in the top ten percent of anything."

Ed manufactured a grim chuckle.

"But getting drafted was the best thing that could've happened to me. It got me away from dear old dad. And it gave me the cojones to see through that loser. Got me out of my funk, let me tell you."

Ed stayed silent, but his eyes were locked on Edward.

"So, you asked me if I've killed anyone." Edward gave out a cynical laugh. "I started *before* Vietnam, sonny boy. So killing some gooks was no big deal after that. In fact, I got pretty good at killing." He looked at Ed with raised eyebrows.

Ed exhaled heavily. "You mean, you've ..." He couldn't finish the sentence.

"You're asking if I've killed anyone since the war? Is that what you're asking, Mr. model-citizen? That's none of your eff-ing business." Edward now leaned back in his chair and seemed to relax. "Let's just say that sometimes people cross me. There are people who think they're superior to me, want to rub it in. I get very angry when that happens. That's all I'm saying about that, sonny boy."

Ed didn't know what to say. Those shared memories about deep-sea fishing, baseball, Spud and John Muir seemed distant and irrelevant. He looked into the eyes of this man, this mysterious, frightening, offensive man. This man who disgusted him. This man he loved. This man he didn't know. This man who was him.

Chapter 35

Ed was now alone again, in his chair at the edge of the Grand Ballroom, shaken by his most recent interaction with Edward. Dammit, he was a scientist, a practitioner of reason, a professional who was trained to use the scientific method to build foundations of understanding. He recalled a line from Feynman, extolling the joys of being a physicist, about "the pleasures of finding things out." Feynman had used his brains and the intellectual tools he had received through his education to develop explanations for complex phenomena that dazzled a whole generation. He explained the Challenger tragedy and that faulty O-ring. Ed was no Feynman, but he was a trained physicist, and he should be able to still his underlying panic and craft a plan to escape this nightmare.

Sure, Ship seemed to be moving toward some kind of rational explanation for his situation, but Ed needed more than a rational explanation. He needed a rescue. When you're in an earthquake, you need more than a technical understanding of plate tectonics.

Maybe it didn't really matter. Who cares if there are multiple realities, if you are experiencing only one of them at a time? Why should he be surprised to learn that there are other exact replicas of himself in parallel universes, when there is a vast continuum of selves existing side by side right here—sometimes blending in, sometimes in conflict, sometimes ignored or denied—sloshing together inside each person, this very complicated, bewildering, contradictory compilation of realities that is each of us.

Ed suspected that each person at this reunion was dealing with multiple realities: the reality of the doting grandfather, living in the world of stories he's inventing for his six-year-old granddaughter's next visit; the reality of the couple married fifty years and all the complexities that includes; the reality of the woman who is living in the memory world of when she was 28 or 18; the reality of the man who made it out to the golf course last Saturday, but is more and more aware that knee replacement surgery looms in his future; the reality of the couple who know that their children have been evaluating senior-housing plans; the reality of the man who doesn't know what to do with himself since retirement; the reality of all of us who do not grasp what lies ahead, or have not reconciled with what lay in the past, or are unprepared for what is before us now.

Ed's shoulders sagged. This didn't help him to understand his strange situation any better or to know what he could do about it.

But then a realization came to him that troubled him even more, like a sudden stab of guilt. Tonight at the old house, they'd spent the whole time talking about their father and had hardly mentioned their mom. They'd ignored her just like their father had. *Dear God.* He wondered how his mom was doing tonight, then he thought about Edward's mom and Eddie's mom, all the same woman, although each had lived different lives. Eddie's mom had buried a teen-age son—how had she survived that? Edward's mom had seen her son thrown in jail, then return from Vietnam with bitterness and anger, and Ed's mom had nurtured her son through his debilitating injury. All of them had been married to a dominating, perhaps abusive, husband.

Mom never remarried and lived with her sister in Santa Rosa for many years before her declining health dictated the move to the graded-care facility at Sycamore. But the good years she'd had after his father's death didn't seem to matter much now. The image of his mom that dominated his mind now was the frail 92-year-old, diminished by dementia.

He'd been so wrapped up in panic for most of the evening that it was just now hitting him. *Who's going to visit her? Be there to help with decisions? Be there to help stand against the loneliness? Be there to receive the love that even a mother beleaguered by dementia can still give? I am essentially gone from her world, probably forever.*

He'd seen her just a few days ago, after getting the middle-of-the-night call from the on-duty nurse that she'd fallen out of bed. It was 4:30 am when he pulled into the parking lot of Sycamore. Sure, Sycamore was an ElderHealth senior-living facility—modern, clean and well-staffed—that made every effort to project the image of "This is not an old folks home." But the ambiance of such places is never one of sunshine and joy. That morning had been no different. In the parking lot, Ed had seen the familiar unmarked van, sent by a local funeral home to collect the body of another departed soul. And in the pre-dawn, the memory-care unit, where his mom lived, was anything but a serene place, where everyone was resting peacefully.

"Good morning, George," one woman, standing in her doorway, bent over her walker, bellowed to Ed as he had passed by.

Cries of agony—"Oh, oh, oh, help me, help me, help me"—came from behind the closed door of another room.

"Hello, hello, how are you?" said a man, waving from his bed through the open door of yet another room.

Another man sat zombie-like in front of a TV blaring cable news.

Caregivers were slouched over in couches, trying to stay awake until the shift change.

At the nurse's station, a woman greeted Ed. "Mr. Turner, sorry to wake you from your night's sleep. Your mom did have a fall, but she's all right. No injuries." She gave him a reassuring, professionally groomed smile. "She'll be glad to see you."

Ed worked his crutches down the hall toward his mom's room, passing the two men from the unmarked van, now leaving one of the rooms, pushing a cart bearing a dark zipped-up body bag. Ed checked the name plaque on the door. Virginia Doolin. He'd seen her in the dining room just last week.

His mom was awake when he poked his head into her small room. "Oh, Eddie"—after all these years of him being Ed, she still called him Eddie—"I knew you'd come."

"How are you feeling, Mom?"

"I'm feeling great. Are you going to drive or am I going to drive?" His mom hadn't driven a car in almost ten years.

"We're not going anywhere today, Mom," he said, working at a cheery tone. He stepped up to her bedside and took her hand in his. "Are you in any pain?"

"Heck, no, slept like a baby." She apparently didn't remember the fall, which was probably a good thing. "So, then how much longer are we going to be staying at this hotel?"

"We're not in a hotel, Mom. You live here." Ed was never sure whether it was best to keep her grounded in reality or let her be in her delusional world.

She looked confused. "Are you sure? I don't remember this place."

Ed surveyed the small room. Aside from the bed, there was an heirloom dresser that Ed remembered from his childhood and a small table and chair, where his mom sat during the day. A door in one corner of the room opened into a handicapped-access bathroom. "See the dresser, Mom? That was always a special thing for you."

His mom smiled in recognition. "Your dad got me that when we first got married. Is he meeting us today?"

Ed stroked her hand.

"I'm so glad you're here, Eddie."

Ed brushed a wisp of thin white hair from her face. "Me, too, Mom. Me, too." He swallowed hard. This place was where the last-stand battle against the onslaught of death was being pitched. This place that was overwhelmed by the inevitability of death, like the final glimpse of a loved-one's face, as she disappeared over the brink of Niagara Falls, needing to surrender, yet putting up a useless, desperate fight. He looked down into his mom's cloudy gray eyes. Yet, this place, this time, was still able to produce moments of pure love.

Chapter 36

Frank Castenado was now pouring himself a cup of lemonade at the refreshments table, near Ed's chair. He took a sip, as he turned toward Ed. "You've had a busy evening," he said with that slight smile.

"You mean my little speech?"

"I wouldn't call it so little."

"And you probably saw Edward."

"The guy who looks like you? Yeah, I saw him."

"How'd you know this was me and not him?" Ed produced a nervous laugh. "Does that question even make sense?"

"You're the one with the cool cord sport coat."

Ed ran a hand along the worn sleeve of his coat, pulled out a loose thread, and laughed. "Anyway, maybe I need to explain about Edward."

"Only if you want to."

"Ha, not sure I want to."

"Then don't. It doesn't matter to me. In Alaska we don't ask a lot of questions. Everybody's got a past. That's usually why they're up there."

"But I think I need to." He'd told so many others. It seemed like telling Frank was the right thing to do.

As he began his account, the voice from behind him interrupted them. "Hey, Mr. Turner, I'm glad I found you."

It was Cody, the bellhop from the Villa Solana. He'd shed his red jacket and wore blue jeans and a faded T-shirt, with the words 'No Waves, No Glory' surrounding two crossed surf boards. "Cody, what are you doing here?"

"My shift just ended, and I thought I'd better head over and check up on you."

"I appreciate that. I was just getting ready to explain everything to Frank here. Frank, Cody." Frank extended a hand that Cody shook.

Frank and Cody pulled up chairs next to Ed.

When Ed finished his story, he said, "It's okay if you think I'm crazy."

"Whether you're crazy or not," said Frank, "isn't for me to decide. Being crazy usually only means you don't quite fit in with what everybody else is doing."

Sounded like something a guy living in the boonies in Alaska might say, thought Ed.

Cody didn't seem terribly upset by the story, or even very surprised. He'd probably seen too many episodes of the *X Files*. "I figured it must have been something pretty spooky, Mr. Turner."

Ed pressed his fingers against his temples. "I just don't understand all this."

"I don't think you need to understand everything, Ed." Frank's voice was soft and slow. "But you do need to pay attention to everything. Up on the Copper River Delta, a lot of things happen that you can't understand. Maybe you don't need to. But you do have to pay attention." Now he gave that slight smile again. "You may never understand the grizzly bear, but you'd sure as hell better pay attention to where she is."

They all shared brief laughter.

Then Ed said, "Anyway, I'm thinking about what that old woman in Alaska said to you, Frank. About not forgetting who you are."

Frank squinted slightly, like he was focused on Ed's words.

"I'm not sure I know who I am, after tonight. I mean, there are three versions of me here. And this version, the one in the cord sport coat, has no driver's license, no Social Security card, no proof that I even exist. I have no identity."

Frank took a sip of lemonade. "Hmm, your driver's license, Social Security and all that—that's not who you are. That's not what that old Eyak woman meant when she told me to never forget who I really am. I'm pretty sure she wasn't saying I needed to memorize my Social Security number. So you lost some numbers. I'd say that's no big deal. If you lost your soul, I'd say that's a different story."

Ed gave out a nervous laugh. "I guess I just don't know what I'm going to do."

"Oh, Mr. Turner," said Cody, as he leaned closer toward Ed. "It's going to be okay."

"Well, you could come work for me," said Frank. He seemed deadly serious.

Ed leaned back in his chair, stunned by Frank's apparent job offer. "But remember, I don't even have any ID."

Frank offered that slight smile again. "People aren't into all that up where I come from. Pieces of paper aren't as important as whether you can work—that's all that matters."

Ed imagined himself on the slippery deck of a fishing boat, bouncing in the swells, clinging to his cane. "But don't you think I'm a little old to work on a fishing boat? I mean, I'm hardly the most mobile guy around."

"Hell, Ed, I'm too old to work on those boats, too. But there's a lot of work to do on shore. I need some smart people who can handle the books, help better organize our operation. I figure a guy who's a physicist and a teacher, too, could handle those things."

Ed managed a weak chuckle. "I must admit it sounds tempting. Alaska. Cool little town. All that beautiful nature. But, I need to stay here for a while. There are some things here I need to …" He let his voice trail off.

Frank smiled again. He'd seen Ed with Ellen at the table tonight. Maybe he understood what Ed was trying to say. "Good luck with that, Ed," he said.

"Maybe you ought to consider it, Mr. Turner," Cody said. "Geez, I'd love to go to Alaska and work as a fisherman."

Now Frank turned his attention toward Cody. "You would?"

"Yeah, I … I mean … geez, a chance to … I don't know anything about it, but yeah …"

Ed now grinned. "I can tell you this, Frank. I've only known Cody for a few hours, but I'm really impressed with him. He saved my ass tonight."

Cody's mouth hung open. "You wouldn't really consider me for a job up in—"

"Why not?"

Cody rubbed his hands together like a starving man watching a steak on the grill. "Man, I always wanted to go up there."

"Why don't you?"

Cody scratched an ear. "Uh, well, I don't know."

"If you want to go, just go. That's what I did. Never regretted it. But maybe you've got a good career going already."

Cody grimaced. "Well, not sure I'd call it a good career. In fact, it's definitely not." He turned to Ed. "What do you think, Mr. Turner? Would you do it if you were me?"

Ed scratched his head with a forefinger, surprised that Cody would seriously consider such a big move so spontaneously. But then that's apparently what Frank had done years ago. He launched out; wasn't that how Frank described it? Ed opened his mouth, but couldn't find words. Cody studied his face, as if what Ed was about to say would make a big difference. *Seriously, why would someone make such a huge decision so ... so ... so impulsively? Why?* Ed had no good answer. But then another question popped into his head that seemed radical and unexpectedly appealing. *Why not?*

Finally, Ed said, "Hell, yes, Cody. This could be a great opportunity. But, of course, you'll have to decide for yourself."

"Yeah, gotta admit it sounds good. But I'm not sure."

"What aren't you sure about?" Ed asked.

"Just everything. It's kind of a big step."

Ed bit his lip. "I've been unsure of just about everything my whole life. And to tell you the truth, too many times I just sort of wound up doing nothing. I hope you don't do that. I'm thinking now it would be better to have made some mistakes than to have done nothing." He wiped his forehead that felt suddenly sweaty.

Cody nodded thank you, let out a nervous laugh, as he turned back to Frank. "Might be ready to try something new."

"The work's hard. But the pay's good."

"I can work hard. What's it like up there?"

"Well, Cordova's a small town, friendly folks. Surrounded by ocean and wild mountains. Salmon, grizzlies, sea otters and wolves. But maybe for you, that's not—"

"Dang, that sounds nice. But why would you take a chance on me, Frank?"

"I judge a person by what I see. That's usually the best way."

"You know, what the hell, I might be interested."

Frank steepled his fingers. "You know, I was about your age when I left SoCal. Needed a break, a fresh start. I know about such things. But maybe you need to think about it."

"Yeah, I think I've already thought about it. I'd need to give a couple week's notice."

"That could work. Here's my contact info." Frank handed Cody a business card. "When you're ready, let me know. We'll arrange to get you up there. Fall season is coming up. Cohos are still running. A busy time. Good time to start."

Ed was reminded of his conversation with Gloria about starting over. Seriously, was launching out in a parallel universe any more extreme than heading off to Alaska to fish for Cohos?

Cody stood and leaned toward Frank, beaming. They shook hands. "Dang it," said Cody, almost squealing, "Thank you. I can't wait to start."

Frank also stood, poured himself another cup of lemonade, nodded to both Ed and Cody, then headed back off into the room, just as Jasmine returned to the table, carrying a platter and a water pitcher. She nodded at Ed.

"Who's that?" Cody whispered.

"That's Jasmine," he said quietly, but Jasmine, who Ed had learned had a talent for overhearing conversations, looked up at them.

"What?" she said, giving Cody a brief glance before settling her eyes on Ed.

"Jasmine, this is Cody. Cody really helped me out earlier this evening."

"Oh," she said, busying herself with straightening dishes on the table.

Cody shuffled awkwardly.

"Jasmine's going into her senior year at Sentinel," said Ed. "She's been a big help in figuring out my situation."

Jasmine shot Ed a dart of a glance, like she was telling him to cool it.

"Nice to meet you, Jasmine," Cody said.

Jasmine nodded but said nothing.

"So, you're working here tonight?"

"Just helping out with refreshments. No big deal." She continued to arrange the dishes, without looking at him.

"How long do you work tonight?"

"I go home at midnight."

"I thought you said you didn't have a car, Jasmine," said Ed.

Jasmine shot Ed another annoyed look. "My dad's supposed to pick me up." She sighed. "If he shows up. Otherwise, it's only a mile."

"I could drive you home," said Cody.

"You don't need to wait."

"I don't mind. Less than an hour."

For the first time Jasmine looked up at Cody, and Ed could see her Adam's apple move as she swallowed. "Whatever," she said.

"Cool," said Cody, as he looked with uncertainty at Ed. He cleared his throat, then looked back at Jasmine. "Guess I'll just hang out for a while, if that's okay."

"Sure," said Jasmine.

Ed smiled as he watched Cody saunter off, pleased to see that Jasmine and Cody were almost as awkward as him in the flirting department. He wondered about the future and the decisions that awaited Cody and Jasmine. In some parallel universe, Jasmine will go to Stanford, on her way to becoming a prominent physicist. In another universe, perhaps she would follow Cody to Cordova, Alaska, raise a big family and work on the fishing boats. Which outcome would be best? Ed shook his head. How the hell was he supposed to know?

Chapter 37

Watching the interaction between Jasmine and Cody brought Ellen back into his mind. Jerry had just put on "Piece of My Heart," and Janis Joplin wailed with raw, desperate pain. God, he didn't need to hear that song now. It was as if Jerry was hammering him with one crushing love song after another, like the left-right-left-right punching barrage from an emboldened boxer sensing the kill.

Standing next to his chair, he turned away from the room, and with his head down, eyes closed, he pounded the wall softly with a clenched fist. When he opened his eyes, he noticed Gloria standing next to him. "You don't need to be here," he said.

She rested a hand on his arm, and he lost it. *Oh, hell, I don't want to cry.* But what began as a mistiness in his eyes now threatened to turn into sobs. He bit hard on his lip and looked away. Gloria waited beside him, making no effort to offer him a tissue or help him avoid a public display of grief. Finally, wiping his arm across his face, he managed a weak laugh. "Oh, God, I'm so sorry."

"I don't know what you should be sorry about, Ed."

"About crying, about falling to pieces."

"You've got some things to cry about, Ed, and I know from experience that crying is often the most healthy thing you can do. I'm surprised you're holding it together as well as you are." Her hand remained on his arm.

Ed continued to wipe his eyes and tried to manage his drippy nose, but said nothing.

"Tomorrow the sun will come up at our house. We'll have coffee. You, Martin and I will sit outside in the sunshine, and we'll sort things out."

"That sounds nice." His voice was almost a whisper.

She patted his arm, then said, "A person who didn't know how he or she could take any more, wrote, *Tears at night, but joy in the morning*. Maybe that sunlight will help us find where the joy may be lurking."

Ed sniffled one last time, then said, "That guy who said tears at night, I suspect he hadn't just been transported into a parallel universe." He gave her a helpless smile.

"Probably not, but I'm not sure." She produced a little laugh. "I think he was more worried about someone running him through with a sword."

"Oh." Then, Ed also laughed.

Ed and Gloria turned and faced the room, as Jerry had just put on Louis Armstrong's "What a Wonderful World." They listened to the song, then Gloria said, "Geez, that song always gets me. Reminds me of things I can so easily overlook."

After more silence, she said, "Remember that old story about putting a frog into a pot of boiling water?"

"Sure."

"The frog, feeling danger, immediately leaps out. But put the frog in a pot of cool water and slowly raise the temperature—the frog will stay in the water until it's cooked."

He turned toward her.

"Maybe it's the same with love and beauty. Any one of us arrives at the rim of the Grand Canyon, steps out and suddenly sees that view, we're blown away. Maybe we want to cry or sing or dance or pray. But, in our everyday world, we see beauty all around us, and because we've become so used to it, we seldom sing and dance. We just take it for granted.

"I must have listened to that song a hundred times before I really heard it. Satchmo sees trees and roses, the sky, clouds, the dark of night, faces of people, friends shaking hands, greeting each other—all those familiar, ordinary things we see every day, things a lot of people probably don't even notice. And he says all those things are really about love. Yes, what a wonderful world. But too often, because we've gotten used to it, like that frog, we don't even notice it. How seldom do we sing and dance and give thanks for all this love?"

Ed knew that what Gloria was saying was true. But perhaps in a Utopian world, not a world like his, with loneliness, physical impairment, not to mention isolation in an alternate reality. "Maybe it's easy for you to talk about all this love and beauty stuff, but you're not in my situation. You've got a husband, you've always had a career, you've got friends. What do you really know about failure?"

Anger flashed briefly in Gloria's eyes. "Maybe I know more about failure than you think, Ed."

"I'm sorry, I didn't mean to—"

"Maybe you think I spout these things about God because I read them in a book." There was an edge in her voice now, the first time he'd heard it.

Ed wanted to look down, but couldn't turn away from her piercing eyes.

"Well, they are in a book. But I know about them because my life has hit bottom at times. I know about shit."

Ed was surprised she said 'shit.'

"I know about them because these are truths that got me through really tough times in my life."

Ed licked his lips, regretting that he had confronted her.

"Ed, I'm sorry if I come across as pompous and preachy to you. I certainly don't intend that. I'm just speaking to you as a fellow beggar who has learned where to find a scrap of bread."

Now, Gloria was quiet, waiting for Ed to speak.

Finally, he said, "Last week I saw a girl with a T-shirt that said, 'I Never Cease to Amaze Myself.' Maybe that was true for that girl, but I doubt it. It certainly isn't true for me."

Gloria pressed an index finger to her lips, like she was giving this serious thought. "Yeah, I agree. The problem with most of us is that we seldom amaze ourselves. Even though, when you get right down to it, I suppose we are pretty amazing."

She shook her head slowly. "I certainly don't have all the answers, Ed. I don't even have very many of the answers. But I do have a few answers. And one thing I am sure of is that God thinks we're amazing." She let this hang there for a moment, then added, "Yet, it seems to me like we try to avoid that truth. Instead, we often go down two other paths." She leaned in closer to Ed. "And they're painful paths, so I don't understand why we choose them. The first way we avoid the truth is to surrender to the inevitability of life—aging, disappointments, failure, loneliness—and we substitute lesser things, like money, possessions, or status for meaning and transcendence. We succumb to the pain, maybe we just fall apart."

Ed nodded.

"It seems to me that the second wrong path we choose is to live in denial about the inevitability of life. We struggle against life, frustrated, angry. We buy all the lotions, workout programs, botox, vitamins, whatever promises that we'll stay young forever.

"When we choose those paths, we replace the ultimate goal of joy and love and meaning with just trying to find some peace—a safe place to hide from ourselves. Does that make sense to you?"

Ed shrugged.

Now Gloria stepped away from him, paced slowly in a tight circle, head down. Then she stopped and faced him. "Succumbing to the pain was the wrong path I chose." She glowered at him now, so intensely that he had to look away.

She waited for him to return his eyes to her. "Twenty-five years ago, I was working hard as an attorney. Too hard. Never had time for marriage or a family. I was hardly some great lawyer, but I was okay. Mostly divorce cases, civil law suits, dealing with people's anger and suffering. It took a toll." Now she paused, as she shook her head slowly, like she was reliving something awful. "The diagnosis of breast cancer came like a bolt out of the blue—just a routine physical, and there it was."

Ed shuffled and licked his dry lips. "Look, Gloria, you don't have to—"

"It was bad, real bad. Double mastectomy, Ed. Lots of chemo."

"Oh, God, Gloria, I'm so sorry."

"I went into a tailspin, didn't have a family or a church to anchor me back in those days."

Ed had no words. It felt like some damn holding back a reservoir of grief had just burst. He opened his mouth to say … something, words of consolation or wisdom … but all that came out was a troubled breath.

"With so much time away from work, I got let go from the law partnership, so I was out of job, too. I know about nights, Ed, when you scream out, asking why were you born. Begging God to take the pain away, but it doesn't go away."

"I'm so sorry." He'd already said that, but he had no other words.

"My next door neighbor would come and sit with me. She didn't say much, but it meant a lot. She got me going back to church. That was the turning point for me." She stood with her hands on her hips, shaking her head. "I learned that life can go on. That there can be joy ahead, no matter how bleak your situation may be."

Now Gloria's features softened, as she let out a huge cathartic sigh. "Five years later I was in seminary—who would have ever thought?—and three years after that I was ordained. I married Martin Herrera, who I'd met in seminary. He was an administrator on the staff there." She gazed out into the room, as if searching for him, then turned her eyes back to Ed. "It was at church that I met Ellen, who's been a good friend. Oh yes, Ed, priests need somebody there for them, too. It's true that I have Jesus, but sometimes I need somebody with flesh."

Ed was aware that he didn't have anyone with flesh. "Look, Gloria, I'm sorry. I didn't—"

"Oh, shut up, Ed." She now smiled and gave him a gentle punch on the shoulder. "Look out into that room. Everyone here's had some bad things in their life. You don't get to be 68 without it. It isn't just me, and it isn't just you.

"So you're not just some do-gooder project, Ed. You're another human being like me, who needs help. Yes, I'm here for the reunion. I came to see these people. Have fun. And I am. But I also can't turn my back on someone who is suffering. I just can't."

Ed wanted to hug Gloria, but held back.

After a long silence, Gloria said, "So, what about you, Ed?" She again looked him hard in the eye. "What has formed you? For some people, they've been shaped by which cable news network they watch nonstop. Others, by hobbies. Or addictions. But what about you, Ed?" She watched him for a moment, and when he couldn't respond, she said, "I suspect the reasons you're so out of water here is that you are the same person you were in your other reality. I mean, everything around you may be new, but who you are, everything that is unique about you, that apparently has not changed. Is that not true?"

"What about Edward?"

Gloria looked out into the room, where Edward was wandering among the tables. She shook her head slowly, then produced a little laugh. "Yeah, that's crazy, isn't it? I mean, totally freaking crazy." She chewed her lip, as if pondering how to address this. "You and Edward have identical DNA, probably the exact same fingerprints, and at one time before fifty years ago, you were the same person." She shook her head again. "But life has shaped you, Ed, made you who you are. You are a unique person. Edward has become someone else, his own unique person. Yes, this is strange. But it's what it is.

"So, you are Ed Turner. And Ed Turner is a unique, complex, and yes, amazing person, the same amazing person in whatever universe he may find himself in. Maybe there are other Ed Turners, but this one is a unique, and dare I say, beloved Ed Turner."

Ed's mouth fell open as he followed her words.

"One more thing, Ed. Maybe you're feeling lost in this reality. Maybe you're longing for your old reality. Even though, I suspect, that reality wasn't perfect either. Ed, it's not trying to find the perfect world that matters, it's how you live in the one you're in."

Ed considered this. Yes, that old reality wasn't perfect. In fact, will anyone even miss him in that reality? Maybe only Ship. He'd wonder what happened to Ed. Kidnapped? Crashed his car and it wasn't found? Collapsed and was not identified? Murdered? Run away? No, Ship would never expect him to run away. He looked at Gloria and said, "Maybe God is punishing me."

"I don't think that's the way God works."

"But look at my life. Look at what's happened to me."

"I am, Ed. You found Ellen—"

"But she's gone."

"You don't know that."

"And I'm stuck in this limbo."

"But I got to meet you because of that, Ed. And so did Jasmine and Dottie."

Ed felt tears welling up behind his eyes again. "Why would God love me?"

"Because, Ed, you are his child. God will never turn his back on you or me, no matter what losers we might be, because we are his children." Gloria sighed, then said, "People hold onto the image of this angry old man throwing down lightning bolts. I think we need to get rid of that picture and see how God really is. See that God loves us so much that he'd come to earth and live among us as a vulnerable human, subjected to everything we are, even death. That's the kind of God I believe in, Ed. That's the kind of God I think you're waiting to know."

"I've been waiting for a long time, that's for sure."

Gloria pursed her lips, like she wanted to cry, too. "Your words remind me of another line from Scripture." She let out a soft giggle. "I'm sorry if I'm always thinking about lines from Scripture, but there's a passage that says, *My soul waits for the Lord, more than watchmen for the morning, more than watchmen for the morning.*"

Ed exhaled a nervous sigh. "Maybe that is who I've been."

Gloria grasped his forearm and squeezed. "And, Ed, maybe the morning has come."

All Ed could do was look into Gloria's eyes. Those intense, penetrating, inquiring, eyes. As he was beginning to reply, Jasmine appeared before them.

"Hey, Jasmine," said Gloria.

Jasmine nodded. "Gloria." Then she focused on Ed. "Sorry about interrupting, but Ed, I think we have a problem."

Chapter 38

Ed turned toward Jasmine with annoyance. She'd interrupted his conversation with Gloria, but mainly, the last thing he needed now was another problem.

"So, Ed, there are still some unsettled things about the theory, aren't there?"

"Like?"

"Like why aren't there more Ed Turners here tonight?"

"You're kidding, right?"

"I mean there's only three, if you include"—she grimaced—"the dead guy."

"There's not enough already?" He forced a hollow laugh.

"Like, why aren't there ten thousand?"

"Huh?"

"Seriously, Ed, if it's like Ship said—that every decision leads to a new parallel universe—then there should have been a new universe created that day for every decision, like did you order cheese on that burger or not? Get it?"

Gloria watched this interaction patiently, with what looked like amusement.

Ed scratched his chin. "Hmmm. Yes. Why are there only three? Good question." Jasmine had real promise as a scientist. She saw any inconsistency in the data as a problem. Looking at small inconsistencies had been, in fact, what led to the discovery of quantum mechanics. Furthermore, and this made him smile, Jasmine's worry about a 'problem' trumped anything else that might be going on around her at the moment. And that could cause unintentional rude behavior, on occasion, as had just been the case. He chuckled to himself. Physicists, lost in their scientific ponderings, were often considered rude by others. *Jasmine will fit right in.*

"And also," Ed added, "I'm still concerned about Ship's speculation about the mutual induction analogy."

"Still don't like that, huh?" Jasmine said.

"No, no, the analogy is fine. Clever, in fact. But Ship's talk about some collective imprinting of everybody's thoughts on my mind—that was a little far-fetched, don't you think?"

"Yeah, maybe so. He said we needed to talk to a—" She stopped abruptly, her eyes locked on something across the room. "So, there's your guy over there."

Ed followed Jasmine's gaze to Lennie Berger, talking to a woman who was backing away from him. Ed shook his head. "Not sure he'd talk to me."

"Well, he sure as hell won't talk to me. And FYI, I'm not talking to him either." She grimaced, then said. "But I'm thinking Feynman would say you should. We need to hear what a shrink has to say about our ideas." She added, with a little smile, "It's for science."

Ed rolled his eyes, gave Gloria a see-you-later nod, then launched off into the room.

"Uh, Dr. Berger," Ed said from behind Lennie. He would call him Dr. Berger for now.

Lennie turned, and his mouth opened when he saw Ed. He cleared his throat, glanced at his watch like he had an appointment he needed to get to, then said, "What is it?"

"I need to talk with you, Dr. Berger. It's important."

Lennie grunted with disgust. "So impersonating the dead wasn't enough for you, huh? Now you've brought in a stunt double. Not sure I appreciate your sick humor, Turner."

Ed was certain that what really bothered Lennie Berger was that Ellen had left with him. "I'm desperate, Dr. Berger. I'm in the midst of a real crisis. And I need your help. Now." As Lennie edged away, he added, "Please, Dr. Berger." Yes, he was begging, and this made him slightly nauseous, but it might be what it would take to get Lennie to talk with him.

Lennie looked around, like he was searching for an exit in case he needed to flee this lunatic, then said, "Let's talk here. Not sure I want to be alone with you."

Ed nodded with fake understanding. Then he told Lennie the whole story, even though he'd already told him parts of it earlier, but that had been when Lennie was more engaged with the charming Ellen. *Oh God, Ellen.* He had to refocus to get back on track. He tried to tell his story quickly, to hook Lennie before he threw up his hands and walked away in disgust. He made sure to invoke the opinions of the "MIT-trained physicist, Professor Shipley Jameson," conveniently neglecting any mention of the less-than-prestigious Muir College.

When he had finished, Lennie glanced at his watch again, then exhaled an impatient breath. "Look, Turner, I told you I am a man of science. I don't deal in speculation and conjecture. I deal with data and tested theories. Furthermore, I'm not sure I believe anything you're telling me."

"Dr. Berger, I'm a physicist. I too prefer data and tested theories. But right now, I need your conjectures, your educated conjectures. I need your help. Like I said, I am desperate."

"I'm sorry I cannot help you, Turner." He began to back away.

"I will not accept that answer, Dr. Berger." Ed maintained eye contact, unblinking, with Lennie. "This is a life-and-death situation for me."

Lennie licked his lips, then sighed. "Okay, then. Let's find a place to sit."

Ed and Lennie sat alone at the round table. Ed sat upright, hands folded in front of him, like the attentive model student. Lennie leaned forward slightly, his fingers steepled, like he was preparing to present a learned opinion, which Ed hoped he was. "So, the TGA creates a temporary state of amnesia. Of course, you already know that. But a TGA can mimic some of the symptoms of dementia, in that the diminution of short-term memory—key data about your identity, date, home address and phone number, for example—removes a—let's call it an intellectual rudder—a means to keep you navigating a straight course through reality." Lennie cracked his first smile. "Hope you don't mind my nautical metaphor." This was similar to what Ship had conjectured.

"Not at all, Dr. Berger," said Ed. "My mother suffers from dementia, so I understand."

"In a TGA the brain may be open to other memories imprinting themselves on one's perception of reality. This is common among those who struggle with dementia."

Like Ed's mother believing she could still drive, like wondering what hotel she was in, when she was in fact in her own room.

"When you've lost the rudder, that imprinting is possible." He pushed his glasses back upon his nose. "Have you ever heard of a phenomenon called the amplitude of memory?"

Ed shook his head.

"It's like looking at the Chicago skyline. Your eyes are naturally drawn to the tallest skyscrapers. There are thousands of buildings, but your eyes are naturally drawn to the Willis Tower and the Hancock Building. If memories from 1968 were imprinting themselves into your consciousness—caused by the collective effect of the hundred or so people on the other side of the door, centered in their memories of 1968, then it's not surprising that your brain would be drawn to the most commanding memory from that year—the tallest skyscraper—which was the accident. And your brain, having lost its rudder, through the TGA, mimicking the effects of dementia, could have likely landed on that time and place, unruddered, as it were, by reality. Your brain could have been ripe for reliving the decisions you made that day afresh, actually re-enacting them."

Lennie pursed his lips, like he was trying to connect things together in his mind. "I don't know about the quantum things you've mentioned—and I admit, they sound far-fetched, but then you asked me to speculate, and that's what I'm doing. Anyway, if there is some probability of you flipping into another reality, or more likely, being convinced that you had flipped into another reality"—he raised his eyebrows at this; all that was lacking was a patronizing pat on the head—"I guess I could see that being possible."

Memory amplitude? That would explain the ten-thousand-Eds question that Jasmine worried about. Only the decisions involving the accident would be revisited, my Willis Tower of 1968. He glanced toward the rear of the room, where Jasmine stood, wringing her hands, eyes glued on him. "That's very helpful, Dr. Berger. Can you say more about the collective effects? That's a part I don't understand."

Lennie laughed, and Ed smiled in response, although he didn't see anything funny. "I'm thinking of things like mass hysteria and mass hallucinations. Very strange phenomena that have been around for a long time. I recall ..." Lennie paused to laugh again, as if what he was about to say was hilarious. "As far back as the middle ages, there have been reports of strange mass psychological effects. For example, I recall reading about a nun in a convent who began to meow like a cat at a certain time each day. The other nuns, of course, denounced this crazy behavior. But here's what's weird. Within a month, all the nuns, a hundred of them, also began to meow at the same time each day. As you might imagine, this struck terror in the surrounding community. There are lots of such examples. Many of them modern. Bizarre stories of a person presenting symptoms of an illness, and soon nearly everyone in the community had begun to present the same symptoms, even though medical people could find nothing wrong with any of them. In any case, Turner, what I'm suggesting is that a mental state in one individual, or a group of individuals, can in fact be imprinted upon others. It's not well understood, but its existence is unquestioned by the professional community." Lennie produced a self-satisfied smile.

Like Jasmine's mutual induction analogy of a current carrying wire inducing a current into an adjacent wire.

"So there you are, Turner, your brain a blank slate in the presence of a strong collective focus on the year 1968 by the many attendees of the reunion. I guess it's not hard to imagine your mind being imprinted with that focus. Then the memory amplitude effect took you right to a certain moment in 1968, the accident. And if what your physicist contact says is true, your brain could be restored to the chemical state it was in when the decisions involved at the time of your accident were first made. And ..." He threw his hands in the air, as if saying, 'whatever.' "Perhaps those decisions got remade, and, to use your language, parallel universes that were created at those moments could reconnect."

Amazingly, Lennie and Ship, and Jasmine, had put it all together. "Thank you, Dr. Berger, that's very helpful." This was all still speculation, with no proof, but it was credible speculation. It had the ring of truth about it.

Lennie gave out a chuckle. "This is probably all bullshit. I'm not sure I believe any of it. My best guess is that you're experiencing some bizarre, possibly dangerous, psychotic episode."

Ed had heard that part before. Now glancing over Lennie's shoulder, he said, "I noticed Lila Panovsky staring at you, maybe checking you out. Did you know her?"

Lennie casually turned his head in her direction and caught her eye. She gave him that my-dad's-a-dentist smile. When he turned back to Ed, he said, "Hmm. Not sure."

"Yeah, I knew her from the photo club, got a selfie with her a little earlier. Great lady."

"Maybe I'd better head over and say hello." Lennie stood, then gave Ed a wink, like they were a couple of wild bucks out on the prowl. Ed worked to suppress a laugh. "By the way, you can call me Lennie."

"Good luck, doctor," Ed said. "And thank you."

As Lennie hurried across the room toward Lila, Ed leaned his chin on the back of one hand, like Rodin's *The Thinker.*

He reviewed it in his mind. *I arrived at the Villa Solana, just as the invitation had said. A brief amnesia attack, the TGA, produced by my anxiety about the reunion, left my brain a blank slate, much in the way that short-term-memory loss in elderly persons, like my mom, permits delusions. A little later, Edward, in his universe, also experienced a TGA—being the same person, it was not surprising that Edward and I both suffered from TGAs.*

Nearby, the large group of people, focused on our graduation year, 1968, created a collective or mass-psychological effect—like Jasmine's mutual induction analogy—that imprinted that period of time on Edward's and my brains. Then, the phenomenon of memory amplitude ensured that our brains would lock into the moments of the accident. I was effectively reliving that moment, having no mental rudder to steer me away from it.

All this re-established the quantum state in my brain as it was that day, somehow removing the decoherence of the wave functions and allowing two, three actually, parallel universes to reconnect, after being separated for fifty years. The quantum probabilities that had guided the decisions I faced during the accident were being reproduced—whether to jump from the car as Edward did, whether to stay with the car as Eddie did, or whether to drag myself out.

All this was, of course, unlikely, but it was certainly plausible. In fact, he was now convinced that this was exactly what happened. All three of those parallel universes had intersected, which they had not done since they separated on that fateful day fifty years ago. Schrodinger's cat is either alive or dead. And so, he had come into the world, Eddie's world, in which the cat was dead. And yet, he and Edward were here, both very much alive.

Chapter 39

"Holy crap, Ed. We nailed it!" Jasmine shrieked after Ed had presented Gloria and her with the complete explanation. She put up a hand for a high five. The three of them were sitting around one of the tables, otherwise empty. People were still avoiding Ed.

"So, are we going to write a paper about this? A scholarly paper like Feynman would? I mean, you and me and Ship? And I guess that shrink, too."

"Hmm. Maybe we should."

"That would be so awesome. Maybe in some fancy journal. You'll have to figure out which one. My first scholarly paper!"

Ed grinned. He didn't say this to Jasmine, but it would be his first scholarly paper, too. In any universe.

"You don't seem so happy, Ed," Jasmine said.

"Oh, I am pleased that we've got an explanation, but meanwhile I'm still here in this strange place with two other Ed Turners."

"Well, I can tell you this much," said Jasmine. "One of them's dead, so he doesn't count. One of them's a creep. Then there's you." She pointed a finger at him. "And you're just right." She crossed her arms over her chest and smiled.

Ed nodded, still unconsoled.

Gloria said, "You've gotten to see and learn things tonight that few other people ever get to see. I guess I share Jasmine's enthusiasm."

Ed now sat back and studied Gloria and Jasmine. These two strangers, no, friends, good friends. If he ever got together with Ellen, he thought, he just might visit Gloria's church.

Gloria added, "It was a scientist, I believe, who said that 'when an astronomer looks through a telescope into the deep reaches of space, the most significant thing in the known universe—or dare I say, universes—is still immediately behind the eyes of that astronomer.' I think that scientist was saying that the human brain is the most incredible thing there is. And tonight, you, Ed, are learning more about it than perhaps any other person ever has. And Jasmine and I" —she and Jasmine exchanged smiles—"we are privileged to witness it."

Then Jerry announced to the room, "Okay, boys and girls, the last time we heard some of these songs together, they were checkin' our IDs to see if we could get a beer. Now they're checkin' 'em to see if we qualify for the senior citizen discount." There were howls of laughter. "So, here's the number one song from 1968. Enjoy, my friends, enjoy."

Ed had heard "Hey Jude" a million times. Could sing all the words. But he realized now that he'd never listened carefully to what Lennon and McCartney were really saying to their friend, Jude. It was right there. *Don't be afraid.*

He'd always been so afraid. And like Jude, he'd found her! He needed to go and get her. Yes, he'd figure this all out tomorrow with Gloria. He said it again to himself. *I will go and get her.* And Edward? *Don't be afraid, Ed, don't be afraid.*

When the song was over, Ed reached over and took one of Gloria's hands in his left hand and one of Jasmine's hands in his right. "I am so fortunate to have such good friends." Then he said, "I need to talk to Edward."

"Need to talk to me?" Edward stepped from behind Ed toward the other side of the table and faced him. There was contempt written all over his face.

Chapter 40

"We'll leave you two to talk," said Gloria. She stood and Jasmine followed her lead. They disappeared into the crowd.

Edward took a seat across the table from Ed. "Didn't mean to chase your girlfriends away," he sneered.

Ed exhaled heavily and shook his head slowly.

Edward's arms were on the table, his hands clenching into fists and then unclenching, like Ed had seen him do earlier. Then his hands opened and he laid them flat. "Okay, so I'm sorry. Is that what you want to hear? Does that make you feel better?" He ran the back of his hand across his mouth, like a caveman who's just polished off a big chunk of meat. "So sometimes I blow up around guys like you. Okay?"

"Guys like me?" Ed said, keeping his voice soft.

"People who think they're superior to me, rubbing it in. I could have gotten an education. You should know that, you're proof of that. But you piss me off even more than the others. Because … because you're me."

Ed leaned forward. "Look, Edward, I don't feel superior to—"

"Oh, you don't have to say anything. It's just that here I am at sixty-freaking-eight, and I get to have what I could have been rubbed in my face. Could have had a degree. A professional career. People respecting me. Me respecting myself. Can you see how that would affect me?"

"Look, I don't—"

"Shit, I'm just starting to realize I have no job—well, I had no job in the other universe either." He offered an angry sneer. "God, I have no identity, proof I even exist. What am I going to do?"

Ed shook his head. "I don't know." He considered sharing with Edward what he'd learned from Lennie, but he knew Edward wouldn't listen. "I'm just hoping the people here might be able to help."

"Ah, now I get it, sonny boy. Buttering up little Miss Hey-look-I'm-a-priest so she can help you out. And you're probably gonna kiss old Denny's ass, too, hoping he can get you on down at Home Depot. Don't know what your angle is with the Goth chick." Edward laughed, as he stroked his chin between his thumb and forefinger. "You're a more cunning bastard than I thought. Maybe I underestimated—"

"Oh, come on. I'm not trying to butter up anyone. Besides, there are other things to worry about."

Now Edward leaned back in his chair with a skeptical look. "Like?"

"Like who's gonna look out for our mom, or should I say our moms, back in our universes, now that we're gone? I'm worried about her. Who'll visit her?"

Edward looked away, like this conversation had suddenly become uninteresting.

Now Ed leaned forward and fiddled with one of the decorative pens on the table. The little hula dancer jiggled atop the pen, reminding him of Ellen writing on his hand. He set the pen down. "If we ever get back, I think you should visit mom more often, Edward. I know it's not easy, but my visits mean a lot to her."

"Oh, aren't you the wonderful son? More shit to rub in my face—must make you feel good, makes up for being a crip."

"No, Edward, I just—"

"Listen, asshole, you don't have to go to the depressing dump I have to visit. And I told you I don't have the cash to move her into a ... anyway, I don't need you or anyone else trying to put some guilt trip on me."

"Look Edward, I told you earlier I don't have the money either. Those places—"

Ed stopped mid-sentence when he saw Ellen enter the Grand Ballroom. He stood abruptly, nearly toppling over his cane in his excitement.

Ellen stood by the door, scanning the room, hopefully looking for him, as Ed made his way toward her, leaving Edward sitting at the table with a befuddled look.

"God, Ellen ... you came back."

They stood in silence, eyes locked on each other. Then Ellen said, "I couldn't stay away, Ed. I must know what's going on."

Ellen's eyes, shadowed with darkness from exhaustion or crying, searched him. Ed wanted to touch her, to again feel his face against her, to hold her. He reached out toward her, but then pulled back. She needed answers, not his touch, not yet. "I think I understand it better now," he said. Her silence and intense eyes encouraged him to go on. He told her about the explanation that Ship, Lennie and Jasmine had developed. "Look, I still don't understand everything, but I—"

"What about him?"

Ed turned toward Edward, still sitting at the table, but now watching Ellen and him. Talking fast, he launched into an explanation of Edward's presence, telling her how Edward had jumped from the car and wound up with only a broken ankle, while he had stayed with the car to miss the oncoming vehicle and crashed into a tree.

Ellen's face was filled with incredulity. "I need to talk to him," she said.

"I'm not sure that's a good idea. He's difficult to talk to. He's angry and unpredictable, like a coiled snake ready to strike." He cleared his throat.

"You don't trust me."

Who he didn't trust was himself. He didn't trust that he could handle Ellen being with the slim, ambulatory, confident Edward. "Oh, no, it's not that, it's just that—"

"I don't need your permission, dammit, to talk to him." Her face flashed with anger.

"Of course not." He cleared his throat again. "Like I said, he's difficult. I don't want you to have to—"

"Can we talk to him together?"

"Like I said, he's—"

"Obviously, I shouldn't have come." She spun and started for the door.

Ed started after her. "No, Ellen, don't go. Please. Just listen to me." Ellen turned and faced him. "Look, I'm sorry. It's just that I'm afraid. I'm afraid of what's happening to me tonight. I'm afraid of Edward, too. But mainly I'm afraid of losing you. Please stay. Of course, we can talk to Edward."

Ellen gave Ed a wary nod, then they made their way back to the table, where Edward sat alone, waiting for them.

Edward stood and extended a hand to Ellen. "Why, Ellen, I'm so glad you came back. I was really worried that I had missed seeing you." All the rage in Edward's face had been replaced with a gentle cordiality. He held onto her hand a few seconds too long, Ed thought.

"Come sit next to me, Ellen. I want to see you up close. We've got a lot of catching up to do."

Chapter 41

Ellen flashed Ed an off-balance look, then took a chair next to Edward.

Ed tried to craft his words, but Edward was ahead of him. Leaning toward Ellen, he said, "I know this must be really confusing for you, and I'm so sorry. But you must know that it is really pretty confusing for Ed and me, too." He shot Ed a kind smile.

What the—? What a bullshit artist.

Ellen spoke up, looking first at Ed, then Edward. "I've got to know more about you, why you're both here." There was urgency in her voice.

When they didn't immediately answer, she said, "So which of you is the real Eddie Turner?"

"I think we both are," said Ed. "But there's more to—"

"I can't accept that," she said.

Ed began to speak again, began to explain once more how the many-worlds phenomenon had caused them to be here, but Edward cut in. "I understand. Ed here's got some theory, you've probably heard it. Maybe it's true, maybe not. Who knows? Main thing is, Ellen, we are here now. It's like you and I are back in high school, chatting away in Mrs. Klinewell's geometry class. God, I can't believe it's really you."

Ellen looked over at Ed, her mouth open, her eyes wide. But she said nothing.

Ed felt his heart pounding in his chest, felt the need for air. "Ellen," he said, "You need to understand that Edward and I may be the same person, or at least we used to be, but we are really different. Gloria explained that to me." Citing Gloria should get her attention, he thought. "She said—"

"Sure, Ed, Gloria is a fine priest, and I'm sure she had some good things to say. But the main thing is that Ellen is here now." Edward returned his eyes to Ellen's face. "And now, maybe I'll finally get the chance to tell her how I felt back then, but never said it, how I still feel. God, I guess that sounds silly, after all these years, huh, Ellen?"

Ellen had her hands flat on the table, like she needed the support. "No, it doesn't sound silly, Eddie."

Oh, God, she's calling him Eddie. Ed thought about Edward's earlier comments about jumping Ellen's bones, his boasting about all the hot chicks he'd made it with. He needed to do something. He needed to protect her from Edward. No, that was wrong. Ellen was able to make her own decisions. She didn't need some male protecting her. He needed to respect her integrity, her intelligence. *But she doesn't know what Edward really thinks about her.*

And just who would Ed be protecting Ellen from? Himself? His own lust, which he knew was real, was unleashed in Edward with skill and poise that Ed lacked. Maybe he should just leave them alone and take a step back. But he couldn't. Edward might be displaying the lust that Ed felt also, but there was more. Maybe love. Where was the love in Edward? Had that died out on Highway 50, as he watched that couple suffer? Had it died in some rice paddy in Vietnam?

Now Edward leaned closer toward Ellen. She seemed hypnotized. Her lips parted slightly.

"God, Ellen, I hope you'll forgive me. I'm not usually so forward, but tonight, right now, I just ..." Then he leaned forward and kissed Ellen on the lips. It was a slow kiss, gentle as a feather floating in the breeze. She didn't move.

Edward pulled back, but only slightly, obviously ready to move in again for a deeper kiss. His eyes searched her face.

Ed needed to do something. He had had enough of sitting on the sidelines watching. Long ago Eddie Turner had left Ellen. *I won't do it again.*

Ed stamped his cane of the floor, hard. Ellen and Edward turned toward him. "We have things to talk about."

Ellen leaned back in her chair, as she wiped her lips with the back of her hand, perhaps embarrassed. Edward's eyes flashed at Ed. Ah, yes, the real Edward was returning.

Ed crossed his arms and looked from face to face. "Edward, you need to tell Ellen about the accident." This should stop the kissing for a while, thought Ed.

Ellen looked at Edward, as if expecting an answer.

Edward's eyes flashed anger at Ed, then he turned back to Ellen, with a smile. "Why would you want to hear about—"

"I do want to hear about it, Edward," she said. "I want to hear about everything."

Edward shot Ed another angry glance. "You didn't already tell her?"

"Not everything."

Edward licked his lips. "Look, Ellen, I don't think it helps to dig up painful old—"

"Please, Edward, I need to know. I need to know why you both are here. Start with the accident."

Edward pinched his lips together like he didn't want to talk about it. "So there was the accident up in the mountains. I'm guessing you know that."

"Go on," Ellen said,

"So I jumped out when the car hit the guard rail and the door sprung open. But, hell, we're here at the reunion, let's not—"

"I want to know everything." Ellen's voice was now more insistent.

Edward raised his hands in disgust. "Shit. Whatever." He rubbed his chin with the back of his hand, in a quick, nervous motion, and his eyes were now darting, like Ed had seen them do earlier. "So I jumped. Broke my ankle. While good old Ed obviously lacked the balls to—"

"Tell her what happened next, Edward." Ed knew he was trying to discredit Edward in Ellen's eyes, and this was a desperate, and not admirable, thing to do.

"So you just couldn't handle it, could you, sonny boy, that Ellen and I were sharing something nice?"

"Go on," said Ellen.

Edward looked down at the table and fiddled with a Pez dispenser. "So there was a collision."

"And?"

"Two people were killed. Look, Ellen, it hurts me to dig that up tonight. I heard them suffering. It's been a burden on my heart ever since." Now he was trying the old sympathy ploy.

Ellen was wide-eyed and breathing hard. She turned to Ed. "So why didn't you jump, too?"

Before Ed could speak, Edward cut in. "Old Ed's going to tell you he stayed in the car to avoid the collision, but the truth is, Ellen, and you need to know it, Ed lacked the courage to jump. Plain and simple, he was a coward." Now Edward leaned back and gave Ed a sorry-you're-such-a-loser look.

"I don't believe that, Edward," said Ellen.

Edward stood up. "Okay, I've had about enough of this shit. Ellen, surely you can see through this crap. Ed's jealous. Jealous because he's a cripple and I'm not."

"That's not true," blurted Ed. But, of course, there was truth in his words.

"And he's pissed. When you showed up, he was on my ass about not visiting our mother more, about why I should be hanging around some depressing nursing home, like he does. Just because I have a life and he—"

"And our mother has a life, too, Edward. She needs us."

Edward leaned toward Ed, his clenched fists on the table. "Maybe it makes you feel superior to hang out in some filthy—"

"She doesn't have to be in some filthy place, Edward." Ed felt the heat in his face. He took a deep breath. "I told you about the ElderHealth program."

Ellen added, "That's the Sandy Kaseman program."

"That's right. Sandy Kaseman made those places possible. Surely, you've heard of her, Edward."

"So, now you're insinuating I'm a dumbshit, too, because I never heard of this, who? Sandy Kaseman? Well, I shouldn't have to spell it out to you, but I've got the same brain as you. I could have been a physicist, too. I could be spouting all your oh-look-at-me-and-my-quantum bullshit. Anyway, I've never heard of this Sandy Kaseman."

Ellen and Ed exchanged uncertain glances.

Edward chewed the inside of his cheek for a moment, then gave out a little laugh. "Only Kaseman I ever heard of was the one killed in the accident."

Ed felt like a bucket of ice water had been thrown in his face. He looked at Ellen, whose face had suddenly paled. "What?"

"Oh, don't get your panties in a bunch, Ed. That Kaseman was a man. I presume your Sandy Kaseman is a woman."

Ellen exhaled a sigh of relief. "Yes, in fact, Sandy Kaseman is a woman."

"Bill Kaseman, that was his name. Poor bastard. He and his girlfriend were law students at Berkeley. I only had that factoid rubbed in my face about a million times. I won't be forgetting that any time soon."

"And his girlfriend?" Ed asked.

"Name was Sandra Richards. Okay, enough about—" He stopped, as if a realization had suddenly hit him.

Ellen wobbled for a moment, and Ed worried that she might collapse. Trembling, she said, "Bill Kaseman? Oh my God. He's an immigration attorney in San Francisco. He married Sandy Richards."

Ed couldn't speak. In his universe, Sandra Richards had lived through the day of the accident and became a national hero. In Edward's universe she died that day. He wanted to cry.

Edward opened his mouth to speak, but said nothing. He reached for a glass of water.

Ellen, obviously working hard to steady herself, leveled a steely gaze at Edward. "Sandy Kaseman eventually became a state assemblyman, where she led many reforms, including improvement of senior care facilities, like the one Ed's mom lives in." Now she turned to Ed and sagged. "I didn't come here to learn this. I'm leaving now. And don't try to stop me." She stood and headed for the door.

Ed struggled to his feet and followed her. Halfway to the door, Ellen turned and faced him. "I said, don't follow me. I mean it, Ed. I can't be a part of this craziness anymore."

He reached toward her. "But Ellen, I stayed with the car, I avoided the other car. Ellen, please don't—"

"I don't want to hear any more. I can't take this. Now leave me alone." She turned and continued toward the exit.

Gloria appeared from the crowd and spoke to Ellen. They exchanged a hug and walked toward the door together, arm in arm.

Ed wanted to follow, but he knew he had to let her go. If there was any hope at all, it would not be found in a parking-lot confrontation now. He leaned forward on his cane with both hands, fearing that his knees were about to buckle.

When Ed returned to the table, Edward was seated and the color had returned to his face. It had become red.

"You're responsible for this, Edward. You've hurt Ellen. I've had enough of your two-faced—"

"You shouldn't have messed with me, sonny boy." Then Edward stood, placed both hands under the lip of the table and violently over-turned it. Ed had to jump back quickly, almost stumbling over his cane, as Good & Plentys, noisemakers and the pens with little hula dancers went flying in all directions.

Chapter 42

Ed looked around the room apologetically, as all eyes were upon them. "I'm sorry," he said softly, over and over again. Edward stood across the toppled table from him, his eyes filled with hate. Or was it pain? It took only seconds for Ed to conclude that he needed to put some space between Edward and himself.

He backed away from the table, which conveniently served as a barrier between him and Edward, who seemed about to lunge at him.

Ed hurried as best he could through the crowd, not making eye contact with the many he felt upon him. At the rear of the room, he paused at the refreshments table, where he'd spent much of the evening. Fearing an even uglier confrontation with Edward, he didn't stop there. Making it to the hotel entrance would require passing many of his glowering classmates again. Instead, he tottered toward the door to the service hallway, where he'd taken the earlier calls from Ship.

The service corridor ran alongside the Grand Ballroom. It was plain and gray with unpainted concrete floors that reflected the harsh light of the ceiling fluorescent tubes.

He needed to think, but his brain was overloaded with panic. Ellen was gone again, maybe for good. And, God, the dying screams of Sandy Kaseman on that icy highway.

Edward would surely be looking for him, and it wouldn't take him long to find his hiding place. He recalled Edward's words about killing, about blowing up when people angered him. He felt his body trembling, his knees growing wobbly.

God, this frightening person is actually me. How do I get that through my thick skull? The person I love most, the person I hate most, the person I know best, the person I most need to know better. Here I am, with a different version of me, yet truly me. Hell, not the person I could have become, but the person I actually did become, in another reality.

Since the accident, Ed had fantasized about what might have been if he'd escaped the crash without injury. He had envisioned a healthy, ambulatory Ed Turner, with a world of possibilities before him. And now here he actually was, the real thing. Not some 'might-have-been' or 'could-have-been' Ed Turner, but the way he really was.

Ed leaned his back against the wall and stared into the bright fluorescents. In the silence he could hear their hum. He shook his head in disgust. *My regrets and shame have always controlled my life, a life filled with so many 'if onlys.' If only I hadn't been such a dork in high school. If only I'd jumped from the car. If only I hadn't dropped out of Davis. If only ... if only I'd kissed Ellen tonight.*

In our fantasies the 'if onlys' take us to different outcomes, where there are no shame and regrets. And yet, here was Edward, whose life was one of Ed's greatest 'if onlys,' right before him. And he, too, was filled with shame and regrets.

Ed took a few slow steps down the hallway. The recurring ugly images kept replaying: the wounded Ellen leaving again,

Edward's frightening rage, the dying screams of the Kasemans. He leaned against the wall again and wept.

He raised his head. *That's what I'll do. Find Frank. Tell him I'll take the Alaska job.* Gloria had asked him earlier why he didn't start over—this would be his answer. He felt suddenly calmed by the image of standing on the bow of the Alaska ferry, the cool breeze blowing his hair, looking north up into the high glacier-encrusted peaks that surrounded the narrow inside passage, through which the vessel crept. Maybe he'd sleep in a tent on the deck tonight, with the young mountaineers, wanderers and vagabonds. The Aurora would animate the dark sky with greens and reds, there'd be laughter and singing, and someone would pass around a flask of brandy.

"There you are," bellowed Edward from behind him. Ed spun quickly. Edward stood just inside the doorway. "You bastard, you didn't think you could shake me this easy, did you? Underestimating me again."

Ed looked around, contemplating an escape route, but there was no way he could outrun Edward. Edward blocked the doorway back into the ballroom, and it was unclear what lay in the other direction, at the end of the hallway, which made a right-angle turn just a few feet behind him.

Ed backed away slowly. Breathing heavily, he said, "It shouldn't come to this, Edward. We are the same person. I bear you no hard feelings."

"No hard feelings," laughed Edward. "I'm not sure you consider me worthy of feelings at all." He slowly approached Ed.

"We can't be taking this out on each other, Edward."

"Oh, really?" Edward continued to approach Ed slowly, like a stealthy fox closing in on its prey before its lethal lunge.

"You certainly were taking it out on me back at the table, in front of Ellen. Humiliating me. So, now I'll be taking it out on you, and I'm going to take it out on you good. You're the version of me I always hated, the person I could have been, should have been. I never thought I'd actually meet that person; he was always just a dream, a nightmare, really. And so here I am, face to face with my worst nightmare."

Ed continued to back away. He wasn't sure what Edward had in mind, but he feared the worst. "I'm not your nightmare, Edward, I'm just a person. A person with his own problems, fears, nightmares. I'm not someone you should hate."

"Oh, God—you telling me who I should hate. You've just got to be the superior one, got to have the last word. Well, you are about to have your last words, that is true."

"Edward, let's just—"

"I could've been something. I could've started out without that damned black shadow hanging over my life. I could've missed that meat grinder of a war that chewed up any decency and gentleness that had been inside me. I could've missed all that." Edward stepped closer to Ed, his arms rigid at his side, his fists clenching and unclenching. His eyes were red and wet, like he was about to explode. "You have no idea, do you, sonny boy, how many nights I'd wake up in cold sweats. You have no idea what it's like to be a failure, to be a nobody."

Ed clutched the cane in one hand, his other extended toward Edward, palm up. "No, Edward, that's not—"

Jasmine entered the hallway, pushing the refreshments cart, piled with dirty dishes. She stopped abruptly when she saw them.

Edward glanced over his shoulder at her, apparently not regarding the tiny girl as enough of a threat to warrant even turning around. "I'm gonna mess you up good, asshole, and now your little friend will get to witness it."

Jasmine shrieked, "You leave him alone or—"

"Jasmine, get out of here," barked Ed. "You shouldn't be here."

Now Edward turned toward Jasmine, glowered at her, then he looked down at the service cart. He stepped toward the cart and removed a long carving knife. He waved the knife, dirty with strings of dried beef clinging to it, at Ed. "Oh, look what I found." He gave out a little chuckle. "Showtime," he said, ignoring Jasmine and now moving briskly toward Ed. He lowered the knife to his side, as if preparing to attack.

As Ed braced for the attack, Jasmine, with blinding speed, launched herself onto Edward's back. With her legs wrapped around his waist, she pummeled the side of Edward's head with her fists. "Leave him alone. Leave him alone," she cried with fury.

Ed watched helplessly, as Edward spun violently, the knife slashing through the air. Jasmine was thrown against a wall. She hit hard, crumpling on the floor for just a moment before springing up, ready to fight. Edward turned toward her with the knife.

"No, Edward," screamed Ed. Edward turned back toward him too late. Ed planted the feet of the quad cane firmly into Edward's face, one foot smashing his nose and evoking a loud grunt. Edward went down, writhing and holding his bloody face.

"Run, Jasmine. Get help." When Jasmine hesitated, he commanded even louder, "Now! Jasmine, go!"

Jasmine looked around, uncertain for only a moment, before she sped for the door.

Ed's options flashed through his mind. He could also head for the door back to the ballroom, but Edward's writhing body blocked the way. Edward still grasped the knife. Getting around him with the cane would be too risky. No, he needed to buy time until help arrived. Edward was stirring and beginning to awkwardly make his way to his feet. Maybe Ed should hit him again.

With one hand against the wall for support, he raised the cane and stepped toward Edward. Edward looked hard at him, no fear in his face, as Ed aligned the cane, preparing to strike. A long second passed—he couldn't do it. He lowered the cane, turned and hobbled down the hall toward the other exit.

Ed surprised himself with his speed. Terror is a great motivator. He made the turn in the hallway and saw the exit just ahead, double doors with push bars. He couldn't risk looking around. Edward would quickly be upon him.

Ed arrived at the double doors and leaned into a push bar. Locked. He pushed the bar on the other door. Also locked. *Damn.* He turned. No Edward yet, but he was trapped here.

There was another door on the side of the hallway between him and the right-angle turn. Why hadn't he seen that before?

He got to the door, and it opened. He could hear Edward approaching from around the corner.

Ed stepped into the darkness on the other side of the door, and only then realized that it was not another hallway, but rather a service closet. Edward was nearly upon him. He pulled the door closed and hunkered as best he could against the back wall, amidst various large metal implements. Vacuum cleaners? Sweepers? Buckets? It was pitch dark inside the closet, except for a blue LED, probably the charging light for some appliance. He felt for a lock button on the door handle, but there was none.

Ed gasped for breath, but he had to discipline himself to be silent. It was inevitable that Edward would find him. Soon. Maybe help would arrive before then. But there hadn't been enough time. He tried to hold his breath.

He heard Edward's footsteps in the hallway, passing by the closet. *Maybe he'll think I made it through the double doors and locked them behind me. Maybe he would—*

But then he heard the footsteps again, returning to the closet entrance. Now, Edward was just on the other side of the door. Ed tried to lift his cane, but it was caught on something. He pulled again, and something fell from a shelf, producing a loud crashing sound. The cane was still stuck. He flailed, trying to find anything that could serve as a weapon. His hands found a large sponge. A can of some cleaning product. Essentially nothing.

Then the door flew open. The light from the hallway backlit Edward's head so that his face was dark. "You in here, sonny boy?" Edward said with an innocent, inquisitive lilt. "It's judgment day."

Edward stepped into the closet and pulled the door closed behind him.

Chapter 43

It seemed like an eternity that they were alone in the silence, although it was probably less than ten seconds. Finally, Edward said, "I don't want this to go too fast."

"You'll never get away with this." *God, that was the wrong thing to say.*

"What do you mean I won't get away with it? Neither one of us really exists."

The few seconds of extra time had allowed Ed's eyes to adjust to the dim blue light from the LED. He could now make out the vague outline of Edward, and he could pick up the flicker of the light off the shiny blade.

"This might be the last chance we each have to learn about ourselves," said Ed, surprised at how calm and in control he sounded. He was shaking inside.

Edward was quiet. Maybe he was thinking about Ed's words. Finally, he said, "Maybe I don't want to learn about myself. Maybe that's what this is about."

"But we are the same person, Edward. Why would you want to kill yourself?" Ed immediately regretted his words. People kill themselves all the time. Edward had the opportunity to rid himself of a part of his life—his nightmare?—once and for all. "Killing me just eliminates another person. It won't change anything about you."

Now Ed could see the reflection of the blue LED in Edward's eyes and a dim relief of his face. Edward said nothing.

"Edward, I'm the guy who went to see the Yankees, the M and M boys, caught the big halibut, listened to Chick Hearn and Vin Scully. Do you want to kill that?"

"You're trying to manipulate me. Don't think I can't see that." Then his voice shook as he said, "I didn't want those people to die."

"I know, Edward, I know."

"But you didn't jump out."

"Yes, I did. I am you. I did jump out," said Ed, his voice trembling. "Edward, I've spent years wishing I had jumped out."

"But you stayed in the car and those people didn't die." His voice had softened. Ed kept his eye on the shiny blade, watching for any slight movement.

Edward continued. "But you had to rub it in on me. How could you? Beating me down in front of Ellen. You think that didn't hurt? You think that didn't just add to the guilt I've been bearing all my life?" His voice had now regained its angry edge. He was talking himself back into his rage.

Maybe Eddie Turner was destined to die in this reality, no matter what decision was made on that day. Oh God, I cannot let myself die here. If there was to be a lunge by Edward, Ed would try to move quickly to the right, avoid the blade, if possible, and seize hold of Edward's arm. Edward was no doubt more fit than Ed, but Ed had good upper body strength, also. Living a life on crutches will do that for you. He was determined to put up a fight—he wouldn't go down without a struggle. "I'm sorry. I'm sorry that I did that. You didn't need to hear that. I know. I'm not blaming you, any more than I'm blaming me. For God's sake, Edward, we were just kids. How the hell were we supposed to know what to do?" He was gasping for air. "We were just kids."

In the dim glow of the blue light, Ed saw Edward lower the knife. "Oh, shit, I can't do this. Damn you, you win again."

Was this a ploy to drag the game out longer? But then Ed heard something hit the floor. The knife? How could he know?

As Ed risked a glance to the floor to see if he could see the knife, there was a sudden flash of light, as the closet door flew open. Edward spun toward the opening.

In an instant, Edward was gone. Simply vanished.

Chuck Barlow stood there in the opening, as Ed gasped for air. "Sorry, gents, I thought this was the john."

Ed's heart was pounding so hard, he thought his veins might explode. Now he heard others coming behind Chuck. He heard Jasmine's voice. "This way, Denny."

Then everything went black.

Chapter 44

"Here come the Lakers, two on one, left to right across your radio dial," Chick Hearn said, his voice rising with the urgency of the moment. "NBA finals for '68 and it doesn't get any better than this. Jerry West—Zeke from Cabin Creek—dribble-drives across the midcourt stripe. Two seconds left. He's got Baylor open underneath! Lob pass into Elgin. He goes up, hangs, and puts it in!" Eddie rose up off the bed, staring at the dim yellow dial of the clock radio, as the final seconds of the game ticked off. "Ladies and gentlemen, the Lakers have just put this game in the refrigerator against the Celtics!"

Ed stirred as his consciousness returned. He wanted to stay in his room, there with Jerry, Elgin and Chick. He opened his eyes in complete darkness. *What?* Where was he? Then he was jolted upright, as he remembered. The closet. He was on the floor. He felt for his cane, but couldn't locate it in the darkness. He struggled to his knees, then pushed the door open.

Edward was gone. Dear God, he had seen him vanish. *Was this just an illusion induced by terror?*

The harsh fluorescent light from the hallway was blinding. Where was Edward? Had he gone to another universe?

But I'm still here. Ed could hear the laughter on the other side of the door back into the ballroom, just down the hall. Now he tried to stand, as he felt for the quad cane again. He couldn't find it. He fell forward out into the hallway.

He glanced at his wrist—*no Garmin*—then patted his pants pockets. *No phone, wallet or keys.* He was still here.

He cried out, "Jasmine!" then waited a second. "Denny! Gloria! Dottie!" No answer.

But the laughter in the Grand Ballroom. They were still there. He was still here. "Dear God," he pleaded, "I need to still be here."

Ed reviewed the recent events. He was certain he'd been unconscious. Long enough to have that Lakers dream from 1968. Edward was gone. He'd seen him vanish. It had happened when Chuck Barlow startled them. Had Edward had another TGA? Had this allowed him to leave this reality? Apparently so. But where would Edward go? There could be many parallel universes for him to shift into.

But he, Ed, was still here. The hallway, the familiar hallway leading to the Grand Ballroom. The laughter on the other side of the door. The absence of his belongings from his original reality. He had not gone back to his original universe. He was still here, and he was amazed at what a great sense of relief this caused.

But where were Jasmine and Denny? He'd heard Jasmine calling to Denny just before he blacked out. Why weren't they here?

He crawled to the door into the Grand Ballroom and, grasping the handle with both hands, was able to lift himself to a standing position. Getting the door open without falling took some effort. Slowly he pulled the door open. Indeed the room was filled with people, animated conversations, laughter. He was back. He was safe.

He stepped into the room, holding onto the door for support.

But something was wrong. These weren't his people. They were much younger. He saw no one he recognized.

He couldn't breathe, as the panic ripped through him like a buzz saw. He reached out a hand into the room and called again, "Jasmine! Denny! Gloria! Dottie!"

He took a step forward and went down hard, on his face.

Chapter 45

"Are you okay, sir?" A bearded young man with a concerned look leaned over him.

"The reunion. I'm trying to get back to my reunion … I must have …"

"Just breathe, sir. You took quite a tumble."

"The Sentinel reunion. I must have come in through the wrong door."

The man shot a desperate I-could-use-some-help-here glance around the room. "Sorry, sir, there's no reunion here—this is the CMA Convention."

"No, no. The Sentinel High School Fiftieth. I'm part of it. I … I … I'm one of the students."

"Why don't you just stay still for a bit, make sure you're breathing okay. Like I said, this is the CMA Convention."

"Huh?"

"California Microbrewers Association."

Ed stared at the man, trying to comprehend.

"Seriously, man, you don't look so good. Here, let me get you into a chair. Maybe if you sit down—"

"No, I'm okay, really." It began to sink into him. *God, no. God, no. God, no.* "Gloria. Where's Gloria? I've got to talk to Gloria."

Now a young woman joined the bearded man beside Ed, who had just been helped into a chair. "What's the matter, Zach?" she said to the man.

"Not sure, just found him here on the floor. Seems to be lost."

The woman gave Ed a kind look. "I'm so sorry, sir. Should we call somebody? A doctor?"

"I've got to get back to the reunion."

"Do you have some family we can call?"

"No family."

The woman shot Zach a helpless look. "What should we do with him?"

"Oh, God, I need to get back. I need to find Jasmine and Gloria. Can you find somebody to help me?"

Zach gave Ed a caring pat on his shoulder. "We'll find you some help, sir."

It was now clear. He had left that universe. The universe of Ellen and Jasmine and Denny and Gloria. It was gone. That world was gone. They were all gone.

Chapter 46

There are three main north-south routes connecting LA and San Francisco. The most scenic route, US 101, follows the coast, occasionally cutting inland to pass through beautiful small cities. The highway's usually bounded either by green mountains or lush wine-country valleys or the Pacific. The second route, California 99, cuts right up the middle of the Central Valley, passing small towns of people who work the vast agricultural fields, the muscle of the State, putting food on the table for much of the country. Ed followed the third route, I-5, along the western shoulder of the Central Valley, far from the teeming farms to the east and far from the rugged mountains of the Coast Range to the west. Long, straight and boring, with little to see. It was perfect.

In the middle of the night there was even less to see—only some lonely interchange every half-hour or so with a Shell and a McDonald's.

This was just the way Ed wanted it. Flat and empty. This was the world to which he was returning, the world to which he belonged, the reality in which he owned a car, had a home, a phone number. A place where there were records of his existence.

The microbrewers—Zach and the woman, her name was Lori—had gotten Ed back over to the Villa Solana, after he realized that his car, his crutches and all his other possessions were probably there. Zach and Lori found a wheelchair in the Villa Solana lobby and pushed Ed up to the front desk. Indeed, his crutches, keys, watch, phone and wallet had all been found earlier in the evening out front and turned into the lost and found. The woman at the desk also pointed out that Ed had a room reserved for the night, already paid for. Ed opted not to stay. Indeed, it was his native universe to which he had returned.

Once he had his crutches, Ed, with trepidation, made his way into the main conference room of the hotel. In his universe, this is where the reunion had been held. He wasn't sure if he wanted to go in, but he pushed the big doors open and stepped into room. Everyone was gone. After all, it was now after one. A cleaning crew was already working on the room. He saw one banner still lying on the floor: "Welcome Titans, Class of '68."

Out in the parking lot, his Volvo was just where he'd left it. He scanned the lot just in case there might also be a Roadtrek, but the lot was now nearly empty. Yes, he should stay the night here, but he wasn't sleepy and, if he left now, he could be home by dawn.

Now, well north of the Grapevine, the high mountain pass separating the LA basin from the Central Valley, he thought about the upcoming dawn. There would be a dawn in this universe, and there would a dawn in that other universe.

In that other reality, he'd considered Frank's offer to launch out to Alaska. An exciting fresh start. But what he really wanted was to rise from his bed at Gloria's. She, Martin and he would have coffee on the patio, just like she'd promised. And they'd figure things out, like she'd said. She'd call Ellen. Maybe Ellen and Ralph would be soon pulling the Roadtrek into Gloria's driveway. And there they'd be in the morning light, facing each other. He'd take her in his arms. It wouldn't be long before they'd be heading out, with Ralph, of course, for a new adventure. Maybe Lake Tahoe. Maybe he'd go on one of those mission trips with her, to some remote reservation in North Dakota. He'd never been there either. Maybe he could teach basic physics to the high school students there. When they got home, maybe he'd go to church with Ellen to hear Gloria explain more to him about God. The watchman for the morning would have finally seen the dawn.

Then there'd be lunch meetings with Denny—there'd be lots of laughter and the sharing of good stories about the past. Oh, the laughter. God, how much laughter he'd missed in his life. Maybe Denny would get Ed a job down at Home Depot. They would've somehow gotten around the detail that Ed had no Social Security number.

And, of course, he'd stay in touch with Jasmine. Maybe it was time he re-read *The Feynman Lecture Series*. She would need some professional guidance from a mentor, if she was getting ready to head off to Stanford.

Life would be good. *Oh, God, life would be so good.*

He had to shake off those memories. He needed to banish all the thoughts that had flowed through his mind the past few hours. All of them, all the people he'd met—hell, even Chuck Barlow and Lennie Berger—all of them gone.

But mostly Ellen. *Oh God, Ellen.* Her hair against his face, her body pressing into his, her voice saying his name. He could smell her hair. All of it was gone. Unreachable. Off in another universe.

A more practical question now troubled him. With the efforts of Ship, Jasmine and Lennie, he had a plausible explanation for how he'd made the initial transition to the parallel universe in which Eddie had died. But what had caused him to return? And why did he return to his native reality?

Most likely, Edward had suffered another TGA when they had been surprised by Chuck Barlow, and he likely suffered one when he witnessed Edward's dematerializing before his eyes. But why would that cause the return? And why would the jump be to his original universe instead of some other universe?

During the first semester of his Physics 101 course, Ed would demonstrate the concept of stable and unstable equilibrium. For the first demonstration, he placed a marble in the bottom of a salad bowl, then invited a student to tap the marble so that it moved from its initial position. The marble would quickly roll back to its initial resting place at the bottom of the bowl. This was an example of stable equilibrium. Then he would bring out a basketball and ask a student to place a marble atop the basketball. With some effort, the student was able to do this, and the marble would stay in place as long as it wasn't disturbed. But if the marble was tapped—even if it was a tiny tap—it rolled off the basketball, away from its initial position. An example of unstable equilibrium.

Maybe that was the case with him. Yes, there may be many parallel universes and perhaps under unusual circumstances, like he experienced tonight, one could shift to such universes. But these were places of unstable equilibrium, universes where the slightest tap would send him back to his native universe. Perhaps there is only one universe to which each of us naturally belongs, the place of stable equilibrium.

He didn't need Ship to explain this to him, using some arcane quantum mechanics theory. He knew he was right.

If it was inevitable that he would return to his native universe, then perhaps it was best that it would be so soon. Not on some future night, maybe months from now, when he was alone with Ellen, looking into her eyes at sunset, talking about future plans over a bottle of cabernet, when he was about to take her into his arms.

Ed switched on the radio. A late night DJ said, "And now here's an oldie from 1968 to take you all back." Ed slammed his hand against the power button.

He ran his hand along the leatherette surface of the steering wheel, shifted uncomfortably in the old Volvo seats and watched headlights in the oncoming lanes of I-5. He looked at the dimly illuminated clock on the dash—3:20—and noted the pungence of the dry dusty fields of the Central Valley. This is reality, he thought.

But there were other realities, also. Maybe in another universe, he was already settled into the bed in Gloria's guest room. Maybe he was heading out tonight with Frank, preparing to catch a morning flight to Anchorage, then a commuter plane over to Cordova. Those realities were just as real as this one. And maybe there was a reality in which he was now snuggling closer to Ellen in the back of her Roadtrek, falling asleep bathed in the warm scent of her. Then a chilling thought. Maybe there was another reality in which Edward did not drop the knife in the service closet, and by now a coroner had already removed the body of the man with no ID.

Who was he kidding? This was real. Those other worlds were fantasies. Get your head out of that dream world. You're a physicist, not a starry eyed child. He shook his head in disgust and turned on the radio again, scanned until he found something classical, something more timeless. He turned the volume up as loud as it would go.

And so he was home. He stared out the windshield at the dark empty night. It didn't feel like home. The highway went on forever, empty, revealing nothing new, nothing interesting, just like the rest of his life promised to be. Through the side window he glimpsed black silhouettes of barren hills speeding by, like the high dark swells on an angry sea.

Sometime around four, he stopped for gas at a place off the interstate, in the middle of nowhere. Not another soul was in sight. He inserted his credit card into the pump. He had a credit card. He was once again part of the world. Credit cards, driver's license, Social Security number, an address and phone number. He recalled what Frank had said to him about identity. All these numbers meant was that there was information associated with him stored in a database somewhere. Was that what is meant by identity? That's what he had. It was all he had. He knew there was more, like Frank said. Maybe identity only exists in the caring others have for you. Isn't it about the people you touch and who touch you? Ultimately, identity is about love.

There were still hours to go, and his only companions were his thoughts. Edward. Tonight he had met himself. The same person, yet so different. Maybe this was the manifestation of all the different people inside each of us, the many different facets, the different sides. Everybody knows that. The light side and the shadow side. The better self and the not-so-good self. The diligent self and the lazy self. The forgiving self and the unforgiving self. The smart self and the clueless self. The bold self and the shy self. The self I love and the self I hate.

Ed pondered those different selves that were on display the day of the accident: the self that valued personal survival above all else and became Edward. The self that decided to stay in the car after the crash, unwilling to fight through the pain to drag himself from beneath the crumpled dash that had crushed his legs. Eddie. And then, there was the self who stayed with the car to avoid a collision with an oncoming vehicle and crashed, but then had the courage to pull his badly injured body from the wreckage.

That self. Ed. Ed, who, unbeknownst to himself, had saved the lives of Sandy and Bill Kaseman and changed the course of history for the better. That self who'd spent his life with regrets and self-incrimination.

That self, Ed now realized, was a hero.

Chapter 47

Ed's garden had long been his sanctuary. Although it was no more than a good-sized room, and it was part of a crowded condo complex, the garden area was surrounded by a six-foot-high gray-block wall that gave him plenty of privacy.

It would be an exaggeration to say that Ed strolled in his garden—it was just thirty feet from the sliding-glass patio door to the back wall—yet he drew pleasure moving among the plants. The regimen of caring for them was what he needed now to avoid recent memories too painful to bear.

He knew the history, health and care needs of each plant. In the center of the garden area were the vegetables, the Celebrity and cherry tomatoes, the radishes, carrots and the sweet potato plants. Although he only had a few plants of each type, they provided more produce than he could use. He had no one to share with, other than Ship, and he'd often show up at breakfast, carrying a grocery bag full of veggies, usually received reluctantly by Ship with a groan and a muted thank you.

Along the back wall was a small section of native plants. A patch of yarrow, with their brilliant white flowers, reminded him of a wildflower meadow. Several California wild rose plants formed a red-flowery thicket in the corner, and Ed kept them separated from his walking path out of respect for their abundant thorns. The crown jewel of Ed's native-plant area was the Manzanita. Tall and rangy, with smooth reddish bark, it poked its branches above the top of the wall.

Surrounding the vegetable garden, like embracing arms, were the ornamentals, mostly annuals. Zinnias, peonies, asters, marigolds, dahlias (he prided himself in the enormous flowers they produced), and ranunculus.

Ed got his foam kneeling pad and a pair of pruning shears from a small storage shed next to the back door. It was seven, which gave him some time to be among his plants, which he needed right now, before he'd go see Ship at nine, their usual breakfast time. Ship would be surprised to see Ed, assuming he spent the night in Southern California, but it would be an understatement to say he had a lot to talk about with Ship.

There was no way the plants needed pruning, but it gave Ed pleasure to keep them perfectly trimmed, like a pet owner doting on his French Poodle.

"So, good morning, Carmen. How are you doing?" He said it aloud to the stately camellia, tall against the side wall. He'd been worried about Carmen's yellowing leaves, but they hadn't gotten worse since he was away. Good Lord, he was only away for one day.

Ed examined the lush pink flowers—there were only a few left at the end of the blooming season. Ed knew how to care for Carmen, and so she bloomed most of the year, beginning in late fall, peaking in early Spring, but continuing to mid-July. He knew about keeping the base of the camellia damp at all times, but to never water the foliage in direct sunlight. That would cause brown spots and rot. Feeding was important with camellias. He religiously gave Carmen her first feeding on March 15, using a balanced plant food, perhaps a 10-10-10—those were the percentages of nitrogen, phosphorus and potash that Mrs. Benson had taught him about in her visits during his convalescence so long ago. Carmen's March feeding would be followed by feedings on May 15 and August 15. It was good to have minutia in which to bury himself.

He studied the soft, pink petals of the camellia's luscious blossoms and gently stroked their satiny surfaces. He pulled his hand away. It reminded him of Ellen's skin.

After an hour of trimming the plants, Ed stood and dragged a sprinkler to the middle of the garden. The plants had been watered just two days ago, but things dried out fast in July around here. He stood back and watched the loopy oscillation of the water pattern thrown by the sprinkler. It felt good knowing he was a provider, a responsible and trustworthy caregiver.

He was back in his reality. The place he belonged. Maybe it was like he'd never been away. But that reality—God, he'd only been there a few hours—had seemed so real. Those people were real; they had, in fact, become something more to him. More than what? He sagged. More than this.

He remembered the scene from his chair next to the refreshments table, watching the other attendees. Behind the laughter and jokes and silly memories out there in the room, he knew that almost every one of these people was familiar with the grit of life—not exiled to some small walled garden. He blew out a troubled breath. These were people who at sixty-eight knew about surgery, healthcare, high blood pressure, mortgages going under water, 401ks, parents in nursing homes, children facing divorce, what hospice offers.

Kids that don't call, kids that are dead, grandchildren. Am I still in love? Was I ever in love? Can I still find love?

The reunion attendees weren't gathered around the posters of Fallen Titans, but they knew they were there. Their avoidance of the posters showed how much they knew they were there. And the posters had room for more photos.

All this life made him feel connected. Like he belonged. There had been something there in the Grand Ballroom that Carmen could not provide, that no garden could provide.

Why had he always been such a loner? Most people would rather die than give one of his lectures before a packed house in the arena-like Schrader Lecture Hall or address the hundred emotional attendees during that Vietnam confrontation. He could do those things, but the thought of that now brought him little comfort.

He'd always been awkward and tongue-tied in one-on-ones, except for when he was with a student, explaining, say, mutual induction. Why was that? Maybe it was because his student consultations were about conveying information, about sharing something he knew about. It was business. It was something he was expected to do, paid to do. Not like standing before Ellen, right after that Aretha song, when she'd pulled away slightly and looked at him, with her lips parted, her eyes washing him. Waiting for him. He should have kissed her. That's what she'd wanted. But no, he hadn't kissed her. Even though there was nothing at that moment that he wanted more. Instead, he'd said some lame thing—he couldn't remember what—but it was about as romantic as telling one of his students about mutual induction.

He had driven Ellen away. Twice. He threw the pruning shears down in disgust, and they speared their way into the soil, like an assassin's knife.

He should grab a shower before breakfast, but there'd be time for that later. He glanced down at the Garmin. Almost nine. There on the back of his hand was a little heart with an arrow drawn through it. *Oh, God.* Ellen had drawn that just hours ago. He felt a surge of despair in his chest that threatened to drive him to his knees again. He stepped over to the perimeter of the sprinkler pattern and extended his hand, letting it get soaked, before vigorously rubbing the little heart away.

Chapter 48

Sarah's Café was always quiet on Sunday mornings. The church-going crowd wouldn't drift in until around eleven, so Ed and Ship and a dozen or so other non-churchgoers had the place to themselves. This morning, Ship sat in his usual spot, a booth by the window looking out onto First Street, the Sunday *San Francisco Chronicle* spread across his table. When he saw Ed, he did a double-take. "Uh-oh, you didn't chicken out, did you?"

Ed laughed, shaking his head. "Nope. Just didn't spend the night. Got home a couple hours ago." He sat down opposite Ship, who pulled the massive pile of newspaper sections onto the seat beside him.

"Didn't spend the night? I thought you said you had a hotel room reserved."

"Yeah, I did. I just wanted to get back home."

Ship shook his head. "My, aren't you the world traveler."

Ed pursed his lips and folded his hands on the Formica table top. "You might be surprised." It was good to see Ship again.

The waitress filled their coffee cups, then asked to take their order. They hadn't opened the plastic laminated menus. "The usual?" she said. Ginger was a bony, middle-aged redhead. Ed realized that in all the years he and Ship had been eating here, he'd never called her by her name. He looked up at her now. Lines of worry gave her a perpetual frown, and her face had the leathery look of a chain smoker.

Ship said yes to the usual. Eggs Benedict, which he always ordered on Sundays. He had oatmeal on the other days.

"I think I'll try something different today. I see on the chalkboard you have some special crepes. I'll try those." Then Ed added, "Thanks, Ginger."

Ship leaned back and looked carefully at Ed, like there was something different about him. "What do you mean, I might be surprised? You didn't meet a woman, did you?"

Ed felt his face redden slightly. "Well, as a matter of fact, I did. But that's not—"

"Way to go, Ed!" Ship hoisted his coffee cup for a toast. Ed clinked cups with Ship, then took a sip. God, where was he going to begin with this story? "I want to hear everything. If there are any juicy details, definitely don't leave those out."

"Maybe I should just begin at the beginning." Ed exhaled a great sigh. "This may take a while."

Ship's raised his bushy eyebrows, giving Ed the go-ahead to begin.

"I'll say right up front that you may not believe any of what I'm going to tell you, but ... well, anyway, here's the story." Ed took another sip of coffee, then set the cup down, but still circled it with his hands. "So, I showed up at the Villa Solana. That's the hotel listed on the invitation and where I had my room reserved." That was how he began.

Ship listened attentively, but soon had to interrupt. "Wait, you say that when you came to, all your stuff, even your crutches, was gone?"

"That's right."

"Damn, that's terrible. I knew you had those TGAs, Ed, but I never knew you went unconscious with them."

"I don't, but as you'll see, something else was also happening." Ed told Ship about being redirected to the Golden Foothills Inn, where he learned about Eddie Turner's death fifty years ago.

"Holy shit, Ed. What the hell was going on? Maybe—"

"I need you to just listen for a few minutes, Ship, or we're never going to get through this."

Ship took a sip of coffee."Okay, but this needs to start making sense pretty soon."

"Trust me, it's going to make less sense before it starts making more sense. So, just hold on." Ed had a lot of experience laying out the story to others, including the Ship from the parallel universe, so it was straightforward to lay it all out now.

But he only got a little way before Ship had to interrupt again. "What do you mean, I didn't know you?"

"That's right. Never heard of me. You were barely willing to talk with me."

Ship let out a nervous laugh. "Hey, I do know you, and I'm barely willing to talk with you." They laughed. "Oh, and was I still working at Muir?"

"Yes."

"Damn." They both laughed again. It wasn't clear that Ship was taking this seriously.

"And you were just as ornery as you are now."

"But at least I was alive." He paused. "So, you talked to me and you talked to a psychiatrist? What'd we tell you?"

"At first, you both thought I was crazy."

"Well, at least in that universe I displayed good sense." Ship chuckled again.

"But it became clear that I wasn't crazy. You talked to me about the quantum many-worlds theory."

"I did?" Ship had suddenly turned serious.

"Yes. That's not something I'd make up."

"I know."

A typical Ship insult, but Ed let it slide. He went through the whole sequence of arguments. The TGA leaving his brain a blank slate, the collective psychological focus of the crowd on 1968, the effect of memory amplitude, and the quantum many-worlds reconnection of parallel universes.

"But … but …" sputtered Ship, who then shook his head and slurped down some more coffee. "So, you believe that you entered a parallel universe? And you're not shittin' me? I know you're not much of a joker, but this takes the cake. I mean—"

"Not only was I there in the universe in which I had died fifty years earlier, but another Ed Turner showed up, too. One who wasn't handicapped."

"My God," breathed Ship. He'd been munching on his Eggs Benedict, but now he set his fork down. "You're really serious, aren't you?"

Ed nodded.

Ship scratched his chin. "I always believed that parallel universes could not interact because of the decoherence of the wavefunctions, but what you've told me makes me wonder. I've got to admit, it does sound plausible." Then a smile reappeared on his face. "But, of course it sounds plausible. It was my idea."

"Well, yours and Jasmine's. She's a junior in high school."

Ship looked skeptical.

"She's pretty smart. In fact you connected her up with Jergen Shimsky, so she might have a shot at Stanford."

"I did?"

Ed nodded.

Ship let out a great sigh.

"Of course, she exists in another universe. I'll never see her again. Can you believe, she was reading *The Feynman Lecture Series*?"

"That's good. Probably a bright girl."

"I'll miss her. I could have been her friend. Be a mentor. Encourage her about physics. She's got a pretty hard life." Ed looked down.

Ship's eyes were now locked on Ed, and his disbelieving smile had been wiped away. "Look, Ed, I know I'm a loony old scientist, babbling about things like chaos and Higgs bosons and entanglement. Things most people don't understand or even care to understand. But here's something really important. Sure you left this, what's her name, Jasmine, in that other world. Yes, maybe she needed a friend. A mentor. And yes, if this parallel universe crap is true, you'll never see her again."

Ship paused to dab his mouth with his napkin, then looked out onto First Street, where absolutely nothing was going on. He looked back at Ed. "But can you get this into your brain? There are Jasmines all over the place, all around you, who need a mentor, a friend. And here you sit, day after day, on your lazy ass, feeling sorry for yourself, because you got pushed out of your job. Sit here doing nothing. Sit here while all those Jasmines out there go unhelped. For God's sake, Ed, go volunteer somewhere. Come back to Muir as a part time adjunct. I know you thought that was beneath you.

But, Ed, it's time to come to your senses—do something and stop feeling sorry for yourself."

Deep down, beneath the bravado and joking, this was the real Ship. A caring friend. "Thank you," said Ed.

"Anyway, about this parallel universe stuff, I still think it's probably impossible. Delusion or some kind of concussion is still probably the best explanation."

"Why do you say that, Ship?"

"Well, so I don't have a good explanation, okay? I realize I'm sounding a little like Bohr and his Copenhagen buddies, who didn't have a good reason to reject the many-worlds interpretation, either. But still." He shook his head.

"Gell-Mann," said Ed.

"What about Gell-Mann?"

"Gell-Mann's Totalitarian Principle. Everything not forbidden is compulsory."

Ship's mouth fell open. Then he nodded. "Okay, I get it," he whispered.

They were silent for a while, then Ship said, "And you say you met a woman? What was that about?"

Ed told Ship about Ellen.

Ship's sharp wit seemed to have returned. Not missing the chance for a cheap shot, he cracked, "You're amazing, Ed. You can't find a woman in this world who'll have you, so you have to go find one in a parallel universe."

Ed shared the laugh, then turned serious. "But, of course, I'll never see her again."

Ship leaned toward Ed. "You fool, there are women all around you. Get off your sorry, introverted butt and go meet some of them."

Ed recalled Gloria's words to him. "It's not trying to find the perfect world that matters, it's how you live in the one you're already in." He took another sip of coffee. Meeting other women held no appeal at all.

He had barely touched the crepes, while Ship had nearly polished off his Eggs Benedict. Ed took a sip of coffee and gazed out the window. A man across the street was loading some boxes into an old pickup. A kid wobbled down the sidewalk on a skateboard. He wondered what Ellen was doing this morning.

"Damn it, Ed, I don't mean to be a hard ass about the woman you met. It's exciting to talk about quantum entanglement, but ultimately it's no match for human entanglement."

"I know. Thanks, Ship."

In a more upbeat mood, Ship said, "So, what was I like in this new universe?"

"Still the same curious physicist I know. I only got you to talk with me by mentioning there was some screwy physics going on. I knew you wouldn't be able to resist that."

"Guess some things don't change."

"And you had a woman," Ed added. He suddenly wasn't sure he should have mentioned this.

"A woman?" Ship joked. "I hope it was a gorgeous blonde." He let out a big laugh that Ed thought sounded hollow.

"I didn't see her. She was in the background on the phone."

"Oh? So, then, was I married?"

What should he say? "Hey, you don't even believe all this really happened, and now you want all the details on how Shipley Jameson was doing. Come on."

Ship licked his lips, then said, "Well, was I married? I guess maybe you don't know, huh?"

"Yes, you were married." He couldn't lie to Ship, even if this might hurt him. "She kept calling out for you to come to bed."

"Ooh, the plot thickens."

Ship had not had a relationship with a woman for as long as Ed had known him. He'd always busied himself with physics, but Ed suspected that he must have been lonely. "So, tell me more, Ed. What was her name?"

Ed swallowed hard. He sensed he was getting off into deep water. "Leyla."

Ship's face lost all color and, for a moment, Ed was worried that he might be about to pass out. Ship took a sip of water.

"Leyla?"

"Yes."

"And she was calling me to come to bed?"

Ed wiped a bead of sweat from his forehead. "Yes."

"What else did she say?"

"Ship, I can't remember everything that … hey, I was talking into a cell phone, and I couldn't hear—"

"What else did she say?" Ship's voice had become demanding.

"She said, if I remember this correctly, Come to bed, Ya Hayati. At least, that's what I recall it sounding like, or maybe …" Ed's voice trailed off, as he saw tears form in Ship's eyes.

Now Ship stood, his napkin falling to the floor. He stepped out of the booth and walked toward the rear of the restaurant, where he leaned against the wall, one hand on the top of his head. Ed considered following him, then decided to give Ship some space.

After several minutes, Ship returned and took his seat. He retrieved his napkin from the floor and arranged it on his lap. He breathed out hard. "*Ya Hayati* is Arabic. It means 'my life' or 'my love.'" He swallowed hard, then said, "That's what Leyla used to call me."

Ed's mouth fell open.

Ship stared at his plate, his lips moving silently, like he was talking to himself. "Back at Chicago," he began, then stopped. "God, I've never told anyone about this." He ran a hand through his shaggy hair. "There was a girl, a student from Iran. Leyla." His words were coming out in breathless bits. He shook his head, as he said, "She was a sophomore and I was a new assistant professor. She was in my general physics class. Leyla was a music major, but had to take a science course. I got to know her." He paused, and Ed noticed that he was trembling. "She would play the flute for me. It was so lovely." He pressed his fingertips against his mouth, like he was trying to suppress a sob. "She was so beautiful." He stopped to gaze out the window for a while. Then he said, "We became lovers. It was a terrible decision for us both, a student and a teacher, a recipe for disaster, but we couldn't help ourselves." Ship turned toward the window again. With his gaze on the street, he said, "I think I've said enough."

But after a moment, Ship continued. "The final exam came, and Leyla was poorly prepared. She was bright, studied hard, but she was an artist, not a science type. She was desperate."

There was pleading in Ship's eyes. "If she didn't pass the course, she would lose her scholarship and have to return to Iran." He shook his head. "I gave her some answers to the exam. She didn't ask me for them. Okay? I offered them."

He blew out a trembling sigh. "The department discovered it. Don't know how, but they did. Leyla failed the course. She was expelled from school and sent back to Iran. I never saw her again."

Ship swallowed hard again. "I was fired. I didn't care about losing the job at the time. I was so crushed by the loss of Leyla. In time, I began to look for a new job, but no one would have anything to do with a cheater." He shook his head again. "The only offer I got, after a year of searching, was here at Muir. They apparently were so thrilled to have a professor from Chicago on their faculty that they decided to give me a chance."

Ship manufactured a cynical laugh. "Oh, I went out with a few women, after a while. Never another student. But I never got over Leyla. Physics became my lover, my wife." There was a hollow chuckle. "This is the first time I've talked about it with someone else in all this time. Over thirty years."

Ship gave Ed a helpless look. "So, here I am, sitting here like some pompous ass, giving you advice about some woman you lost. Get over it! Move on!" He looked Ed hard in the eye now. "What a crock of shit."

"Did you ever try to find Leyla?"

"No." Ed had never seen Ship look so wounded, defeated. Then he smiled, "Maybe in some other universe I did. Maybe, in time, that can give me some comfort."

"I'm sorry, Ship."

"I know," Ship said. He reached over and laid a hand on Ed's. "I know."

Chapter 49

Having plans is essential when you live alone. The plans are not needed because your calendar is so full. They're needed because your calendar is not full. Because plans help give one's life structure. Purpose. Even those accustomed to living alone, like Ed, found that the prospect of looking forward into the empty abyss of the future, with absolutely no obligations, no duties, no engagements, was nearly unbearable. So Ed decided that later in the day he would make the trip down to Santa Rosa, to the medical supply store, and trade in his forearm crutches for a quad cane. Then he'd swing over to Sycamore to visit his mother and maybe cap the trip off by hitting Costco for a foot-long. Sure, he had just completed the long drive from Riverside County, and he'd probably crash later, but right now he needed to keep busy.

He could leave for Santa Rosa now, but he'd go later. Deferring the trip gave him something to anticipate. Hardly exciting, but it was something that helped fill the day.

Ed leaned his back against the refrigerator and stared out through the patio door into his garden, reflecting on his breakfast with Ship. As much as he was still reeling from the bizarre events of last night, it was Ship's shocking story about Leyla that commanded his attention now.

Ship had never asked, "How could this be?" He never attempted to theorize how he and Leyla might be together in another universe. If he had asked that question, Ed would have had to confess that he did not know. Why were some things the same and other things different, like the venue for the reunion, in the other universe?

He stroked his chin with a knuckle. Ed's surviving the accident had set many things into motion in this universe. Ellen had not attended his funeral. What might she have done instead and how might her life have been different? Ed's parents did not have to grieve a dead child. How might their subsequent actions have been different? What things did Ed do that the dead Eddie Turner would never have the chance to do? Who knows how the small things we do might affect something large? The butterfly effect? But Ship had shown no interest in exploring the possible underlying physics of the situation. This was so unlike him. But what had he said? Something about quantum entanglement never being as interesting as human entanglement?

His mind turned to the people from last night. It was clear that Edward had vanished from that universe, hopefully to return to his old universe. Thank God, Ed had seen him disappear, giving him the peace of knowing that he would not be left in that reality with Ellen and Jasmine and Gloria. How could Edward have become so filled with anger, been so comfortable with violence? But Edward had dropped the knife at the last moment. *Why was that?* Was there still a trace of good in Edward Turner, a trace of the innocent boy who rooted for the Angels and played with Spud and leapt into the air when he'd caught the big halibut?

Jasmine would miss him for sure. But when she and Denny did not find him in the hallway, she'd be the one most likely to understand. She probably would call Ship and they would speculate about Ed's departure from their world. She'd probably be trying out a new theory, something she'd dug up from *The Feynman Lecture Series*. Ed smiled, knowing that Jasmine would be okay. With Ship and Jergen Shimsky on her side, her future was bright. But, of course, he would never find out.

What will happen to Ellen when she finds me gone? He'd been in that reality just a few hours, but it was long enough to hurt Ellen again. Ed felt his knees crumble beneath him, as he collapsed slowly to the floor, his back sliding along the surface of the refrigerator. *Gloria. Thank God, Ellen has Gloria to help her through this.* Gloria wouldn't understand what happened any better than anyone else, at least from a scientific perspective. But Gloria had something more to offer Ellen. Something that would provide strength and peace. Ed could sure use a good dose of that right now.

The rest of the attendees? They would just conclude that he had left. And many would probably be grateful. Certainly, Chuck Barlow, who witnessed Edward's and his departures, would be too plastered to have delivered a report that anyone would believe.

Ed pulled himself up from the floor and headed for the shower. Unwittingly, he began humming the melody to "Hey Jude." Then he stopped. Remembering to let her into his heart wasn't his problem. It was getting her out of his heart that would be his struggle.

He leaned into the shower, holding onto one of the handicap grab bars, and turned the water on. He wanted the shower hot today, really hot. Hot enough to wash everything away.

It was when he removed the Garmin watch that he saw it. He stared at it for a long time, as the small bathroom filled with steam. It was there on his wrist, in a place that had been covered by the Garmin wristband. A phone number, written in ink.

Dear God, a connection with Ellen from the other universe. She had written it there last night. It was right before Edward appeared. Damn, he should have seen it then. He could have called her after she left. But what difference would it have made anyway?

Might this also be her number in this universe? Ship had the same phone number in this universe; maybe Ellen did, too. But even if it was her number, it would be a different Ellen. Probably married. Or in a relationship, no doubt. Women like her didn't remain single for very long. Or maybe, God forbid, she was dead. He couldn't bear to learn such news. Yes, but the connection with him in high school would be the same. He could call that number. But why would he do that? To set himself up for more disappointment?

He stepped into the shower, and the first thing he did was scrub the number away. He had to move on. Isn't that what Ship had advised? There were other women. God, he was pining away for a woman who didn't exist. This Ellen Barnes, or whatever her name was these days, was a different person from the one he'd met last night. The Ellen Barnes he met last night didn't exist.

After his shower, Ed, dressed but still barefoot, returned to the garden. He sat down in the dirt, still wet from the sprinkler, next to the Celebrity tomatoes. He was instantly aware of the moisture seeping into his pants. Even though he had just showered, it didn't matter. He picked up a handful of the wet dirt and squeezed it tight into a compact clod, then released it.

Now he stared blankly at the tall block wall that enclosed the garden and the two-story apartment building looming beyond it. Atop the highest branch of the Manzanita, a bird had landed. A sparrow.

There are over fifty species of sparrows in North America.

He looked over at Carmen. The blossoms were stunning. Layers of pink, like waves receding to infinity. Colors so subtle they were heartbreaking. Absolute beauty, he thought. Like Ellen's face resting against his chest.

He pulled the phone from his pocket. He stared at the wrist where the number had been written. It was now gone.

Ed smiled. He was a physicist. He remembered numbers.

With muddy fingers, dirt now under his fingernails, he tapped in the number. There was a ring. *God, there actually is such a number here.* He couldn't breathe. It rang again. He began to hope she wouldn't answer or that someone else would answer.

He looked up at Carmen again and thought about the feel of Ellen's warm, moist breath on his neck, as they danced.

By the sixth ring, he decided to hang up. It would be the best thing to do. His finger hovered over the end-call button. He had made the call. He hadn't been a chicken shit, after all.

Then there was a click. The phone was answered. His heart jumped out of his chest. Another click. He'd gotten a machine. "This is Ellen." It was a message. It was her voice. *My God, it's her voice.* "Ralph and I are probably on the road and out of range. Please leave a message."

Ed felt his eyes fill up and his throat close off. He swallowed hard, took a deep breath. "Ellen," he said, "it's Eddie Turner."

*If you enjoyed 68, please consider
posting a customer review at Amazon or Goodreads.*

Discussion Questions
for Book Clubs and Small Groups

1. How do you react to the idea that parallel universes may be possible? Terrified? Invigorated? Or does the idea sound impossible to you?

2. Have you been to a high school reunion? Any specific interesting or surprising experience you wish to share? If you have been to several reunions, how might an early one, say your tenth, differ from a later one like your fiftieth?

3. Ed wonders if class reunions are occasions for people to give honest accountings of their lives. How do you react to that?

4. How did Ed's initial assumptions about the people at the reunion change over the course of the evening?

5. How would you react to meeting an exact replica of yourself? What questions would you ask another version of yourself?

6. Ed and Edward both have regrets. How do they differ from each other's regrets? How are they the same? What do they tell us about our own regrets?

7. Ed had very few acquaintances in his life, other than his friend Ship. Yet, in just one evening at the reunion, he made many new friends. How was that possible? How did Ed react?

8. Why do you think Ed intervened in the arguments between classmates over Vietnam?

9. In Ed's discussion with Denny about the concept of home, he says, "Home may be a place you've never been." What do you think Ed meant by this?

10. Ed says that a class reunion is like a time machine. In what ways is this true? In which ways not?

11. Gloria counseled Ed: "...it's not trying to find the perfect world that matters, it's how you live in the one you're in." How do you react to this?

12. There are over two dozen songs from 1968 mentioned in the book. Was there one or more that connected with you? How did the music help bring attendees back to their graduation year? Is there a song in your life that connects you to a specific event/time?

13. Ed gets advice from a quantum physicist, a psychiatrist and a priest. How do the three sets of advice differ from one another? How did Ed respond/react to the advice?

14. If you were writing an additional chapter beyond the end of the book, what would it contain?

Acknowledgements and References

It is a pleasure to thank Tim Storm for an excellent job critiquing this manuscript. Thanks also to John DeDakis, who critiqued a portion of the book. Thank you to my beta readers Patty Trainor, Bill Dorsey, and Luanne Dorsey. I am especially grateful to my wife, Mary, who patiently read the manuscript several times and was a major contributor to improving the story.

The physics of the many-worlds interpretation of quantum mechanics is presented here with as much accuracy as I could provide. An excellent popular overview of the many-worlds theory may be found in Brian Greene, *The Hidden Reality* (Knopf: New York, 2011), especially Chapter 8, "The Many Worlds of Quantum Measurement," p. 189*ff.* Failures in correctly interpreting the theory rest entirely with the author.

Transient Global Amnesia (TGA) is also a real phenomenon, which I've attempted to describe faithfully. How the many-worlds quantum-mechanics and TGAs might combine with memory amplitude and collective mass psychology to produce a merging of parallel universes is the product of the author's imagination.

I was privileged to hear lectures from famed physicist Richard Feynman. And I was privileged to read some his seminal papers in theoretical physics, including a very complicated theoretical paper on the physics of liquid helium that read like literature. He was an amazing spokesman for science. His important introductory textbook series on physics, *The Feynman Lecture Series*, ©1963 by the California Institute of Technology, is still considered a classic. The book is available for free online at http://feynmanlectures.caltech.edu/. Feynman agreed that volume one was the best.

A number of quotations are used in the book, including:

"Reality is a multiverse ..." John Polkinghorne, *Quantum Theory, A Very Short Introduction*, Oxford University Press, 2002, p. 52.

"We have a few minutes at sunset time ..." Georgia O'Keeffe, biographical video, Georgia O'Keeffe Museum, Santa Fe, NM, 2018.

"Never forget who you are." This was mentioned by the character Frank Castenado, quoting an elderly Eyak in Alaska. (Ernestine Hayes, Tlingit, Juneau, Blonde Indian: An Alaska Native Memoir, *p. 7, University of Arizona Press, 2006.)*

The science fiction story recalled by Ed is "A Sound of Thunder" by Ray Bradbury, which appeared in *Collier's Magazine*, June 28, 1952.

"The problem with physicists is not that they trusted their equations too much ..." Steven Weinberg, *The First Three Minutes, 1977.*

"... when someone looks through a telescope into the deep reaches of space ..." quoted in John Polkinghorne, *The Faith of a Physicist*, p. 28 (Princeton: Princeton University Press: 1994).

"We find ourselves in a bewildering world ..." Stephen Hawking, *A Brief History of Time*, p. 171 (New York: Bantam, 1988).

"Only those who dare to fail greatly can achieve greatly." Robert F. Kennedy, Day of Affirmation Address, University of Capetown, Capetown, South Africa, June 6, 1966

"... the world is all messed up. The nation is sick. Trouble is in the land." from a speech given by Martin Luther King, Jr., April 3, 1968, at the Mason Temple (Church of God in Christ Headquarters) in Memphis, Tennessee, the night before his death.

"Climb the mountains and get their good tidings ..." John Muir, *The Mountains of California*, (1989 by Sierra Club Books; first published January 1st, 1894).

There are several Scripture quotes from Gloria, all from the Psalms. " ... *How deep I find your thoughts, O God!,"* Psalm 139:16-17; *"... tears at night but joy in the morning,"* Psalm 30:5; *"... like watchmen for the morning,"* Psalm 130:6. The translation used is from the Episcopal *Book of Common Prayer, 1979.*

The words to the fictitious Sentinel High School Alma Mater were borrowed from the alma mater of my own high school, Arroyo High School, El Monte, California.

Gladys Stewart was one of many dedicated teachers from my alma mater, Arroyo High School, in El Monte, California. I am very grateful to them all. But Miss Stewart may have been my favorite.

About the Author

Jim Trainor is the author of six books.

He is a former deputy leader of the Physics Division at Los Alamos National Laboratory. He holds a Ph.D. in physics (Univ. of Calif.) and has served at some of the world's top research centers, authoring over sixty articles in physics. He is also an ordained Episcopal priest and has served as a  parish priest to congregations in New Mexico, Texas and Wisconsin. He is active as a speaker on topics in science and spirituality.

Jim grew up in LA and has lived much of his life in the West. He now lives on a lake in the upper midwest with his wife Mary. They have three grown children. When not at his desk writing, he's hiking in the wilderness or paddling his kayak across a lake.

More information on Jim and his books at
www.JimTrainorAuthor.com

Also by Jim Trainor
www.JimTrainorAuthor.com

An old camper van was all Ryan Browning's mother left him when she died last year. Ryan, has just been fired and could be facing prosecution. It might be a good time to hop in that old van and head out on a long road trip, perhaps to never return. When he goes to the bank to close out his account, Ryan meets the lovely customer service rep, Amanda, who has a few issues of her own. Join Ryan and Amanda on a road trip through the scenic west—into a face-to-face encounter with a deadly threat far greater than they can imagine.

For Wil Weathers, who's lost his job and his girlfriend, a backpacking trip might just be a cure for the blues. But while waiting for a late-night bus in a small northern Wisconsin town, Wil finds a body. When he returns with help, in the form of the attractive Sally, the body has disappeared. Come up north, where Wil and Sally now find themselves the target of unknown killers and on a collision course with an eco-terrorist gang preparing to destroy the lives of millions.

Karen hopes that Maui will rekindle the firs in her marriage. But the flames that engulf her are of betrayal and murder, from which there may be no rescue.

The Sand People takes us to beautiful Maui, amidst posh beachfront resorts, then draws us deeper into the Maui most tourists never see: rural onion fields, the county jail, a funeral and a run-down bar far from the beachfront glamour. It blends laughter and tears in grappling with issues that plague our lives: broken relationships, addiction, shame and death -- and pointing toward the victory of hope over failure.

Honorable Mention
Foreward Reviews 2012 Book of the Year

Josh and Evangelina have little in common, until they are thrown together and pursued by unknown killers. In a desperate flight for survival, they take refuge in a run-down nursing home in rural northern New Mexico. In this place of helplessness, they must confront old demons, as they are catapulted toward a final deadly showdown that means reaching for strength that may be beyond their grasp.

We have big questions
about the meaning of life.

Join Jim Trainor, physicist and pastor, in exploring the intersection of science and religious faith. *Grasp* leads you deep into the heart of the matter, bringing together thoughts of great scientific and religious thinkers with the real-life stories of people who have grasped for the truth.

www.ingramcontent.com/pod-product-compliance
Lightning Source LLC
Chambersburg PA
CBHW051335250626
47155CB00007B/2607